Memoirs Of Emma Courtney

MARY HAYS

First published 2015
Copyright © 2015 Aziloth Books

British Library Cataloguing in Publication Data

A catalogue record for this book is available from the British Library

ISBN-13: 978-1-909735-89-7

Printed and bound in Great Britain by Lightning Source UK Ltd., 6 Precedent Drive, Rooksley, Milton Keynes MK13 8PR.

Cover Illustration: *A Portrait of a Young Lady.*
Oil on Canvas. Eugene de Blass (1870s)

CONTENTS

VOLUME II

PREFACE

The most interesting, and the most useful, fictions, are, perhaps, such, as delineating the progress, and tracing the consequences, of one strong, indulged, passion, or prejudice, afford materials, by which the philosopher may calculate the powers of the human mind, and learn the springs which set it in motion - 'Understanding, and talents,' says Helvetius, 'being nothing more, in men, than the produce of their desires, and particular situations.' Of the passion of terror Mrs Radcliffe has made admirable use in her ingenious romances. - In the novel of Caleb Williams, curiosity in the hero, and the love of reputation in the soul-moving character of Falkland, fostered into ruling passions, are drawn with a masterly hand.

For the subject of these Memoirs, a more universal sentiment is chosen - a sentiment hackneyed in this species of composition, consequently more difficult to treat with any degree of originality; - yet, to accomplish this, has been the aim of the author; with what success, the public will, probably, determine.

Every writer who advances principles, whether true or false, that have a tendency to set the mind in motion, does good. Innumerable mistakes have been made, both moral and philosophical: - while covered with a sacred and mysterious veil, how are they to be detected? From various combinations and multiplied experiments, truth, only, can result. Free thinking, and free speaking, are the virtue and the characteristics of a rational being: - there can be no argument which mitigates against them in one instance, but what equally mitigates against them in all; every principle must be doubted, before it will be examined and proved.

It has commonly been the business of fiction to pourtray characters, not as they really exist, but, as, we are told, they ought to be - a sort of *ideal perfection*, in which nature and passion are melted away, and jarring attributes wonderfully combined.

In delineating the character of Emma Courtney, I had not in view these fantastic models: I meant to represent her, as a human being, loving virtue while enslaved by passion, liable to the mistakes and weaknesses of our fragile nature. - Let those readers, who feel inclined to judge with severity the extravagance and eccentricity of her conduct, look into their own hearts; and should they there find no record, traced by an accusing spirit, to soften the asperity of their censures - yet, let them bear in mind, that the errors of my heroine were the offspring of sensibility; and that the result of her hazardous experiment is calculated to operate as a *warning*, rather than as an example. - The philosopher - who is not ignorant, that light and shade are more powerfully contrasted in minds rising above the common level; that, as rank weeds take strong root in a fertile soil, vigorous powers not unfrequently produce fatal mistakes and pernicious exertions; that character is the product of a lively and constant affection - may, possibly, discover in these Memoirs traces of reflection, and of some attention to the phænomena of the human mind.

Whether the incidents, or the characters, are copied from life, is of little importance - The only question is, if the *circumstances*, and situations, are altogether improbable? If not - whether the consequences might *not* have followed from the circumstances? - This is a grand question, applicable to all the purposes of education, morals, and legislation - *and on this I rest my moral* - 'Do men gather figs of thorns, or grapes of thistles?' asked a moralist and a reformer.

Every *possible* incident, in works of this nature, might, perhaps, be rendered *probable*, were a sufficient regard paid to the more minute, delicate, and connecting links of the chain. Under this impression, I chose, as the least arduous, a simple story - and, even in that, the fear of repetition, of prolixity, added, it may be, to a portion of indolence, made me, in some parts, neglectful of this rule: - yet, in tracing the character of my heroine from her birth, I had it in view. For the conduct of my hero, I consider myself less responsible - it was not *his* memoirs that I professed to write.

I am not sanguine respecting the success of this little publication. It is truly observed, by the writer of a late popular novel[1] - 'That an author, whether good or bad, or between both, is an animal whom every body is privileged to attack; for, though all are not able to write books, all conceive themselves able to judge them. A bad composition carries with it its own punishment - contempt and ridicule: - a good one excites envy, and (frequently) entails upon its author a thousand mortifications.'

To the feeling and the thinking few, this production of an active mind, in a season of impression, rather than of leisure, is presented.

1: The Monk.

VOLUME I

To Augustus Harley

Rash young man! - why do you tear from my heart the affecting narrative, which I had hoped no cruel necessity would ever have forced me to review? - Why do you oblige me to recall the bitterness of my past life, and to renew images, the remembrance of which, even at this distant period, harrows up my soul with inconceivable misery? - But your happiness is at stake, and every selfish consideration vanishes. - Dear and sacred deposit of an adored and lost friend! - for whose sake I have consented to hold down, with struggling, suffocating reluctance, the loathed and bitter portion of existence; - shall I expose your ardent mind to the incessant conflict between truth and error - shall I practise the disingenuousness, by which my peace has been blasted - shall I suffer you to run the wild career of passion - shall I keep back the recital, written upon my own mind in characters of blood, which may preserve the child of my affections from destruction?

Ah! why have you deceived me? - Has a six months' absence obliterated from your remembrance the precept I so earnestly and incessantly laboured to inculcate - the value and importance of unequivocal sincerity? A precept, which I now take shame to myself for not having more implicitly observed! Had I supposed your affection for Joanna more than a boyish partiality; had I not believed that a few months' absence would entirely erase it from your remembrance; had I not been assured that her heart was devoted to another object, a circumstance of which she had herself frankly informed you; I should not now have distrusted your fortitude, when obliged to wound your feelings with the intelligence - that the woman, whom you have so wildly persecuted, was, yesterday, united to another.

To The Same

I resume my pen. Your letter, which Joanna a few days since put into my hands, has cost me - Ah! my Augustus, my friend, my son - what has it not cost me, and what impressions has it not renewed? I perceive the vigour of your mind with terror and exultation. But you are mistaken! Were it not for the insuperable barrier that separates you, for ever, from your hopes, perseverance itself, however active, however incessant, may fail in attaining its object. Your ardent reasoning, my interesting and philosophic young friend, though not unconsequential, is a finely proportioned structure, resting on an airy foundation. The science of morals is not incapable of demonstration, but we want a more extensive knowledge of particular facts, on which, in any given circumstance, firmly to establish our data. - Yet, be not discouraged; exercise your understanding, think freely, investigate every opinion, disdain the rust of antiquity, raise systems, invent hypotheses, and, by the absurdities they involve, seize on the clue of truth. Rouse the nobler energies of your mind; be not the slave of your passions, neither dream of eradicating them. Sensation generates interest, interest passion, passion forces attention, attention supplies the powers, and affords the means of attaining its end: in proportion to the degree of interest, will be that of attention and power. Thus are talents produced. Every man is born with sensation, with the aptitude of receiving impressions; the force of those impressions depends on a thousand circumstances, over which he has little power; these circumstances form the mind, and determine the future character. We are all the creatures of education; but in that education, what we call chance, or accident, has so great a share, that the wisest preceptor, after all his cares, has reason to tremble: one strong affection, one ardent incitement, will turn, in an instant, the whole current of our thoughts, and introduce a new train of ideas and associations.

You may perceive that I admit the general truths of your reasoning; but I would warn you to be careful in their particular application; a long train of patient and laborious experiments must precede our deductions and conclusions. The science of mind is not less demonstrative, and far more important, than the science of Newton; but we must proceed on similar principles. The term *metaphysics* has been, perhaps, justly defined - *the first principles of arts and sciences.*[2] Every discovery of genius, resulting from a fortunate combination of circumstances, may be resolved into simple facts; but in this investigation we must be patient, attentive, indefatigable; we must be content to arrive at truth through many painful mistakes and consequent sufferings. - Such appears to be the constitution of man!

To shorten and meliorate your way, I have determined to sacrifice every inferior consideration. I have studied your character: I perceive, with joy, that its errors are the ardent excesses of a generous mind. I loved your father with a fatal and unutterable tenderness: time has softened the remembrance of his faults. - Our noblest qualities, without incessant watchfulness, are liable insensibly to shade into vices - but his virtues and *misfortunes*, in which my own were so intimately blended, are indelibly engraven on my heart.

2. *Helvetius.*

A mystery has hitherto hung over your birth. The victim of my own ardent passions, and the errors of one whose memory will ever be dear to me, I prepare to withdraw the veil - a veil, spread by an importunate, but, I fear, a mistaken tenderness. Learn, then, from the incidents of my life, entangled with those of his to whom you owe your existence, a more striking and affecting lesson than abstract philosophy can ever afford.

CHAPTER I

The events of my life have been few, and have in them nothing very uncommon, but the effects which they have produced on my mind; yet, that mind they have helped to form, and this in the eye of philosophy, or affection, may render them not wholly uninteresting. While I trace them, they convince me of the irresistible power of circumstances, modifying and controlling our characters, and introducing, mechanically, those associations and habits which make us what we are; for without outward impressions we should be nothing.

I know not how far to go back, nor where to begin; for in many cases, it may be in all, a foundation is laid for the operations of our minds, years - nay, ages - previous to our birth. I wish to be brief, yet to omit no one connecting link in the chain of causes, however minute, that I conceive had any important consequences in the formation of my mind, or that may, probably, be useful to your's.

My father was a man of some talents, and of a superior rank in life, but dissipated, extravagant, and profligate. My mother, the daughter of a rich trader, and the sole heiress of his fortunes, allured by the specious address and fashionable manners of my father, sacrificed to empty shew the prospect of rational and dignified happiness. My father courted her hand to make himself master of her ample possessions: dazzled by vanity, and misled by self-love, she married him; - found, when too late, her error; bitterly repented, and died in child bed the twelfth month of her marriage, after having given birth to a daughter, and commended it, with her dying breath, to the care of a sister (the daughter of her mother by a former marriage), an amiable, sensible, and worthy woman, who had, a few days before, lost a lovely and promising infant at the breast, and received the little Emma as a gift from heaven, to supply its place.

My father, plunged in expense and debauchery, was little moved by these domestic distresses. He held the infant a moment in his arms, kissed it, and willingly consigned it to the guardianship of its maternal aunt.

It will here be necessary to give a sketch of the character, situation, and family, of this excellent woman; each of which had an important share in forming the mind of her charge to those dispositions, and feelings, which irresistibly led to the subsequent events.

CHAPTER II

Mr and Mrs Melmoth, my uncle and aunt, married young, purely from motives of affection. Mr Melmoth had an active, ardent mind, great benevolence of heart, a sweet and chearful temper, and a liberal manner of thinking, though with few advantages of education: he possessed, also, a sanguine disposition, a warm heart, a generous spirit, and an integrity which was never called in question. Mrs Melmoth's frame was delicate and fragile; she had great sensibility, quickness of perception, some anxiety of temper, and a refined and romantic manner of thinking, acquired from the perusal of the old romances, a large quantity of which, belonging to a relation, had, in the early periods of her youth, been accidentally deposited in a spare room in her father's house. These qualities were mingled with a devotional spirit, a little bordering on fanatacism. My uncle did not exactly resemble an Orlando, or an Oroondates, but he was fond of reading; and having the command of a ship in the West India trade, had, during his voyages in fine weather, time to indulge in this propensity; by which means he was a tolerable proficient in the belles lettres, and could, on occasion, quote Shakespeare, scribble poetry, and even philosophize with Pope and Bolingbroke.

Mr Melmoth was one-and-twenty, his bride nineteen, when they were united. They possessed little property; but the one was enterprizing and industrious, the other careful and œconomical; and both, with hearts glowing with affection for each other, saw cheering hope and fairy prospects dancing before their eyes. Every thing succeeded beyond their most sanguine expectations. My uncle's cheerful and social temper, with the fairness and liberality of his dealings, conciliated the favour of the merchants. His understanding was superior, and his manners more courteous, than the generality of persons in his line of life: his company was eagerly courted, and no vessel stood a chance of being freighted till his had its full cargo.

His voyages were not long, and frequent absences and meetings kept alive between him and my aunt, the hopes, the fears, the anxieties, and the transports of love. Their family soon increased, but this was a new source of joy to Mr Melmoth's affectionate heart. A walk or a ride in the country, with his wife and little ones, he accounted his highest relaxation: - on these occasions he gave himself up to a sweet and lively pleasure; would clasp them alternately to his breast, and with eyes overflowing with tears of delight, repeat Thomson's charming description of the joys of virtuous love -

> 'Where nothing strikes the eye but sights of bliss,
> All various nature pressing on the heart!'

This was the first picture that struck my young imagination, for I was, in all respects, considered as the adopted child of the family.

This prosperity received little other interruption than from my uncle's frequent absences, and the pains and cares of my aunt in bringing into the world, and nursing, a family of children. Mr Melmoth's successful voyages, at rather earlier than forty years of age, enabled him to leave the sea, and to carry on an extensive mercantile employment in the metropolis. - At this period his health began to be injured by the progress of a threatening internal disorder; but it had little effect either on his spirits or activity. His business every day became wider, and his attention to it was unremitted, methodical, and indefatigable. His hours of relaxation were devoted to his family and social enjoyment; at these times he never suffered the cares of the counting-house to intrude; - he was the life of every company, and the soul of every pleasure.

He at length assumed a more expensive style of living; took a house in the country (for the charms of which he had ever a peculiar taste) as a summer residence; set up an equipage, increased the number of his servants, and kept an open and hospitable, though not a luxurious, table.

The hours fled on downy pinions; his wife rested on him, his children caught sunshine from his smiles; his domestics adored him, and his acquaintance vied with each other in paying him respect. His life, he frequently repeated, had been a series of unbroken success. His religion, for he laid no stress on forms, was a sentiment of grateful and fervent love. - '*God is love,*' he would say, 'and the affectionate, benevolent heart is his temple.'

CHAPTER III

It will now be necessary, for the development of my own particular character, again to revert to earlier periods. - A few days before my birth, my aunt had lost (as already related) a lovely female infant, about four months old, and she received me, from the hands of my dying mother, as a substitute. - From these tender and affecting circumstances I was nursed and attended with peculiar care. My uncle's ship (it being war time) was then waiting for a convoy at Portsmouth, where he was joined by his wife: she carried me with her, and, tenderly watchful over my safety, took me on all their little excursions, whether by sea or land: I hung at her breast, or rested in her arms, and her husband, or attendant, alternately relieved her. - Plump, smiling, placid, happy, I never disturbed her rest, and the little Emma was the darling of her kind guardians, and the plaything of the company.

At the age at which it was thought necessary to wean me, I was sent from my tender nurse for that purpose, and consigned to the care of a stranger, with whom I quickly pined myself into a jaundice and bilious fever. My aunt dare not visit me during this short separation, she was unable to bear my piercing cries of anguish at her departure. If a momentary sensation, at that infantine period, deserve the appellation, I might call this my first affectionate sorrow. I have frequently thought that the tenderness of this worthy woman generated in my infant disposition that susceptibility, that lively propensity to attachment, to which I have through life been a martyr. On my return to my friends, I quickly regained my health and spirits; was active, blythsome, ran, bounded, sported, romped; always light, gay, alert, and full of glee. At church, (whither on Sunday I was accustomed to accompany the family) I offended all the pious ladies in our vicinity by my gamesome tricks, and avoided the reprimands of my indulgent guardians by the drollery and good humour which accompanied them.

When myself and my little cousins had wearied ourselves with play, their mother, to keep us quiet in an evening, while her husband wrote letters in an adjoining apartment, was accustomed to relate (for our entertainment) stories from the Arabian Nights, Turkish Tales, and other works of like marvellous import. She recited them circumstantially, and these I listened to with ever new delight: the more they excited vivid emotions, the more wonderful they were, the greater was my transport: they became my favourite amusement, and produced, in my young mind, a strong desire of learning to read the books which contained such enchanting stores of entertainment.

Thus stimulated, I learned to read quickly, and with facility. My uncle took pleasure in assisting me; and, with parental partiality, thought he discovered, in the ardour and promptitude with which I received his instructions, the dawn of future talents. At six years old I read aloud before company, with great applause, my uncle's favourite authors, Pope's Homer, and Thomson's Seasons, little comprehending either. Emulation was roused, and vanity fostered: I learned to recite verses, to modulate my tones of voice, and began to think myself a wonderful scholar.

Thus, in peace and gaiety, glided the days of my childhood. Caressed by my aunt, flattered by her husband, I grew vain and self-willed; my desires were impetuous, and brooked no delay; my affections were warm, and my temper irascible; but it was the glow of a moment, instantly subsiding on conviction, and when conscious of having committed injustice, I was ever eager to repair it, by a profusion of caresses and acknowledgements. Opposition would always make me vehement, and coercion irritated me to violence; but a kind look, a gentle word, a cool expostulation - softened, melted, arrested, me, in the full career of passion. Never, but once, do I recollect having received a blow; but the boiling rage, the cruel tempest, the deadly vengeance it excited, in my mind, I now remember with shuddering.

Every day I became more attached to my books; yet, not less fond of active play; stories were still my passion, and I sighed for a romance that would never end. In my sports with my companions, I acted over what I had read: I was alternately the valiant knight - the gentle damsel - the adventurous mariner - the daring robber - the courteous lover - and the airy coquet. Ever inventive, my young friends took their tone from me. I hated the needle: - my aunt was indulgent, and not an hour passed unamused: - my resources were various, fantastic, and endless. Thus, for the first twelve years of my life, fleeted my days in joy and innocence. I ran like the hind, frisked like the kid, sang like the lark, was full of vivacity, health, and animation; and, excepting some momentary bursts of passion and impatience, awoke every day to new enjoyment, and retired to rest fatigued with pleasure.

CHAPTER IV

At this period, by the command of my father, I was sent to boarding school. - Ah! never shall I forget the contrast I experienced. I was an alien and a stranger; - no one loved, caressed, nor cared for me; - my actions were all constrained; - I was obliged to sit poring over needle work, and forbidden to prate; - my body was tortured into forms, my mind coerced, and talks imposed upon me, grammar and French, mere words, that conveyed to me no ideas. I loved my guardians with passion - my tastes were all passions - they tore themselves from my embraces with difficulty. I sat down, after their departure, and wept - bitter tears - sobbed convulsively - my griefs were unheeded, and my sensibility ridiculed - I neither gave nor received pleasure. After the rude stare of curiosity, ever wounding to my feelings, was gratified, I was left to sob alone.

At length, one young lady, with a fair face and a gentle demeanour, came and seated herself beside me. She spoke, in a soft voice, words of sympathy - my desolate heart fluttered at the sound. I looked at her - her features were mild and sweet; I dried my tears, and determined that she should be my friend. - My spirits became calmer, and for a short time I indulged in this relief; but, on enquiry, I found my fair companion had already a selected favourite, and that their amity was the admiration of the school. - Proud, jealous, romantic - I could not submit to be the second in her esteem - I shunned her, and returned her caresses with coldness.

The only mitigation I now felt to the anguish that had seized my spirits, was in the hours of business. I was soon distinguished for attention and capacity; but my governness being with-held, by an infirm constitution, from the duties of her office, I was consigned, with my companions, to ignorant, splenetic, teachers, who encouraged not my emulation, and who sported with the acuteness of my sensations. In the intervals from school hours I sought and procured books. - These were often wantonly taken from me, as a punishment for the most trivial offence; and, when my indignant spirit broke out into murmurs and remonstrance, I was constrained to learn, by way of penance, chapters in the Proverbs of Solomon, or verses from the French testament. To revenge myself, I satirized my tyrants in doggrel rhymes: my writing master also came in for a share of this little malice; and my productions, wretched enough, were handed round the school with infinite applause. Sunk in sullen melancholy, in the hours of play I crept into corners, and disdained to be amused; - home appeared to me to be the Eden from which I was driven, and there my heart and thoughts incessantly recurred.

My uncle from time to time addressed to me - with little presents - kind, pleasant, affectionate notes - and these I treasured up as sacred relics. A visit of my guardians was a yet more tumultuous pleasure; but it always left me in increased anguish. Some robberies had been committed on the road to town. - After parting with my friends, I have laid awake the whole night, conjuring up in my imagination all the tragic accidents I had ever heard or read of, and persuading myself some of them must have happened to these darling objects of my affection.

Thus passed the first twelvemonth of my exile from all I loved; during which time it was reported, by my school-fellows, that I had never been seen to smile. After the vacations, I was carried back to my prison with agonizing reluctance, to which in the second year I became, however, from habit, better reconciled. I learned music, was praised and encouraged by my master, and grew fond of it; I contracted friendships, and regained my vivacity; from a forlorn, unsocial, being, I became, once more, lively, active, enterprising, - the soul of all amusement, and the leader of every innocently mischievous frolic. At the close of another year I left school. I kept up a correspondence for some time with a few of my young friends, and my effusions were improved and polished by my paternal uncle.

CHAPTER V

This period, which I had anticipated with rapture, was soon clouded by the gradual decay, and premature death, of my revered and excellent guardian. He sustained a painful and tedious sickness with unshaken fortitude; - with more, with chearfulness. I knelt by his bedside on the day of his decease; and, while I bathed his hand with my tears, caught hope from the sweet, the placid, serenity of his countenance, and could not believe the terrors of dissolution near.

'The last sentiment of my heart,' said he, 'is gratitude to the Being who has given me so large a portion of good; and I resign my family into his hands with confidence.'

He awoke from a short slumber, a few minutes before his death. - 'Emma,' said he, in a faint voice, (as I grasped his cold hand between both mine) turning upon me a mild, yet dying, eye, 'I have had a pleasant sleep - Be a good girl, and comfort your aunt!' -

He expired without a groan, or a struggle - 'His death was the serene evening of a beautiful day!' I gazed on his lifeless remains, the day before their interment, and the features still wore the same placid, smiling benignity. I was then about fourteen years of age, - this first emotion of real sorrow rent my heart asunder!

The sensations of Mrs Melmoth were those of agonizing, suffocating anguish: - the fair prospect of domestic felicity was veiled for ever! This was the second strong impression which struck my opening mind. Many losses occurred, in consequence of foreign connections, in the settlement of Mr Melmoth's affairs. - The family found their fortunes scanty, and their expectations limited: - their numerous fair-professing acquaintance gradually deserted them, and they sunk into œconomical retirement; but they continued to be respectable, because they knew how to contract their wants, and to preserve their independence.

My aunt, oppressed with sorrow, could be roused only by settling the necessary plans for the future provision of her family. Occupied with these concerns, or absorbed in grief, we were left for some time to run wild. Months revolved ere the tender sorrows of Mrs Melmoth admitted of any mitigation: they at length yielded only to tender melancholy. My wonted amusements were no more; a deep gloom was spread over our once cheerful residence; my avidity for books daily increased; I subscribed to a circulating library, and frequently read, or rather devoured - little careful in the selection - from ten to fourteen novels in a week

CHAPTER VI

My father satisfied himself, after the death of my beloved uncle, with making a short and formal visit of condolence to the family, and proposing either my return to school, or to pay an annual stipend (which Mr and Mrs Melmoth had hitherto invariably refused) for defraying the expenses of my continuance and board with the amiable family by which I had been so kindly nurtured. I shrunk from the cold and careless air of a man whom I had never been able to teach my heart either to love or honour; and throwing my arms round the neck of my maternal aunt, murmured a supplication, mingled with convulsive sobs, that she would not desert me. She returned my caresses affectionately, and entreated my father to permit me to remain with her; adding, that it was her determination to endeavour to rouse and strengthen her mind, for the performance of those pressing duties - the education of her beloved children, among whom she had ever accounted her Emma - which now devolved wholly upon her.

My father made no objection to this request; but observed, that notwithstanding he had a very favourable opinion of her heart and understanding, and considered himself indebted to her, and to her deceased husband, for their goodness to Emma, he was nevertheless apprehensive that the girl had been weakened and spoiled by their indulgence; - that his own health was at present considerably injured; - that it was probable he might not survive many years; - in which case, he frankly confessed, he had enjoyed life too freely to be able to make much provision for his daughter. It would therefore, he conceived, be more judicious to prepare and strengthen my mind to encounter, with fortitude, some hardships and rude shocks, to which I might be exposed, than to foster a sensibility, which he already perceived, with regret, was but too acute. For which purpose, he desired I might spend one day in every week at his house in Berkley square, when he should put such books into my hands [he had been informed I had a tolerable capacity] as he judged would be useful to me; and, in the intervals of his various occupations and amusements, assist me himself with occasional remarks and reflections. Any little accomplishments which Mrs Melmoth might judge necessary for, and suitable to, a young woman with a small fortune, and which required the assistance of a master, he would be obliged to her if she would procure for me, and call upon him to defray the additional expense.

He then, looking on his watch, and declaring he had already missed an appointment, took his leave, after naming Monday as the day on which he should constantly expect my attendance in Berkley square.

Till he left the room I had not courage to raise my eyes from the ground - my feelings were harrowed up - the tone of his voice was discordant to my ears. The

18

only idea that alleviated the horror of my weekly punishment (for so I considered the visits to Berkley square) was the hope of reading new books, and of being suffered to range uncontrolled through an extensive and valuable library, for such I had been assured was Mr Courtney's. I still retained my passion for adventurous tales, which, even while at school, I was enabled to gratify by means of one of the day-boarders, who procured for me romances from a neighbouring library, which at every interval of leisure I perused with inconceivable avidity.

CHAPTER VII

The following Monday I prepared to attend Mr Courtney. On arriving at his house, and announcing my name, a servant conducted me into his master's dressing-room. I appeared before him with trembling steps, downcast eyes, and an averted face.

'Look up, child!' said my father, in an imperious tone. 'If you are conscious of no crime, why all this ridiculous confusion?'

I struggled with my feelings: the tone and manner in which I was addressed gave me an indignant sensation: - a deeper suffusion than that of modesty, the glow of wounded pride, burnt in my cheeks: - I turned quick, gazed in the face of Mr Courtney with a steady eye, and spoke a few words, in a firm voice, importing - that I attended by his desire, and waited his direction.

He regarded me with somewhat less *hauteur*, and, while he finished dressing, interrogated me respecting the books I had read, and the impression they had left on my mind. I replied with simplicity, and without evasion. He soon discovered that my imagination had been left to wander unrestrained in the fairy fields of fiction; but that, of historical facts, and the science of the world, I was entirely ignorant.

'It is as I apprehended,' said he: - 'your fancy requires a *rein* rather than a *spur*. Your studies, for the future, must be of a soberer nature, or I shall have you mistake my valet for a prince in disguise, my house for a haunted castle, and my rational care for your future welfare for barbarous tyranny.'

I felt a poignant and suffocating sensation, too complicated to bear analyzing, and followed Mr Courtney in silence to the library. My heart bounded when, on entering a spacious room, I perceived on either side a large and elegant assortment of books, regularly arranged in glass cases, and I longed to be left alone, to expatiate freely in these treasures of entertainment. But I soon discovered, to my inexpressible mortification, that the cases were locked, and that in this intellectual feast I was not to be my own purveyor. My father, after putting into my hands the lives of Plutarch, left me to my meditations; informing me, that he should probably dine at home with a few friends, at five o'clock, when he should expect my attendance at the table.

I opened my book languidly, after having examined through the glass doors the titles of those which were with-held from me. I felt a kind of disgust to what I considered as a task imposed, and read a few pages carelessly, gazing at intervals through the windows into the square. - But my attention, as I proceeded, was soon forcibly arrested, my curiosity excited, and my enthusiasm awakened. The hours passed rapidly - I perceived not their flight - and at five o'clock, when summoned to dinner, I went down into the dining-room, my mind pervaded with republican ardour, my sentiments elevated by a high-toned philosophy, and my bosom glowing with the virtues of patriotism.

I found with Mr Courtney company of both sexes, to whom he presented me on my entrance. Their easy compliments disconcerted me, and I shrunk, abashed, from the bold and curious eyes of the gentlemen. During the repast I ate little, but listened in silence to every thing that passed.

The theatres were the first topic of conversation, *Venice Preserved* had been acted the preceding evening, and from discussing the play, the conversation took a political turn. A gentleman that happened to be seated next me, who spoke fluently, looking around him every moment for approbation, with apparent self-applause, gave the discourse a tone of gallantry, declaring - 'Pierre to be a noble fellow, and that the loss of a mistress was a sufficient excuse for treason and conspiracy, even though the country had been deluged in blood and involved in conflagration.'

'And the mistresses of all his fellow citizens destroyed of course;' - said a gentleman coolly, on the opposite side of the table.

Oh! that was not a consideration, every thing must give place when put in competition with certain feelings. 'What, young lady,' (suddenly turning to me) 'do you think a lover would not risque, who was in fear of losing you?'

Good God! what a question to an admirer of the grecian heroes! I started, and absolutely shuddered. I would have replied, but my words died away upon my lips in inarticulate murmurs. My father observed and enjoyed my distress.

'The worthies of whom you have been reading, Emma, lived in ancient times. Aristides the just, would have made but a poor figure among our modern men of fashion!'

'This lady reads, then,' - said our accomplished coxcomb - 'Heavens, Mr Courtney! you will spoil all her feminine graces; knowledge and learning, are unsufferably masculine in a woman - born only for the soft solace of man! The mind of a young lady should be clear and unsullied, like a sheet of white paper, or her own fairer face: lines of thinking destroy the dimples of beauty; aping the reason of man, they lose the exquisite, *fascinating* charm, in which consists their true empire; - Then strongest, when most weak -

> *"Loveliest in their fears -*
> *And by this silent adulation, soft,*
> *To their protection more engaging man."*

'Pshaw!' replied Mr Courtney, a little peevishly - 'you will persuade Emma, that the age of chivalry is not yet over; and that giants and ravishers are as common now, as in the time of Charlemagne: a young woman of sense and spirit needs no other protection; do not flatter the girl into affectation and imbecility. If blank paper be your passion, you can be at no loss; the town will supply quires and reams.'

'There I differ from you,' said the gentleman on the opposite side of the table; 'to preserve the mind a blank, we must be both deaf and blind, for, while any inlet to perception remains, your paper will infallibly contract characters of some kind, or be blotted and scrawled!'

'For God's sake! do not let us begin to philosophise,' retorted his antagonist, who was not to be easily silenced.

'I agree with you,' - rejoined the other - '*thinking* is undoubtedly very laborious, and *principle* equally troublesome and impertinent.'

I looked at him as he finished speaking, and caught his eye for a moment; its expression methought was doubtful. The man of fashion continued to expatiate in rhetorical periods - He informed us, that he had fine feelings, but they never extended beyond selfish gratification. For his part, he had as much humanity as any man, for which reason he carefully avoided the scene or the tale of distress. He, likewise, had his opinions, but their pliability rendered them convenient to himself, and accommodating to his friends. He had courage to sustain fatigue and hardship, when, not his country, but vanity demanded the exertion. It was glorious to boast of having travelled two hundred miles in eight and forty hours, and sat up three nights, to be present, on two succeeding evenings, at a ball in distant counties.

'This man,' I said to myself, while I regarded him with a look of ineffable scorn - 'takes a great deal of pains to render himself ridiculous, he surely must have a vile heart, or a contemptible opinion of mankind: if he be really the character he describes, he is a compound of atrocity and folly, and a pest to the world; if he slanders himself, what must be that state of society, the applause of which he persuades himself is to be thus acquired?' I sighed deeply; - in either case the reflection was melancholy; - my eyes enquired - 'Am I to hate or to despise you?' I know not whether he understood their language, but he troubled me no more with his attentions.

I reflected a little too seriously: - I have since seen many a prating, superficial coxcomb, who talks to display his oratory - *mere words* - repeated by rote, to which few ideas are affixed, and which are uttered and received with equal apathy.

CHAPTER VIII

During three years, I continued my weekly visits to Berkley square; I was not always allowed to join the parties who assembled there, neither indeed would it have been proper, for they were a motley group; when permitted so to do, I collected materials for reflection. I had been educated by my aunt, in strict principles of religion; many of Mr Courtney's friends were men of wit and talents, who, occasionally, discussed important subjects with freedom and ability: I never ventured to mingle in the conversations, but I overcame my timidity sufficiently to behave with propriety and composure; I listened attentively to all that was said, and my curiosity was awakened to philosophic enquiries.

Mr Courtney now entrusted me with the keys of the bookcases, through which I ranged with ever new delight. I went through, by my father's direction, a course of historical reading, but I could never acquire a taste for this species of composition. Accounts of the early periods of states and empires, of the Grecian and Roman republics, I pursued with pleasure and enthusiasm: but when they became more complicated, grew corrupt, luxurious, licentious, perfidious, mercenary, I turned from them fatigued, and disgusted, and sought to recreate my spirits in the fairer regions of poetry and fiction.

My early associations rendered theology an interesting subject to me; I read ecclesiastical history, a detail of errors and crimes, and entered deeply into polemic divinity: my mind began to be emancipated, doubts had been suggested to it, I reasoned freely, endeavoured to arrange and methodize my opinions, and to trace them fearlessly through all their consequences: while from exercising my thoughts with freedom, I seemed to acquire new strength and dignity of character. I met with some of the writings of Descartes, and was seized with a passion for metaphysical enquiries. I began to think about the nature of the soul - whether it was a composition of the elements, the result of organized matter, or a subtle and etherial fire.

In the course of my researches, the Heloise of Rousseau fell into my hands. - Ah! with what transport, with what enthusiasm, did I peruse this dangerous, enchanting, work! - How shall I paint the sensations that were excited in my mind! - the pleasure I experienced approaches the limits of pain - it was tumult - all the ardour of my character was excited. - Mr Courtney, one day, surprised me weeping over the sorrows of the tender St Preux. He hastily snatched the book from my hand, and, carefully collecting the remaining volumes, carried them in silence to his chamber: but the impression made on my mind was never to be effaced - it was even productive of a long chain of consequences, that will continue to operate till the day of my death.

My time at this period passed rapidly and pleasantly. My father never treated me with affection; but the austerity of his manner gradually subsided. He gave me, occasionally, useful hints and instructions. Without feeling for him any tenderness, he inspired me with a degree of respect. The library was a source of lively and inexhaustible pleasure to my mind; and, when admitted to the table of Mr Courtney, some new character or sentiment frequently sharpened my attention, and afforded me subjects for future enquiry and meditation. I delighted to expatiate, when returning to the kind and hospitable mansion of my beloved aunt, (which I still considered as my home) on the various topics which I had collected in my little emigrations. I was listened to by my cousins with a pleasure that flattered my vanity, and looked up to as a kind of superior being; - a homage particularly gratifying to a young mind.

CHAPTER IX

The excellent woman, who had been my more than mother, took infinite pains to cure the foibles, which, like pernicious weeds, entangled themselves with, and sometimes threatened to choak, the embryo blossoms of my expanding mind. Ah! with what pleasure do I recall her beloved idea to my memory! Fostered by her maternal love, and guided by her mild reason, how placid, and how sweet, were my early days! - Why, my first, my tenderest friend, did I lose you at that critical period of life, when the harmless sports and occupations of childhood gave place to the pursuits, the passions and the errors of youth? - With the eloquence of affection, with gentle, yet impressive persuasion, thou mightest have checked the wild career of energetic feeling, which thou hast so often remarked with hope and terror.

As I entered my eighteenth year, I lost, by a premature death, this tender monitor. Never shall I forget her last emphatic, affectionate, caution.

'Beware, my dear Emma,' said this revered friend, 'beware of strengthening, by indulgence, those ardent and impetuous sensations, which, while they promise vigour of mind, fill me with apprehension for the virtue, for the happiness of my child. I wish not that the canker-worm, Distrust, should blast the fair fruit of your ripening virtues. The world contains many benevolent, many disinterested, spirits; but civilization is yet distempered and imperfect; the inequalities of society, by fostering artificial wants, and provoking jealous competitions, have generated selfish and hostile passions. Nature has been vainly provident for her offspring, while man, with mistaken avidity, grasping more than he has powers to enjoy, preys on his fellow man: - departing from simple virtues, and simple pleasures, in their stead, by common consent, has a wretched semblance been substituted. Endeavour to contract your wants, and aspire only to a rational independence; by exercising your faculties, still the importunate suggestions of your sensibility; preserve your sincerity, cherish the ingenuous warmth of unsophisticated feeling, but let discernment precede confidence. I tremble even for the excess of those virtues which I have laboured to cultivate in your lively and docile mind. If I could form a wish for longer life, it is only for my children, and that I might be to my Emma instead of reason, till her own stronger mind matures. I dread, lest the illusions of imagination should render those powers, which would give force to truth and virtue, the auxiliaries of passion. Learn to distinguish, with accuracy, the good and ill qualities of those with whom you may mingle: while you abhor the latter, separate the being from his errors; and while you revere the former, the moment that your reverence becomes personal, that moment, suspect that your judgment is in danger of becoming the dupe of your affections.'

Would to God that I had impressed upon my mind - that I had recalled to my remembrance more frequently - a lesson so important to a disposition like mine! - a continual victim to the enthusiasm of my feelings; incapable of approving, or disapproving, with moderation - the most poignant sufferings, even the study of mankind, have been insufficient to dissolve the powerful enchantment, to disentangle the close-twisted associations! - But I check this train of overwhelming reflection, that is every moment on the point of breaking the thread of my narration, and obtruding itself to my pen.

CHAPTER X

Mr Courtney did not long survive the guardian of my infancy: - his constitution had for some years been gradually impaired; and his death was hastened by a continuance of habitual dissipation, which he had not the resolution to relinquish, and to which his strength was no longer equal. It was an event I had long anticipated, and which I contemplated with a sensation of solemnity, rather than of grief. The ties of blood are weak, if not the mere chimeras of prejudice, unless sanctioned by reason, or cemented by habits of familiar and affectionate intercourse. Mr Courtney refusing the title of father, from a conviction that his conduct gave him no claim to this endearing appellation, had accustomed me to feel for him only the respect due to some talents and good qualities, which threw a veil over his faults. Courage and truth were the principles with which he endeavoured to inspire me; - precepts, which I gratefully acknowledge, and which forbid me to adopt the language of affection, when no responsive sympathies exist in the heart.

My eyes were yet moist with the tears that I had shed for the loss of my maternal friend, when I received a hasty summons to Berkley square. A servant informed me, that his master was, at length, given over by his physicians, and wished to speak to Miss Courtney, before his strength and spirits were too much exhausted.

I neither felt, nor affected, surprize at this intelligence, but threw myself, without reply, into the carriage which had been dispatched for my conveyance.

On entering the house, a gloomy silence seemed to reign throughout the late festive apartments; but, as I had seldom been a partaker of the festivity, the contrast struck me less forcibly than it might otherwise have done. My name was announced, and I was conducted, by the housekeeper, to the chamber of her dying master, who, supported on pillows, breathed with difficulty, but appeared to be free from pain, and tolerably composed. I met the physician in the ante-chamber; who, on my requesting earnestly to know the situation of his patient, informed me - That an internal mortification had taken place, and that he could not survive many hours.

Approaching the bed, considerably shocked at the intelligence I had received, Mr Courtney, in a low and faint voice, desired me to draw a chair near him. I obeyed in silence.

'Emma,' said he, 'I am about to quit a world, in which I have experienced little sincere enjoyment; yet, I leave it reluctantly. Had I been more temperate in my pleasures, perhaps, they might have been less destructive, and more protracted. I begin to suspect, that I have made some great mistakes; but it is now too late for retraction, and I will not, in my last moments, contradict, by my example, the lesson of fortitude, with which it has been a part of my plan to inspire you. You have now, unprotected, the world to encounter; for, I will frankly confess, that my affection for you has not been strong enough to induce me to forego my own more immediate gratification: but I have never deceived you. Your mother, when she married, reserved for her private expenses a thousand pounds, which, on her deathbed, she desired might be invested in the funds on your account. This request I religiously complied with, and there it has remained untouched; and, being purchased in your name, you may claim it whenever you please. I have appointed you no guardians; for, already in your nineteenth year and possessing an understanding superior to your sex and age, I chose to leave you unfettered, and at your own discretion. I spared from my pleasures what money was requisite to complete your education; for having no fortune to give you, and my health being precarious, I thought it just to afford you every advantage for the improvement of those talents which you evidently possess, and which must now enable you to make your way in the world; for the scanty pittance, that the interest of your fortune will produce, is, I doubt, insufficient for your support. Had I lived, it was my intention to have established you by marriage; but that is a scheme, to which, at present, I would not advise you to trust. Marriage, generally speaking, in the existing state of things, must of necessity be an affair of *finance*. My interest and introduction might have availed you something; but mere merit, wit, or beauty, stand in need of more powerful auxiliaries. My brother, Mr Morton[3], called on me this morning: - he has agreed, for the present, to receive you into his family, where you must endeavour to make yourself useful and agreeable, till you can fix on a better and more independent plan. Finding me in so low a state, your uncle would have waited a few days in town, to have seen the result, and in case of the worst, to have taken you down with him, but pressing business urged his departure. I would advise you, immediately after my decease, to set out for Morton Park. Proper persons are appointed to settle my affairs: - when every thing is turned into money, there will, I trust, be sufficient to discharge my just debts; but do not flatter yourself with the expectation of a surplus. Your presence here, when I am no more, will be equally unnecessary and improper.'

This was said at intervals, and with difficulty; when, seeming quite exhausted, he waved his hand for me to leave the room, and sunk into a sort of dose, or rather stupor, which continued till within some minutes of his decease.

Mr Courtney had been, what is called, a man of pleasure: - he had passed thro' life without ever loving any one but himself - intent, merely, on gratifying

3: *Mr Courtney's brother had taken the name of Morton, to qualify himself for the inheritance of an estate, bequeathed to him by a distant relation.*

the humour of the moment. A superior education, and an attentive observance, not of rational, but, of social man, in an extensive commerce with the world, had sharpened his sagacity; but he was inaccessible to those kindlings of the affections - those glowings of admiration - inspired by real, or fancied, excellence, which never fail to expand and advance the minds of such as are capable of sketching, with a daring hand, the dangerous picture: - or of those philosophic and comprehensive views, which teach us to seek a reflected happiness in benevolent exertions for the welfare of others. My mother, I suspected, had been the victim of her husband's unkindness and neglect: wonder not, then, that my heart revolted when I would have given him the tender appellation of father! If he coldly acknowledged any little merits which I possessed, he regarded them rather with jealousy than approbation; for he felt that they tacitly reproached him.

I will make no comment on the closing scene of his life. Among the various emotions which had rapidly succeeded each other in my mind, during his last address, surprize had no place; I had not then his character to learn.

CHAPTER XI

The small pittance bequeathed to me was insufficient to preserve me from dependence. - *Dependence*! - I repeated to myself, and I felt my heart die within me. I revolved in my mind various plans for my future establishment. - I might, perhaps, be allowed to officiate, as an assistant, in the school where I had been placed in my childhood, with the mistress of which I still kept up an occasional correspondence; but this was a species of servitude, and my mind panted for freedom, for social intercourse, for scenes in motion, where the active curiosity of my temper might find a scope wherein to range and speculate. What could the interest of my little fortune afford? It would neither enable me to live alone, nor even to board in a family of any respectability. My beloved aunt was no more; her children were about to be dispersed, and to form various connections.

Cruel prejudices! - I exclaimed - hapless woman! Why was I not educated for commerce, for a profession, for labour? Why have I been rendered feeble and delicate by bodily constraint, and fastidious by artificial refinement? Why are we bound, by the habits of society, as with an adamantine chain? Why do we suffer ourselves to be confined within a magic circle, without daring, by a magnanimous effort, to dissolve the barbarous spell?

A child in the drama of the world, I knew not which way to turn, nor on what to determine. I wrote to Mr Morton, to enquire on what terms I was to be received by his family. If merely as a visitor for a few weeks, till I had time to digest my plans, I should meet, with pleasure, a gentleman whose character I had been taught to respect; but I should not consider myself as subject to control. I ought, perhaps, to have been satisfied with Mr Morton's answer to my interrogatories.

He wished to embrace the daughter of his brother, his family would be happy to render Morton Park agreeable to her, as long as she should think proper to favour them by making it her residence. The young ladies expected both pleasure and improvement from the society of their accomplished kinswoman, &c.

I believe I was unreasonable, the style of this letter was civil, nay kind, and yet it appeared, to me, to want the vivifying principle - what shall I say? - dictated merely by the head, it reached not the heart.

The trials of my mind, I foreboded, were about to commence, I shrunk from the world I had been so willing to enter, for the rude storms of which I had been little fitted by the fostering tenderness of my early guardians. Those ardent feelings and lively expectations, with all the glowing landscapes which my mind had sketched of the varied pleasures of society, while in a measure secluded from its enjoyments, gradually melted into one deep, undistinguished shade. That sanguine ardour of temper, which had hitherto appeared the predominant feature of my character, now gave place to despondency. I wept, I suffered my tears to flow unrestrained: the solemnity of the late events had seized my spirits, and the approaching change filled me with solicitude. I wandered over the scenes of my past pleasures, and recalled to my remembrance, with a sad and tender luxury, a thousand little incidents, that derived all their importance from the impossibility of their renewal. I gazed on every object, *for the last time* - What is there in these words that awakens our fanaticisms? I could have done homage to these inanimate, and, till now, uninteresting objects; merely because I should *see them no more.*

How fantastic and how capricious are these sentiments! Ought I, or ought I not, to blush while I acknowledge them? My young friends, also, from whom I was about to separate myself! - how various might be our destinies, and how unconscious were we of the future! Happy ignorance, that by bringing the evils of life in succession, gradually inures us to their endurance.

> *'Had I beheld the sum of ills, which one*
> *By one, I have endured - my heart had broke.'*

CHAPTER XII

The hour at length came, when, harrassed in body and in mind, I set out for Morton Park. I travelled alone, and reached the end of my journey at close of day. I entreated Mr Morton, who hastened to hand me from the carriage, and welcome my arrival, that I might be permitted to retire to my apartment, pleading fatigue, and wishing to wave the ceremony of an introduction to the family till the next morning. My request was obligingly granted, and a servant ordered to attend me to my chamber.

Many years had elapsed since I had seen this family, and my judgment was then so immature, that our meeting at the breakfast table had with each of us, I believe, the force of a first impression. You know my *fanaticism* on these occasions. I will attempt an imperfect sketch of the group, assembled in the saloon, to whom I was severally presented on my entrance, by the lord of the domain. Mr Morton, himself, to whom precedence is due, seemed to be about fifty years of age, was of the middle stature, his features regular, and his countenance placid: he spoke but little, but that little was always mild and often judicious. He appeared not to be void of benevolent affections, and had the character of a humane landlord, but his virtues were, in a great measure, sunk in an habitual indolence of temper; he would sometimes sacrifice his principles to his repose, though never to his interest. His lady - no, I will not describe her; her character will, it may be, unfold itself to you in future - Suffice it to say, that her person was gross, her voice loud and discordant, and her features rugged: she affected an air of openness and pleasantry; It may be prejudiced, perhaps she did not *affect it*. Sarah Morton, the eldest of the daughters, was about my age, she was under the middle height, fair, plump, loquacious; there was a childish levity in her accent and manners, which impressed strangers with an unfavourable opinion of her understanding, but it was an acquired manner, for she was shrewd and sensible. Ann, the second daughter was a little lively brunette, with sharp features and sparkling black eyes; volatile, giddy, vain and thoughtless, but good humoured and pretty. The other children were much younger.

Two gentlemen joined us at our repast, visitors at Morton park. Mr Francis, the elder, was in his fortieth year, his figure slender and delicate, his eye piercing, and his manner impressive. It occurred to me, that I had somewhere seen him before, and, after a few minutes recollection, I recognized in him a gentleman who had occasionally visited at my father's, and whom I have already mentioned as the antagonist of the man of fashion, whose sentiments and volubility excited my youthful astonishment and indignation. Mr Montague the younger, the son of a medical gentleman residing in a neighbouring county, seemed about one and twenty, tall, elegantly formed, full of fire and vivacity, with imperious manners, an impetuous temper, and stubborn prejudices.

The introduction of a stranger generally throws some kind of restraint over a company; a break is made in their usual topics and associations, till the disposition and habits of the intruder have, in some degree, unfolded themselves. Mrs Morton took upon herself to entertain; she exhibited her talents on various subjects, with apparent self-approbation, till a few keen remarks from Mr Francis arrested the torrent of her eloquence. The young ladies scrutinized me with attention; even the lively Ann, while she minutely observed me, ceased to court play from Mr Montague, who attended to me with the air, and addressed me in the language of gallantry. I sometimes caught the penetrating eye of Mr Francis, and his glance seemed to search the soul.

After breakfast, Mr Morton having retired to his dressing-room, and the younger part of the company strolling into the pleasure grounds, whither I declined accompanying them, I took an opportunity, being ever desirous of active and useful employment, of offering my assistance to Mrs Morton, in the education of her younger children; proposing to instruct them in the rudiments either of music, drawing, French, or any other accomplishment, for which my own education had capacitated me. Mr Francis remained standing in a window, his back towards us, with a book in his hand, on which he seemed intent.

'If,' replied Mrs Morton, 'it is your wish, Miss Courtney, to procure the situation of governess in any gentleman's family, and it is certainly a very laudable desire in a young woman of your *small fortune*, Mr Morton will, I have no doubt, have it in his power to recommend you: but in the education of my family, I desire no interference; it is an important task, and I have my peculiar notions on the subject: their expectations are not great, and your *elegant* accomplishments might unfit them for their future, probable, stations.'

The manner in which this speech was uttered spoke yet more forcibly than the words. - I felt my cheeks glow.

'I was not asking favours, Madam, I was only desirous of being useful.'

'It is a pity, then, that your discernment had not corrected your vanity.'

The housekeeper entering, to consult her mistress on some domestic occasion, Mrs Morton quitted the room. Mr Francis closed his book, turned round, and gazed earnestly in my face: before sufficiently mortified, his observation, which I felt at this moment oppressive, did not relieve me. I attempted to escape, but, seizing my hand, he detained me by a kind of gentle violence.

'And why this confusion, my dear Miss Courtney; do you blush for having acted with propriety and spirit?' I burst into tears - I could not help it - 'How weak is this, how unworthy of the good sense you have just manifested.'

'I confess it, but I feel myself, at this moment, a poor, a friendless, an unprotected being.'

'What prejudices! poverty is neither criminal, nor disgraceful; you will not want friends, while you continue to deserve them; and as for protection,' (and he smiled) 'I had not expected from Emma Courtney's spirited letter to Mr Morton, and equally proper retort to his lady's impertinence, so plaintive, so feminine a complaint. - You have talents, cultivate them, and learn to rest on your own powers.'

'I thank you for your reproof, and solicit your future lessons.'

'Can you bear the truth?'

'Try me.'

'Have you not cherished a false pride?'

It is too true, thought I, and I sighed.

'How shall I cure this foible?'

'By self-examination, by resolution, and perseverance.'

'Be to me instead of a conscience.'

'What, then, is become of your own?'

'Prejudice, I doubt, has blinded and warped it.'

'I suspect so; but you have energy and candor, and are not, I hope, of a temper to despond.'

The return of the family terminated this singular conversation. The young ladies rallied me, on being found *tête-à-tête* with the philosopher; Mr Montague, I thought looked displeased. I stole out, while the party were dressing for dinner, and rambled into the gardens, which were extensive, and laid out with taste.

CHAPTER XIII

I judged my visit here would not be very long. I scarcely knew whether I was most inclined to like or to fear Mr Francis, but I determined, if possible, to cultivate his friendship. I interrogated myself again and again - From whence this restlessness, this languor, this disgust, with all I hear and see? - Why do I feel wayward, querulous, fastidious? Mr Morton's family had no hearts; they appeared to want a sense, that preyed incessantly on mine; I could not love them, and my heart panted to expand its sensations.

Sarah and Ann became jealous of me, and of each other; the haughty, yet susceptible, Montague addressed each in turn, with a homage equally fervent for the moment, and equally transient. This young man was bold, ardent, romantic, and enterprizing, but blown about by every gust of passion, he appeared each succeeding moment a different character: with a glowing and rapid imagination, he had never given himself time to reason, to compare, to acquire principles: following the bent of a raised, yet capricious fancy, he was ever in pursuit of meteors, that led him into mischief, or phantoms, that dissolved at his approach.

Had my mind been more assured and at ease, I could have amused myself with the whimsical flights of this eccentric being - One hour, attracted by the sportive graces of Ann, he played with and caressed her, while the minutes flew rapidly on the light wing of amusement, and, till reminded by the grave countenance of Mr Morton, seemed to forget that any other person was present. The next minute, disgusted by her frivolity, all his attention was absorbed by the less fascinating, but more artful and ingenious, Sarah. Then, quitting them both, he would pursue my steps, break in upon my meditations, and haunt my retreats, from whence, when not disposed to be entertained by his caprice, I found it not difficult to drive him, by attacking some of his various prejudices: - accustomed to feel, and not to reason, his tastes and opinions were vehement and uncontrollable.

From this society, so uncongenial to my reflecting, reasoning, mind, I found some resource in the conversation of Mr Francis. The pride of Montague was evidently piqued by the decided preference which I gave to the company of his friend; but his homage, or his resentment, were alike indifferent to me: accustomed to speak and act from my convictions, I was but little solicitous respecting the opinion of others. My understanding was exercised by attending to the observations of Mr Francis, and by discussing the questions to which they led; yet it was exercised without being gratified: he opposed and bewildered me, convicted me of error, and harrassed me with doubt.

Mr Francis soon after prepared to return to town. I was affected at the idea of his departure; and felt, that in losing his society, I should be deprived of my only rational recreation, and should again be exposed to Mrs Morton's illiberal attacks, who appeared to have marked me out for her victim, though at present restrained by the presence of a man, who had found means to inspire, even her, with some degree of respect.

Mr Francis, on the evening preceding the day on which he purposed leaving Morton Park, passing under the open window of my chamber, in which I was sitting with a book to enjoy the refreshing breeze, invited me to come down, and accompany him in a ramble. I immediately complied with his request, and joined him in a few minutes, with a countenance clouded with regret at the idea of his quitting us.

'You are going,' said I, as I gave him my hand (which he passed under his arm), 'and I lose my friend and counsellor.'

'Your concern is obliging; but you are capable of standing alone, and your mind, by so doing, will acquire strength.'

'I feel as if this would not be the case: the world appears to me a thorny and pathless wilderness; I step with caution, and look around me with dread. - That I require protection and assistance is, I confess, a proof of weakness, but it is nevertheless true.'

'Mr Montague,' replied he, with some degree of archness in his tone and manner, 'is a gallant knight, a pattern of chivalry, and appears to be particularly calculated for the defender of distressed damsels!'

'I have no inclination to trust myself to the guidance of one, who seems himself entangled in an inextricable maze of error, and whose versatile character affords little basis for confidence.'

'Tell me what it is you fear; - are your apprehensions founded in reason?'

'Recollect my youth, my sex, and my precarious situation.'

'I thought you contemned the plea of sex, as a sanction for weakness!'

'Though I disallow it as a natural, I admit it as an artificial plea.'

'Explain yourself.'

'The character, you tell me, is modified by circumstances: the customs of society, then, have enslaved, enervated, and degraded woman.'

'I understand you: there is truth in your remark, though you have given it undue force.'

I hesitated - my heart was full - I felt as if there were many things which I wished to say; but, however paradoxical, the manners of Mr Francis repressed, while they invited, confidence. I respected his reason, but I doubted whether I could inspire him with sympathy, or make him fully comprehend my feelings. I conceived I could express myself with more freedom on paper; but I had not courage to request a correspondence, when he was silent on the subject. That it would be a source of improvement to me, I could not doubt, but prejudice with-held me from making the proposal. He looked at me, and perceived my mind struggling with a suggestion, to which it dared not give utterance: he suspected the truth, but was unwilling to disturb the operations of my understanding. We walked for some time in silence: - my companion struck into a path that led towards the house - listened to the village clock as it struck nine - and observed, the hour grew late. He had distinguished me, and I was flattered by that distinction; he had supported me against the arrogance of Mrs Morton, retorted the sly sarcasms of Sarah, and even helped to keep the impetuous Montague in awe, and obliged him to rein in his offensive spirit, every moment on the brink of outrage. My heart, formed for grateful attachment, taking, in one instant, a hasty retrospect of the past, and a rapid glance into futurity, experienced at that moment so desolating a pang, that I endeavoured in vain to repress its sensations, and burst into a flood of tears. Mr Francis suddenly stopped, appeared moved, and, with a benevolent aspect and soothing accents, enquired into the cause of an emotion so sudden and unexpected. I wept a few minutes in silence, and my spirits seemed, in some measure, relieved.

'I weep,' (said I), 'because I am *friendless*; to be esteemed and cherished is necessary to my existence; I am an alien in the family where I at present reside, I cannot remain here much longer, and to whom, and whither, shall I go?'

He took my hand - 'I will not, at present, say all that it might be proper to say, because I perceive your mind is in a feeble state; - My affairs call me to London; - yet, there is a method of conversing at a distance.'

I eagerly availed myself of this suggestion, which I had wished, without having the courage to propose.

'Will you, then, allow me, through the medium of pen and paper, to address, to consult you, as I may see occasion?'

'Will I? yes, most cheerfully!'

'Propose your doubts and state your difficulties, and we shall see,' (smiling) 'whether they admit of a solution.'

Thanking him, I engaged to avail myself of this permission, and we proceeded slowly to the house, and joined the party in the supper room. I never once thought of my red and swoln eyes, till Sarah, glancing a look half curious, half sarcastic, towards me, exclaimed from Shakespear, in an affected tone,

'Parting is such sweet sorrow!'

Mr Francis looked at her sternly, she blushed and was silent; Mr Montague was captious; Ann mortified, that she could not by her little tricks gain his attention. Mrs Morton sat wrapped in mock dignity; while Mr Morton, and his philosophic friend, canvassed the principles upon which an horizontal mill was about to be constructed on the estate of the former. After a short and scanty meal, I retired to my apartment, determined to rise early the next morning, and make breakfast for my friend before his departure.

CHAPTER XIV

Mr Francis had ordered his horse to be ready at five o'clock. I left my chamber at four, to have the pleasure of preparing for him the last friendly repast, and of saying *farewell*. He was serene and chearful as usual, I somewhat more pensive; we parted with great cordiality, he gave me his address in town, and engaged me to write to him shortly. I accompanied him through the Park to the porter's lodge, where the servant and horses waited his coming. My eyes glistened as I bade him adieu, and reiterated my wishes for his safety and prosperity, while his features softened into a more than usual benignity, as he returned my salutation.

I wandered thoughtfully back towards the house, but the rich purple that began to illumine the east, the harbinger of the rising sun, the freshness of the morning air, the soft dews which already glittered on every fragrant plant and flower, the solemn stillness, so grateful to the reflecting mind, that pervaded the scene, induced me to prolong my walk. Every object appeared in unison with my feelings, my heart swelled with devotional affections, it aspired to the Author of nature. After having bewildered ourselves amid systems and theories, religion, in such situations, returns to the susceptible mind as a *sentiment* rather than as a principle. A passing cloud let fall a gentle, drizzling shower; sheltered beneath the leafy umbrage of a spreading oak, I rather heard than felt it; yet, the coolness it diffused seemed to quench those ardent emotions, which are but too congenial with my disposition, while the tumult of the passions subsided into a delicious tranquillity.

How mutable are human beings! - A very few hours converted this sublime complacency into perturbation and tumult. Having extended my walk beyond its accustomed limits, on my return, I retired, somewhat fatigued to my apartment, and devoted the morning to my studies. At the dinner hour I joined the family, each individual of which seemed wrapped up in reserve, scarcely deigning to practise the common ceremonies of the occasion. I was not sufficiently interested in the cause of these appearances to make any enquiries, and willingly resigned myself, in the intervals of the entertainment, to meditation.

When the table was cleared, and the servants had withdrawn, perceiving the party not sociably inclined, I was about to retire - when Mrs Morton observed, with features full of a meaning which I did not comprehend, that -

'Their guest, Mr Francis, had, no doubt, left Morton Park gratefully impressed by the *kindness* of Miss Courtney.'

Montague reddened - bit his lips - got up - and sat down again. The young ladies wore an air not perfectly good-humoured, and a little triumphant. Mr Morton looked very solemn.

'I hope so, Madam,' I replied, somewhat carelessly. 'I felt myself indebted to Mr Francis for his civilities, and was solicitous to make him all the return in my power - I wish that power had been enlarged.'

She held up her hands and eyes with an affected, and ridiculous, gesture.

'Mr Francis,' said Montague, abruptly, 'is very happy in having inspired you with sentiments so partial.'

'I am not partial - I am merely just. Mr Francis appeared to me a rational man, and my understanding was exercised and gratified by his conversation.'

I was about to proceed, but my uncle (who seemed to have been tutored for the occasion) interrupted me with much gravity.

'You are but little acquainted, Emma, with the customs of society; there is great indecorum in a young lady's making these distinctions.'

'What distinctions, my dear Sir! - in preferring a reasonable man to fools and coxcombs.'

'Forgive me, my dear - you have a quick wit, but you want experience. I am informed, that you breakfasted with Mr Francis this morning, and attended him through the Park: - this, with your late walk yesterday evening, and evident emotion on your return, let me tell you, child, wears an indecorous appearance: - the world is justly attentive to the conduct of young women, and too apt to be censorious.'

I looked round me with unaffected surprise - 'Good God! - did I suppose, in this family, it was necessary to be upon my guard against malicious constructions?'

'Pray,' - interrupted Sarah, pertly - 'would you not have expressed some surprize, had I shewed Mr Montague similar attentions?'

I looked at her, I believe, a little too contemptuously. - 'Whatever sentiments might have been excited in my mind by the attentions of Miss Morton to Mr Montague, *surprise*, assuredly, would not have been among them.'

She coloured, and Montague's passions began to rise. I stopped him at the beginning of an impertinent harangue, by observing -

'That I did not think myself accountable to him for my conduct; - before I should be solicitous respecting his opinions, he must give me better reasons, than he had hitherto done, to respect his judgment.'

Ann wept, and prattled something, to which nobody thought it worth while to attend.

'Well, Sir,' continued I, turning to Mr Morton, 'be pleased to give me, in detail, what you have to alledge, that I may be enabled to justify myself.'

'Will you allow me to ask you a question?'

'Most certainly.'

'Has Mr Francis engaged you to correspond with him?'

I was silent a few moments.

'You hesitate!'

'Only, Sir, how to answer your question. - I certainly intend myself the pleasure of addressing Mr Francis on paper; but I cannot strictly say *he engaged* me so to do, as it was a proposal he was led to make, by conjecturing my wishes on the subject.'

Again, Mrs Morton, with uplifted hands and eyes - 'What effrontery!'

I seemed not to hear her. - 'Have you any thing more to say, my dear uncle?'

'You are a strange girl. It would not, perhaps, be proper before this company to enquire' - and he stopped.

'Any thing is proper, Sir, to enquire of me, and in any company - I have no reserves, no secrets.'

'Well, then, I think it necessary to inform you, that, though a sensible, well educated, liberal-minded, man, Mr Francis has neither estate nor fortune, nor does he practise any lucrative profession.'

'I am sorry for it, on his own account; and for those whom his generosity might benefit. But, what is it to me?'

'You affect to misunderstand me.'

'I *affect* nothing.'

'I will speak more plainly: - Has he made you any proposals?'

The purport of this solemn, but ludicrous, preparation, at once flashed upon my mind, the first time the thought had ever occurred. I laughed - I could not help it.

'I considered Mr Francis as a *philosopher*, and not as a *lover*. Does this satisfy you, Sir?'

My uncle's features, in spite of himself, relaxed into a half-smile.

'Very platonic - sweet simplicity!' - drauled out Mrs Morton, in ironical accents.

'I will not be insulted, Mr Morton!' quitting my seat, and rising in temper. - 'I consider myself, merely, as your visitant, and not as responsible to any one for my actions. Conscious of purity of intention, and superior to all disguise or evasion, I was not aware of these feminine, indelicate, unfriendly suggestions. If this behaviour be a specimen of what I am to expect in the world - the world may do its will - but I will never be its slave: while I have strength of mind to form principles, and courage to act upon them, I am determined to preserve my freedom, and trust to the general candour and good sense of mankind to appreciate me justly. As the brother of my late father, and as entitled to respect from your own kind intentions, I am willing to enter into any explanations, which *you, Sir*, may think necessary: - neither my motives, nor my actions, have ever yet shrunk from investigation. Will you permit me to attend you in your library? It is not my intention to intrude longer on your hospitality, and I could wish to avail myself of your experience and counsels respecting my future destination.'

Mr Morton, at my request, withdrew with me into the library, where I quickly removed from his mind those injurious suspicions with which Mrs Morton had laboured to inspire him. He would not hear of my removal from the Park - apologized for what had passed - assured me of his friendship and protection - and entreated me to consider his house as my home. There was an honest warmth and sincerity in his manner, that sensibly affected me; I could have wept; and I engaged, at his repeated request, not to think, at present, of withdrawing myself from his protection. Thus we separated.

How were the virtues of this really good man tarnished by an unsuitable connection! In the giddy hours of youth, we thoughtlessly rush into engagements, that fetter our minds, and affect our future characters, without reflecting on the important consequences of our conduct. This is a subject on which I have had occasion to reflect deeply; yet, alas! my own boasted reason has been, but too often, the dupe of my imagination.

CHAPTER XV

Nothing, here, occupied my heart - a heart to which it was necessary to love and admire. I had suffered myself to be irritated - the tumult of my spirits did not easily subside - I was mortified at the reflection - I had believed myself armed with patience and fortitude, but my philosophy was swept before the impetuous emotions of my passions like chaff before the whirlwind. I took up my pen to calm my spirits, and addressed myself to the man who had been, unconsciously, the occasion of these vexations. - My swelling heart needed the relief of communication.

To Mr Francis

'I Sought earnestly for the privilege of addressing you on paper. My mind seemed to overflow with a thousand sentiments, that I had not the courage to express in words; but now, when the period is arrived, that I can take up my pen, unawed by your penetrating glance, unchecked by your poignant reply, and pour out my spirit before you, I feel as if its emotions were too wayward, too visionary, too contradictory, to merit your attention.

'Every thing I see and hear is a disappointment to me: - brought up in retirement - conversing only with books - dwelling with ardour on the great characters, and heroic actions, of antiquity, all my ideas of honour and distinction were associated with those of virtue and talents. I conceived, that the pursuit of truth, and the advancement of reason, were the grand objects of universal attention, and I panted to do homage to those superior minds, who, teaching mankind to be wise, would at length lead them to happiness. Accustomed to think, to feel, to kindle into action, I am at a loss to understand the distinction between theory and practice, which every one seems eager to inculcate, as if the degrading and melancholy intelligence, which fills my soul with despondency, and pervades my understanding with gloom, was to them a subject of exultation.

'Is virtue, then, a chimera - does it exist only in the regions of romance? - Have we any interest in finding our fellow creatures weak and miserable? - Is the Being who formed them unjust, capricious, impotent, or tyrannical?

'Answer these questions, that press heavily on my mind, that dart across it, in its brightest moments, clouding its sun-shine with a thick and impenetrable darkness. Must the benevolent emotions, which I have hitherto delighted to cherish, turn into misanthropy - must the fervent and social affections of my heart give place to inanity, to apathy - must the activity of a curious and vigorous mind sink into torpor and abhorred vacuity?

'While they teach me to distrust the existence of virtue, they endeavour to impose on me, in its stead, a fictitious semblance; and to substitute, for the pure gold of truth, a paltry tinsel. It is in vain I ask - what have those to do with "*seeming*," who still retain "that which *passeth shew*?" However my actions may be corrupted by the contagious example of the world, may I still hold fast my integrity, and disdain to wear the *appearance* of virtue, when the substance shall no longer exist.

'To admire, to esteem, to love, are congenial to my nature - I am unhappy, because these affections are not called into exercise. To venerate abstract perfection, requires too vigorous an exertion of the mental powers - I would see virtue exemplified, I would love it in my fellow creatures - I would catch the glorious enthusiasm, and rise from created to uncreated excellence.

'I am perplexed with doubts; relieve the wanderings of my mind, solve the difficulties by which it is agitated, prepare me for the world which is before me. The prospect, no longer beaming with light, no longer glowing with a thousand vivid hues, is overspread with mists, which the mind's eye vainly attempts to penetrate. I would feel, again, the value of existence, the worth of rectitude, the certainty of truth, the blessing of hope! Ah! tell me not - that the gay expectations of youth have been the meteors of fancy, the visions of a romantic and distempered imagination! If I must not live to realize them, I would not live at all.

'My harrassed mind turns to you! You will not ridicule its scruples - you will, at least, deign to reason with me, and, in the exercise of my understanding, I shall experience a temporary relief from the sensations which devour me, the suspicions that distress me, and which spread over futurity a fearful veil.

'*Emma.*'

I walked to the next market town, and left my letter at the post-house, - I waited impatiently for a reply; my mind wanted *impression*, and sunk into languor. The answer, which arrived in a few days, was kind, because it was prompt, my sickly mind required a speedy remedy.

To Emma Courtney.

'Why will you thus take things in masses, and continually dwell in extremes? You deceive yourself; instead of cultivating your reason, you are fostering an excessive sensibility, a fastidious delicacy. It is the business of reason to compare, to separate, to discriminate. Is there no medium - extraordinary exertions are only called forth by extraordinary contingences; - because every human being is not a hero, are we then to distrust the existence of virtue?

'The mind is modified by the circumstances in which it is placed, by the accidents of birth and education; the constitutions of society are all, as yet, imperfect; they have generated, and perpetuated, many mistakes - the consequences of those mistakes will, eventually, carry with them their antidote, the seeds of reproduction are, even, visible in their decay. The growth of reason is slow, but not the less sure; the increase of knowledge must necessarily prepare the way for the increase of virtue and happiness.

'Look back upon the early periods of society, and, taking a retrospective view of what has been done, amidst the interruptions of barbarous inroads, falling empires, and palsying despotism, calculate what yet may be achieved: while the causes, which have hitherto impeded the progress of civilization, must continue to decrease, in an accelerated ration, with the wide, and still wider, diffusion of truth.

'We may trace most of the faults, and the miseries of mankind, to the vices and errors of political institutions, their permanency having been their radical defect. Like children, we have dreamt, that what gratifies our desires, or contributes to our convenience, to-day, will prove equally useful and satisfactory to-morrow, without reflecting on the growth of the body, the change of humours, the new objects, and the new situations, which every succeeding hour brings in its train. That immutability, which constitutes the perfection of what we (from the poverty of language) term the *divine mind*, would inevitably be the bane of creatures liable to error; it is of the constancy, rather than of the fickleness, of human beings, that we have reason to complain.

'Every improvement must be the result of successive experiments, this has been found true in natural science, and it must be universally applied to be universally beneficial. Bigotry, whether religious, political, moral, or commercial, is the canker-worm at the root of the tree of knowledge and of virtue. The wildest speculations are less mischievous than the torpid state of error: he, who tamely resigns his understanding to the guidance of another, sinks at once, from the dignity of a rational being, to a mechanical puppet, moved at pleasure on the wires of the artful operator. - *Imposition* is the principle and support of every varied description of tyranny, whether civil or ecclesiastical, moral or mental; its baneful consequence is to degrade both him who is imposed on, and him who imposes. *Obedience*, is a word, which ought never to have had existence: as we recede from conviction, and languidly resign ourselves to any foreign authority, we quench the principle of action, of virtue, of reason; - we bear about the semblance of humanity, but the spirit is fled.

'These are truths, which will slowly, but ultimately, prevail; in the splendour of which, the whole fabric of superstition will gradually fade and melt away. The world, like every individual, has its progress from infancy to maturity - How many follies do we commit in childhood? how many errors are we precipitated into by the fervour and inexperience of youth! Is not every stable principle acquired through innumerable mistakes - can you wonder, that in society, amidst the aggregate of jarring interests and passions, reformation is so tardy? Though civilization has been impeded by innumerable obstacles, even these help to carry on the great work: empires may be overturned, and the arts scattered, but not lost. The hordes of barbarians, which overwhelmed ancient Rome, adopted at length the religion, the laws, and the improvements of the vanquished, as Rome had before done those of Greece. As the stone, which, thrown into the water, spreads circles still more and more extended; - or (to adopt the gospel similitude) as the grain of mustard seed, growing up into a large tree, shelters the fowls of heaven in its branches - so will knowledge, at length, diffuse itself, till it covers the whole earth.

'When the minds of men are changed, the system of things will also change; but these changes, though active and incessant, must be gradual. Reason will fall softly, and almost imperceptibly, like a gentle shower of dews, fructifying the soil, and preparing it for future harvests. Let us not resemble the ambitious shepherd, who, calling for the accumulated waters of the Nile upon his lands, was, with his flock, swept away in the impetuous torrent.

'You ask, whether - because human beings are still imperfect - you are to resign your benevolence, and to cherish misanthropy? What a question! Would you hate the inhabitants of an hospital for being infected with a pestilential disorder? Let us remember, that vice originates in mistakes of the understanding, and that, he who seeks happiness by means contradictory and destructive, is *emphatically the sinner*. Our duties, then, are obvious - If selfish and violent passions have been generated by the inequalities of society, we must labour to counteract them, by endeavouring to combat prejudice, to expand the mind, to give comprehensive views, to teach mankind their true interest, and to lead them to habits of goodness and greatness. Every prejudice conquered, every mistake rectified, every individual improved, is an advance upon the great scale of virtue and happiness.

'Let it, then, be your noblest ambition to co-operate with, to join your efforts, to those of philosophers and sages, the benefactors of mankind. To waste our time in useless repinings is equally weak and vain; every one in his sphere may do something; each has a little circle where his influence will be availing. Correct your own errors, which are various - weeds in a luxuriant soil - and you will have done something towards the general reformation. But you are able to do more; - be vigilant, be active, beware of the illusions of fancy! I suspect, that you will have much to suffer - may you, at length, reap the fruits of a wholesome, though it should be a bitter, experience.

'- Francis.'

I perused the letter, I had received, again and again; it awakened a train of interesting reflections, and my spirits became tranquillized.

CHAPTER XVI

Early one fine morning, Ann tapped gently at the door of my chamber; I had already risen, and invited her to enter.

'Would I accompany her to breakfast, with a widow lady, who resided in a village about two miles from Morton Park, an occasional visitant in the family, a lady with whom, she was certain, I should be charmed.'

I smiled at her ardour, thanked her for her kindness, and readily agreed to her proposal. We strolled together through an adjacent wood, which, by a shady and winding path, conducted us towards the residence of this vaunted favourite of my little companion.

On our way, she entertained me with a slight sketch of the history of Mrs Harley and her family. She was the widow of a merchant, who was supposed to possess great property; but, practising occasionally as an underwriter, a considerable capture by the enemy (during war time) of some rich ships, reduced his fortune; and, by the consequent anxiety, completely destroyed a before debilitated constitution. He died in a few weeks after the confirmation of his loss, and, having neglected to make a will, a freehold estate of some value, which was all that remained of his effects, devolved of course to his eldest son; his two younger sons and three daughters being left wholly unprovided for. Augustus Harley, the heir, immediately sold the estate, and divided the produce, in equal shares, between each individual of the family. His brothers had been educated for commerce, and were enabled, through the generous kindness of Augustus, to carry on, with advantage and reputation, their respective occupations; the sisters were, soon after, eligibly married. Augustus, who had been educated for the law, disgusted with its chicanery, relinquished the profession, content to restrain his expenses within the limits of a narrow income. This income had since received an increase, by the bequest of a distant relation, a man of a whimsical character, who had married, early in life, a beautiful woman, for love; but his wife having eloped from him with an officer, and, in the course of the intrigue, practised a variety of deceptions, he had retired disgusted from society, cherishing a misanthropical spirit: and, on his decease, bequeathed an annual sum of four hundred pounds to Augustus Harley (to whom in his childhood he had been particularly attached) on condition of his remaining unmarried. On his marriage, or death, this legacy passed into another branch of the family. On this acquisition Augustus determined on making the tour of Europe; and, after travelling on the continent for three years, on his return to his native country, alternately resided, either in the village of ...... , with his mother, or in the metropolis, where he divided his time, between liberal studies, and rational recreation. His visits to the country had, of late, been shorter and less frequent: he was the idol of his mother, and universally respected by his acquaintance, for his noble and generous conduct. - 'Ah!' (added the lively narrator) 'could you but see Augustus Harley, you would, infallibly, lose your heart - so frank, so pleasant, so ingenuous are his manners, so intrepid, and yet so humane! Montague is a fine gentleman, but Augustus Harley is more - *he is a man!*'

She began to grow eloquent on this, apparently, exhaustless theme, nor did she cease her panegyric till we came in view of Mrs Harley's mansion.

'You will love the mother as well as the son,' continued this agreeable prattler, 'when you come to know her; she is very good and very sensible.'

Drawing near the house, she tripped from me, to enquire if its mistress had yet risen.

A small white tenement, half obscured in shrubbery, on a verdant lawn, of dimensions equally modest, situated on the side of a hill, and commanding an extensive and variegated prospect, was too interesting and picturesque an object, not to engage for some moments my attention. The image of Augustus, also, which my lively companion had pourtrayed with more than her usual vivacity, played in my fancy - my heart paid involuntary homage to virtue, and I entered the mansion of Mrs Harley with a swelling emotion, made up of complicated feelings - half respectful, half tender - sentiments, too mingled to be distinctly traced. I was introduced into a room that overlooked a pleasant garden, and which the servant called a library. It was hung with green paper, the carpet the same colour, green venetian blinds to the windows, a sopha and chairs covered with white dimity; some drawings and engravings hung on the walls, arranged with exact symmetry; on one side of the room stood a grand piano-forte, opposite to which, was a handsome book-case, filled with books, elegantly bound; in the middle of the apartment was placed a table, covered with a green cloth, on which was a reading desk, some books and pamphlets, with implements for writing and drawing. Nothing seemed costly, yet neatness, order, and taste, appeared through the whole apartment, bespeaking the elegant and cultivated mind of the owner.

After amusing myself for a short time, in this charming retirement, I was summoned by Ann to the breakfast room, where Mrs Harley awaited me. I was interested, at the first glance, in favour of this amiable woman - she appeared to be near fifty, her person agreeable, her countenance animated, her address engaging, and her manners polished. Mutually pleased with each other, the hours passed rapidly; and, till reminded by a significant look from my little friend, I was unconscious that I had made my visit of an unreasonable length.

Mrs Harley spoke much of her son, he was the darling and the pride of her heart; she lamented the distance that separated them, and wished, that her health, and his tenderness, would allow of her residence with him in London. When conversing on this favourite topic, a glow enlivened her countenance, and her eyes sparkled with a humid brightness. I was affected by her maternal love - tender remembrances, and painful comparisons, crowded into my mind - a tear fell, that would not be twinkled away - she observed it, and seemed to feel its meaning; she held out her hand to me, I took it and pressed it to my lips. At parting, she entreated me speedily to renew my visit, to come often without ceremony - I should cheer her solitude - my sympathy, for she perceived I had a feeling heart, would help to console her in the absence of her Augustus.

CHAPTER XVII

On our way home, Ann was in high spirits, congratulating herself upon her sagacity.

'Mrs Harley,' (said she, archly leering in my face) 'will console you for the departure of Mr Francis.'

I smiled without replying. At dinner our visit of the morning was canvassed (Ann had wished me to conceal it, but this I positively refused). Mr Morton spoke of Mrs Harley and her son with great respect, Mrs Morton with a sarcastic sneer, accompanied with a reprimand to her daughter, for the improper liberty she had taken.

I quitted the table, immediately after the desert, to stifle my disgust, and, taking a book, wandered into the pleasure grounds, but incapable of fixing my attention, I presently shut my book, and, sauntering slowly on, indulged in a reverie. My melancholy reflections again returned - How could I remain in a house, where I was every day marked out for insult by its mistress - and where was I to dispose of myself? My fortune was insufficient to allow of my boarding in a respectable family. Mrs Harley came across my mind - Amiable woman! - Would she, indeed, accept of my society, and allow me to soften her solitude! - But her income was little less limited than my own - it must not be thought of. I reflected on the inequalities of society, the source of every misery and of every vice, and on the peculiar disadvantages of my sex. I sighed bitterly; and, clasping my hands together, exclaimed, unconsciously -

'Whither can I go - and where shall I find an asylum?'

'Allow me to propose one,' said a voice, in a soft accent, suddenly, behind me.

I started, turned, and beheld Mr Montague. After some expressions of sympathy for the distress which he had witnessed, apologies for his intrusion, and incoherent expressions of respect and regard, he somewhat abruptly offered his hand and heart to my acceptance, with the impetuosity which accompanied all his sentiments and actions; yet, he expressed himself with the air of a man who believes he is conferring an obligation. I thanked him for his generous proposal -

But, as my heart spake not in his favour - 'I must be allowed to decline it.'

'That heart,' said he, rudely, 'is already bestowed upon another.'

'Certainly not, Mr Montague; if it were, I would frankly tell you.'

He pronounced the name of Mr Francis -

'Mr Francis is a man for whom I feel a sincere respect and veneration - a man whom I should be proud to call my friend; but a thought beyond that, I dare venture to say, has never occurred to either of us.'

He knew not how to conceive - that a woman in my situation, unprepossessed, could reject so advantageous an establishment!

This, I told him, was indelicate, both to me and to himself. Were my situation yet more desolate, I would not marry any man, merely for an *establishment*, for whom I did not feel an affection.

Would I please to describe to him the model of perfection which I should require in a husband?

It was unnecessary; as I saw no probability of the portrait bearing any resemblance to himself.

He reddened, and turned pale, alternately; bit his lips, and muttered to himself. - 'Damned romantic affectation!'

I assumed a firmer tone - methought he insulted me. - 'I beg you will leave me, Sir - I chuse to be alone - By what right do you intrude upon my retirements?'

My determined accent abashed him: - he tried, but with an ill grace, to be humble; and entreated me to take time for consideration.

'There is no need of it. It is a principle with me, not to inflict a moment's suspence on any human being, when my own mind is decided.'

'Then you absolutely refuse me, and prefer the being exposed to the mean and envious insults of the vulgar mistress of this mansion!'

'Of the two evils, I consider it as the least, because it involves no permanent obligation.'

His countenance was convulsed with passion. His love, he told me, was converted into vengeance by my scorn: he was not to be contemned with impunity; and he warned me to beware.

I smiled, I believe, a little too contemptuously. 'You love me not, Sir; I am glad, for your own sake, that you never loved me.'

'My hatred may be more terrible!'

'You cannot intimidate me - I am little accustomed to fear.'

I turned from him somewhat disdainfully: but, instantly recollecting myself, I stepped back, and apologized for the harsh manner into which I had been betrayed by his abrupt address, vehement expostulation, and the previous irritated state of my mind.

'I acknowledge,' said I, 'the disinterestedness of your proposal, and the *distinction* which it implies. Will you allow my own wounded feelings to be an excuse for the too little consideration with which I have treated *your's*? Can you forgive me?' added I, in a conciliating tone, holding out my hand.

The strong emotions, which rapidly succeeded each other in his mind, were painted in his countenance. After a moment's hesitation, he snatched the hand I offered him, pressed it to his lips, and, murmuring a few incoherent words, burst into tears. My spirits were already depressed - affected by these marks of his sensibility, and still more distressed by the recollection of the pain I had occasioned him by my inconsiderate behaviour, I wept with him for some minutes in silence.

'Let us no more,' resumed I, making an effort to recover myself, 'renew these impressions. I thank you sincerely for the sympathy you have manifested for my situation. I am sensible that I have yielded to weak and wayward feelings. - I have youth, health, and activity - I ought not - neither do I despair. - The mortifications I have experienced, since my residence here, will afford me a useful lesson for the future - they have already taught me, what I before merely conjectured, *the value of independence*!'

'Why, then,' interrupted he with quickness, 'do you reject an opportunity of placing yourself out of the reach of insult?'

'Stop, my good friend,' replied I, smilingly looking in his face; 'there is a possibility of exchanging evils. You are yet too young, and too unstable, maturely to have weighed the importance of the scheme you propose. Remember, likewise, that you are, yourself, in a great measure, dependent on the will of your father; and that much reflection is requisite before we fetter ourselves with engagements, that, once entered into, are not easily dissolved.'

'You allow me, then, to hope!'

'Indeed I meant not to imply any such thing. I wish to soften what I have already expressed - but, there are a variety of reasons which oblige me to assure you, that I see no probability of changing my sentiments on the subject.'

'Why, then, this cruel ostentation? I would either love or hate, bless or curse you.'

'You shall do neither, if I can prevent it. If my esteem is of any value to you, you must learn to respect both me and yourself.'

'Esteem! - Is that to be my frigid reward!'

'If *mine* be worthless, propose to yourself *your own* as a recompense.'

'I have already forfeited it, by seeking to move a heart, that triumphs in its cold inflexibility.'

'Is this just - is it kind? Is it, indeed, *my welfare* you seek, while you can thus add to the vexations and embarrassment, which were before sufficiently oppressive? I would preserve you from an act of precipitation and imprudence; - in return, you load me with unmerited reproaches. But it is time to put an end to a conversation, that can answer little other purpose than vain recrimination.'

He was about to speak - 'Say no more - I feel myself, again, in danger of losing my temper - my spirits are agitated - I would not give you pain - Allow me to retire, and be assured of my best wishes.'

Some of the family appearing in sight, as if advancing towards us, favoured my retreat. I quitted the place with precipitation, and retired to my chamber, where I sought, by employing myself, to calm the perturbation of my heart.

CHAPTER XVIII

In a few days I renewed my visit to Mrs Harley: - a strong sympathy united us, and we became almost inseparable. Every day I discovered in this admirable woman a new and indissoluble tie, that bound me to her. Her cultivated understanding afforded an inexhaustible fund of instruction and entertainment; and her affectionate heart spread a charm over her most indifferent actions. We read, we walked, we conversed together; but, with whatever subjects these conversations commenced, some associated idea always led them to terminate in an eulogium on the virtues and talents, or an expression of regret, for the absence of Augustus. There was a portrait of him (drawn by a celebrated artist, which he had lately sent from town as a present to his mother) hung up in the library. I accustomed myself to gaze on this resemblance of a man, in whose character I felt so lively an interest, till, I fancied, I read in the features all the qualities imputed to the original by a tender and partial parent.

Cut off from the society of mankind, and unable to expound my sensations, all the strong affections of my soul seemed concentrated to a single point. Without being conscious of it, my grateful love for Mrs Harley had, already, by a transition easy to be traced by a philosophic mind, transferred itself to her son. He was the St Preux, the Emilius of my sleeping and waking reveries. I now spent almost my whole time in the cottage of my friend, returning to Morton Park late in the evening, and quitting it early in the morning, and sometimes being wholly absent for weeks together.

Six months thus passed away in tranquillity, with but little variation. Mr Montague, during this period, had several times left Mr Morton's, and returned again abruptly: his manners became sullen, and even, at times, ferocious. I carefully avoided encountering him, fearful of exasperating a spirit, that appeared every moment on the verge of excess.

Hastening one evening to my friend, after a longer separation than common, (having been prevailed on by Mr Morton and his daughters to accompany them on a distant visit, where business of Mr Morton's detained us for some days) I ran into the library, as usual, and threw myself into the arms of Mrs Harley, that opened spontaneously to receive me.

'Ah! you little truant,' said she, in a voice of kindness, 'where have you been so long? My son has visited me in your absence; he passed through this part of the country, in his way to the seat of a friend. He staid with me two days, during which I sent half a dozen messages to Morton Park, but you were flown away, it seems, nor could I learn any tidings of you. Augustus,' continued she, without observing the emotions she excited, 'had scarcely quitted the house an hour when you arrived.'

I made no reply; an unaccountable sensation seized, and oppressed, my heart - sinking on the sopha, I burst into a convulsive flood of tears.

My friend was struck: all the indiscretion of her conduct (as she has since told me) flashed suddenly into her mind; she felt that, in indulging her own maternal sensations, she had, perhaps, done me an irreparable injury, and she shuddered at the probable consequences. It was some moments before either of us recovered; - our conversation was that evening, for the first time, constrained, reserved, and painful; and we retired at an early hour to our respective apartments.

I spent the night in self-examination. I was compelled to acknowledge, to myself, that solitude, the absence of other impressions, the previous circumstances that had operated on my character, my friendship for Mrs Harley, and her eloquent, affectionate, reiterated, praises of her son, had combined to awaken all the exquisite, though dormant, sensibilities of my nature; and, however romantic it might appear to others, and did appear even to myself, I felt, that I loved an ideal object (for such was Augustus Harley to me) with a tender and fervent excess; an excess, perhaps, involving all my future usefulness and welfare. 'People, in general,' says Rousseau, 'do not sufficiently consider the influence which the first attachments, between man and woman, have over the remainder of their lives; they do not perceive, that an impression so strong, and so lively, as that of love, is productive of a long chain of effects, which pass unobserved in a course of years, yet, nevertheless, continue to operate till the day of their deaths.' It was in vain I attempted to combat this illusion; my reason was but an auxiliary to my passion, it persuaded me, that I was only doing justice to high and uncommon worth; imagination lent her aid, and an importunate sensibility, panting after good unalloyed, completed the seduction.

From this period Mrs Harley was more guarded in her conduct; she carefully avoided the mention of her son. - Under pretence of having an alteration made in the frame, she removed his picture from the library; but the constraint she put upon herself was too evident and painful; we no longer sought, with equal ardour, an interchange of sentiment, reserve took place of the tender confidence of friendship; a thousand times, while I gazed upon her dear averted countenance, I yearned to throw myself upon her bosom, to weep, to unfold to her the inmost recesses of my mind - that ingenuous mind, which languished for communication, and preyed upon itself! Dear and cruel friend, why did you transfix my heart with the barbed and envenomed arrow, and then refuse to administer the only healing balsam?

My visits to Mrs Harley became less frequent; I shut myself up whole days in my apartment, at Morton Park, or wandered through its now leafless groves, absorbed in meditation - fostering the sickly sensibility of my soul, and nursing wild, improbable, chimerical, visions of felicity, that, touched by the sober wand of truth, would have 'melted into thin air.' 'The more desires I have' (observes an acute, and profound French Philosopher[4]) 'the less ardent they are. The torrents that divide themselves into many branches are the least dangerous in their course. A strong passion is a solitary passion, that concentrates all our desires within one point.'

4: *Helvetius.*

CHAPTER XIX

I had not seen my friend for many days, when, on a dark and stormy night, in the month of January, between nine and ten o'clock, the family at Morton Park were alarmed, by a loud and violent knocking at the hall door.

On opening it, a servant appeared - and a chaise, the porter having unbolted the great gates. drew up to the door. The man delivered a note addressed to Miss Courtney. I was unacquainted with the handwriting, and unfolded it with trepidation. It contained but a few lines, written in a female character, and signed with the name of a lady, who resided about twelve miles from Morton Park, at whose house Mrs Harley sometimes made a visit of a few days. It stated -

'That my friend was seized at the mansion of this lady with an apoplectic fit, from which she had been restored, after some hours of insensibility: that the physicians were apprehensive of a relapse, and that Mrs Harley had expressed a desire of seeing Miss Courtney - A carriage and servants were sent for her conveyance.'

Mr Morton was from home, his lady made no offer of any of her own domestics to accompany me. Montague, who had been at the Park for some days past, solicited permission to be my escort. I hesitated a moment, and would willingly have declined this proposal, but he repeated and enforced it with a vehemence, that, in the present hurried state of my mind, I had not spirits to oppose. Shocked, alarmed, distressed, I wrapped a shawl round me, and sprang into the chaise. Montague stepped in after me, and seated himself by my side; the horses galloped, or rather flew down the avenue, that led to the high road.

We travelled with great swiftness, and in uninterrupted silence for some miles: the darkness was so thick and profound, that I could not discover the road we took, and I began to feel very impatient to arrive at the place of our destination. I questioned my companion respecting his knowledge of our situation, and expressed an apprehension, that we might possibly have missed the way. He made no reply to my interrogation, but, starting as if from a reverie, seized my hand, while his own trembled with a visible agitation, and began once more to urge a suit, which I had hoped the steadiness and consistency of my conduct had induced him entirely to relinquish.

'Is this a time, Mr Montague, for an address of this nature - do you believe, that my favour is to be gained by these proofs of inconsideration? Have some respect for the claims of humanity and friendship, and, in seeking my affection, do not forfeit my esteem.'

He was about to reply, and I could perceive by the few words which he uttered, and by the tone of his voice, that he struggled, in vain, to rein in his quick and irascible spirit; when, in turning a sharp angle of the road, the horses took fright at some object, indistinctly seen, and ran precipitately down a steep hill, with a velocity that threatened immediate destruction.

My companion, forcing open the door, seemed inclined to leap from the carriage, but hesitated, as if unwilling to desert me in so imminent a danger; I exhorted him to think only of providing for his own safety, and, letting down the glasses on the side on which I sat, I resigned myself to my fate. In springing from the chaise, by some means, Montague entangled his coat in the step - he fell, without clearing it, and I felt, with a horror that congealed my blood, the wheel go over him. In a few minutes, I perceived a traveller, at the risque of his own life, endeavouring to stop the horses - the pole of the chaise striking him with great force, he was obliged to relinquish his humane efforts - but this impediment occasioning the restive animals to turn out of the road, they ran furiously up a bank, and overset the carriage. I felt it going, and sitting, with my arms folded, close in the lower corner, fell with it, without attempting to struggle, by which means I escaped unhurt.

The stranger, once more, came to our assistance, and, the mettle of the horses being now pretty well exhausted, my deliverer was enabled to cut the traces, and then hastened to extricate me from my perilous situation. It was some time before I recovered myself sufficiently to thank him for his humanity, and to assure him, that I had received no other injury than from my fears. I then mentioned to him, my apprehensions for the fate of my fellow traveller, entreating that he would return with me in search of him. With this request he immediately complied, leaving the horses in the care of the servants, neither of which had received any material hurt.

We soon discovered the unfortunate Montague, lying in the road, in a melancholy situation: the wheel had gone over one of his legs, the bone of which was broken and splintered in a terrible manner, and, having fainted from the pain, we were at first apprehensive that he was already dead. Turning from this shocking spectacle, a faint sickness overspread my heart, the stranger supported me in his arms, while a violent burst of tears preserved me from swooning. My companion examining the body, perceived signs of life, and, by our united efforts, sense and recollection were soon restored.

I remained with Montague while the stranger returned to the carriage, to enquire what damages it had received, and whether it was in a condition to proceed to the next village, which, the postilion informed him, was near two miles from the spot where the accident had happened, and we were, yet, five miles from the place whither we were going. The axle-tree and one of the hind wheels, upon examination, were found broken, the traces had been cut in pieces, and the horses, had the chaise been in a better condition, were so unmanageable, in consequence of their late fright, that it would have been dangerous to have attempted putting them again into harness.

With this intelligence, our kind friend came back to us - We held a short consultation, on the means most proper to be adopted, and, at length it was determined, that, after placing Montague in the carriage, where he should be sheltered from the inclemency of the elements, and leaving him in the charge of the servants, the traveller and myself should walk onward to the village, and send a chaise, or litter, for the conveyance of our unfortunate companion.

To this proposal Montague assented, at the same time, declaring it to be his intention, to proceed directly across the country, to the house of his father, which could not, he conjectured, be at any great distance, and where he should be assured of meeting with greater attention, and more skilful assistance, than at a petty inn, in a paltry village. Having thus adjusted our plan, and, with the help of the servants. carefully placed Montague in the chaise, we proceeded towards the village.

CHAPTER XX

The night was tempestuous, and, though the moon was now rising, her light was every moment obscured by dark clouds, discharging frequent and heavy showers of rain, accompanied by furious gusts of wind. After walking near a mile we entered upon a wide heath, which afforded no shelter from the weather. I perceived my companion's steps began to grow feeble, and his voice faint. The moon suddenly emerging from a thick cloud, I observed his countenance, and methought his features seemed familiar to me; but they were overspread by a pallid and death-like hue. He stopped suddenly -

'I am very ill,' said he, in a tone of voice that penetrated into my soul, 'and can proceed no further.'

He sunk upon the turf. Seating myself beside him, while his head fell on my shoulder, I threw around him my supporting arms. His temples were bedewed with a cold sweat, and he appeared to be in expiring agonies. A violent sickness succeeded, followed by an hemorrhage.

'Gracious God!' I exclaimed, 'you have broken a blood vessel!'

'I fear so,' he replied. 'I have felt strangely disordered since the blow I received from the pole of the carriage; but, till this moment, I have not been at leisure to attend to my sensations.'

'Do not talk,' cried I, wildly; 'do not exhaust yourself.'

Again the clouds gathered; an impetuous gust of wind swept over the heath, and the rain fell in torrents. Unconscious of what I did, I clasped the stranger to my throbbing bosom, - the coldness of death seemed upon him - I wrapped my shawl around him, vainly attempting to screen him from the piercing blast. He spake not; my terrified imagination already represented him as a lifeless corpse; I sat motionless for some minutes, in the torpor of despair.

From this horrible situation, I was, at length, roused, by the sound of a distant team: breathless, I listened for a few moments; I again distinctly heard it wafted upon the wind; when, gently reclining my charge on the grass, I started from the ground, and ran swiftly towards the highway. The sound approached, and the clouds once more breaking, and discovering a watery moon-light gleam, I perceived, with joy, a waggon loaded with hay. I bounded over a part of the turf that still separated me from the road, and accosting the driver, explained to him, in a few words, as much of my situation as was necessary; and, entreating his assistance, allured him by the hope of a reward.

We returned to my patient; he raised his head on my approach, and attempted to speak; but, enjoining him silence, he took my hand, and, by a gentle pressure, expressed his sense of my cares more eloquently than by words. I assisted the countryman in supporting him to the road. We prepared for him, in the waggon, a soft bed of hay, upon which we placed him; and, resting his head on my lap, we proceeded gently to the nearest village. On our arrival at an indifferent inn, I ordered a bed to be immediately prepared for him, and sent a man and horse express, to the next town, for medical assistance: at the same time, relating in brief the accidents of the night, I dispatched a carriage for the relief of Montague, who was conveyed, according to his wishes, to the house of his father.

Notwithstanding all my precautions, the moving brought on a relapse of the alarming symptoms; the discharge of blood returned with aggravated violence, and, when the physician arrived, there appeared in the unfortunate sufferer but little signs of life; but by the application of styptics and cordials he once more began to revive; and, about five in the morning, I was prevailed on, by the joint efforts of the landlady and the humane Dr ...., to resign my seat at the bed's head to a careful servant, and to recruit my exhausted strength by a few hours' repose.

The vivid impressions, which had so rapidly succeeded each other in my mind, for some time kept me waking, in a state of feverish agitation; but my harrassed spirits were at length relieved by wearied nature's kind restorer, and I slept for four hours profoundly.

On waking, my first enquiry was after my companion, in whose state I felt an unusual degree of interest; and I heard, with pleasure, that the hemorrhage had not returned; that he had rested with apparent tranquillity, and appeared revived. I dressed myself hastily, and passed into his apartment: he faintly smiled on perceiving my approach, and gave me his hand. - The physician had ordered him to be kept quiet, and I would not suffer him to speak; but, contemplating more attentively his countenance, which had the night before struck me with a confused recollection - what were my emotions, on tracing the beloved features of Augustus Harley! His resemblance, not only to the portrait, but to his mother, could not, as I thought, be mistaken. A universal trembling seized me - I hastened out of the apartment with tottering steps, and shutting myself into my chamber, a tide of melancholy emotions gushed upon my heart. I wept, without knowing wherefore, tears half delicious, half agonizing! Quickly coming to myself, I returned to the chamber of my patient, (now more tenderly endeared) which, officiating as a nurse for five days, I never quitted, except to take necessary rest and refreshment.

I had written to Mr Morton a minute account of all that happened, merely suppressing the name of my deliverer: to this letter I received no reply; but had the pleasure of hearing, on the return of my messenger (who was commissioned to make enquiries), that Mrs Harley had suffered no return of her disorder, and was daily acquiring health and strength - I feared, yet, to acquaint her with the situation of her son; not only on the account of her own late critical situation, but, also, lest any sudden agitation of spirits from the arrival of his mother, might, in his present weak state, be fatal to Augustus.

I now redoubled for him my cares and attentions: he grew hourly better; and, when permitted to converse, expressed in lively terms his grateful sense of my kindness. Ah! why did I misconstrue these emotions, so natural in such circumstances - why did I flatter my heart with the belief of a sympathy which did not, could not, exist!

CHAPTER XXI

As my patient began to acquire strength, I demanded of him his name and family, that I might inform his friends of his situation. On his answering 'Harley,' I enquired, smiling -

If he remembered hearing his mother speak of a little *Protegé*, Emma Courtney, whom she favoured with her partial friendship?

'Oh, yes!' - and his curiosity had been strongly awakened to procure a sight of this lady.

'Behold her then, in your nurse!'

'Is it possible!' he exclaimed, taking my hand, and pressing it with his lips - 'My sister! - my friend! - how shall I ever pay the debt I owe you?'

'We will settle that matter another time; but it is now become proper that I should inform your excellent mother of what has happened, which I have hitherto delayed, lest surprise should be prejudicial to you, and retard your recovery.'

I then recounted to him the particulars of the late occurrences, of which he had before but a confused notion; adding my surprise, that I had neither seen, nor heard, any thing from Mr Morton.

He informed me, in his turn, that, having received an express, informing him of his mother's alarming situation, he immediately quitted the seat of his friend, where he was on a visit, to hasten to her; that, for this purpose, riding late, he by some means bewildered himself through the darkness of the evening, by which mistake he encountered our chaise, and he hoped was, in some measure, notwithstanding the accidents which ensued, accessary to my preservation.

I quitted him to write to my friend, whom I, at length, judged it necessary to acquaint with his situation. On the receipt of my letter, she flew to us on the wings of maternal tenderness - folded her beloved Augustus, and myself, alternately to her affectionate bosom, calling us 'her children - her darling children! - I was her guardian angel - *the preserver of her son*! - and *he* only could repay my goodness!' I ventured to raise my eyes to him - they met his - mine were humid with tears of tenderness: a cloud passed over his brow - he entreated his mother to restrain her transports - he was yet too enfeebled to bear these emotions. She recollected herself in an instant; and, after again embracing him, leaning on my arm, walked out into the air, to relieve the tumultuous sensations that pressed upon her heart.

Once more she made me recite, minutely, the late events - strained me in her arms, repeatedly calling me -

'Her beloved daughter - the meritorious child of her affections - the preserver of her Augustus!'

Every word she uttered sunk deep into my soul, that greedily absorbed the delicious poison, prepared for me by the cruel hand of more than maternal fondness.

I mentioned to her my having written to Mr Morton, and my astonishment at his silence.

He had not yet returned, she informed me, to Morton Park; and intimated, that some malicious stories, respecting my sudden disappearance, had been circulated by Mrs Morton through the neighbourhood. She had herself been under extreme solicitude on my account. It was generally believed, from the turn Mrs Morton's malice had given to the affair, that I had eloped with Mr Montague: - the accident which had befallen him had been rumoured; but the circumstances, and the occasion of it, had been variously related. Confiding in my principles, she had waited with anxiety for the elucidation of these mysterious accounts; lamenting herself as the innocent occasion of them, yet assured they would, eventually, prove to my honour. She commended the magnanimity, which her partial friendship imputed to my behaviour, with all the enthusiasm of affection, and execrated the baseness of Mrs Morton, who, having received my letter, must have been acquainted with the real truth.

Her narration gave me many complicated, and painful, sensations; but the good opinion of the world, however desirable it may be, as connected with our utility, has ever been with me but a secondary consideration. Confiding in the rectitude of my own conduct, I composed my spirits; depending on that rectitude, and time, for removing the malignant aspersions which at present clouded my fame. The tale of slander, the basis of which is falsehood, will quietly wear away; and should it not - how unfounded, frequently, are the censures of the world - how confused its judgments! I entreated my friend to say nothing, at present, to her son on this subject; it was yet of importance that his mind should be kept still and tranquil.

We rejoined Augustus at the dinner hour, and spent the day together in harmony and friendship. The physician calling in the evening, Mrs Harley consulted him, whether it would be safe to remove her son, as she was impatient to have him under her own roof. To this the doctor made no objection, provided he was conveyed in an easy carriage, and by short stages. On Mrs Harley's thanking him for his polite and humane attention to his patient, smilingly pointing to me, he replied - 'Her thanks were misplaced.' His look was arch and significant; it called a glow into my cheeks. I ventured, once more, to steal a glance at Augustus: his features were again overspread with a more than usual seriousness, while his eyes seemed designedly averted. Mrs Harley sighed, and, abruptly changing the subject, asked the physician an indifferent question, who soon after took his leave.

CHAPTER XXII

In a few days we returned to the peaceful mansion of my maternal friend. Augustus seemed revived by the little journey, while every hour brought with it an increase of health and spirits. Mrs Harley would not suffer me to speak of going to Morton Park in the absence of its master; neither could Augustus spare his kind nurse: - 'I must stay,' he added, and methought his accents were softened, 'and complete my charitable purpose.' My appearance again in the village, the respectability, and the testimony, of my friends, cleared my fame; and it was only at Morton Park, that any injurious suspicions were affected to be entertained.

The hours flew on downy pinions: - my new *brother*, for so he would call himself, endeavoured to testify his gratitude, by encouraging and assisting me in the pursuit of learning and science: he gave us lectures on astronomy and philosophy -

'While truths divine came mended from his tongue.'

I applied myself to the languages, and aided by my preceptor, attained a general knowledge of the principles, and philosophy, of criticism and grammar, and of the rules of composition. Every day brought with it the acquisition of some new truth; and our intervals from study were employed in music, in drawing, in conversation, in reading the *belles lettres* - in -

'The feast of reason, and the flow of souls.'

The spring was advancing: - we now made little excursions, either on horseback, in a chaise, or in a boat on the river, through the adjacent country. The fraternal relation, which Augustus had assumed, banished restraint, and assisted me in deceiving myself. I drank in large and intoxicating draughts of a delicious poison, that had circulated through every vein to my heart, before I was aware of its progress. At length, part of a conversation, which I accidentally overheard between Mrs Harley and her son, recalled me to a temporary recollection.

I was seeking them in the garden, towards the dusk of the evening, and a filbert hedge separated us. I heard the voice of my friend, as speaking earnestly, and I unconsciously stopped.

'It would be a comfort to my declining years to see you the husband of a woman of virtue and sensibility: domestic affections meliorate the heart; no one ought to live wholly to himself.'

'Certainly not, neither does any one; but, in the present state of society, there are many difficulties and anxieties attending these connections: they are a lottery, and the prizes are few. I think, perhaps, nearly with you, but my situation is, *in many respects, a peculiar one,'* - and he sighed deeply: - Need I enumerate these peculiarities to you? Neither do I pretend to have lived so long in the world without imbibing many of its prejudices, and catching the contagion of its habits.'

'They are unworthy of you.'

'Perhaps so - but we will, if you please, change the subject; this to me is not a pleasant one. What is become of my pupil? It is likely to be a clear night; let us go in, and prepare for some astronomical observations.'

My heart reproved me for listening, I crept back to my chamber - shed one tear - heaved a convulsive, struggling, sigh - breathed on my handkerchief, applied it to my eyes, and joined my friends in the library.

Four months had rapidly passed - 'the spot of azure in the cloudy sky' - of my destiny. Mr Morton, I was informed, had returned to the Park, and Augustus, whose health was now thoroughly restored, talked of quitting the country. I advised with my friends, who agreed with me, that it was now become proper for me to visit my uncle, and, explaining to him the late events, justify my conduct. Mrs Harley and her son offered to accompany me; but this, for many reasons, I declined; taking my leave of them with a heavy heart, and promising, if I were not kindly received, an immediate return.

CHAPTER XXIII

On my arrival at Mr Morton's, the porter informed me, he was ordered by his lady, to deny my entrance. My swelling heart! - a sentiment of indignation distended it almost to suffocation. - At this moment, Anne tripped lightly through the court-yard, and, seeing me, ran to embrace me. I returned her caresses with warmth.

'Ah!' said she, 'you are not, you cannot be, guilty. I have been longing to see you, and to hear all that has happened, but it was not permitted me.' She added, in a whisper, 'I cannot love my mother, for she torments and restrains me - my desire of liberty is stronger than my duty - but I shall one day be able to outwit her.'

'Will not your father, my love, allow me to speak with him? I have a right to be heard, and I demand his attention.'

'He is in his dressing-room,' said Ann, 'I will slide softly to him, and tell him you are here.'

Away she flew, and one of the footmen presently returned, to conduct me to his master. I found him alone, he received me with a grave and severe aspect. I related to him, circumstantially, the occurrences which had taken place during his absence. My words, my voice, my manner, were emphatic - animated with the energy of truth - they extorted, they commanded, they irresistibly compelled assent. His features softened, his eyes glistened, he held out his hand, he was about to speak - he hesitated a moment, and sighed. At this instant, Mrs Morton burst into the room, with the aspect of a fury - her bloated countenance yet more swelled and hideous - I shrunk back involuntarily - she poured forth a torrent of abuse and invective. A momentary recollection reassured me - waiting till she had exhausted her breath, I turned from her, and to her husband, with calm dignity -

'I thank you, Sir, for all the kindness I have received from you - I am convinced you do me justice - *for this I do not thank you*, it was a duty to which I had a claim, and which you owed, not only to me, but, to yourself. My longer continuance in this house, I feel, would be improper. For the present, I return to Mrs Harley's, where I shall respectfully receive, and maturely weigh, any counsels with which you may in future think proper to favour me.'

Mr Morton bowed his head; poor man! his mild spirit was overborne, he dared not assert the dictates of his own reason. I hurried out of the apartment, and hastily embracing Ann, who awaited me in the hall, charging myself with a hundred kisses for Mrs Harley, I took the way to the hospitable mansion of my friend.

I had proceeded about half a mile, when I beheld Augustus, advancing towards me; he observed my tremulous emotions, and pallid countenance; he took my hand, holding it with a gentle pressure, and, throwing his other arm round me, supported my faultering steps. His voice was the voice of kindness - his words spake assurance, and breathed hope - *fallacious hope*! - My heart melted within me - my tremor encreased - I dissolved into tears.

'A deserted outcast from society - a desolate orphan - what was to become of me - to whom could I fly?'

'Unjust girl! have I then forfeited all your confidence - have you not a mother and a friend, who love you - ' he stopped - paused - and added 'with maternal, with *fraternal*, tenderness? to whom would you go? - remain with us, your society will cheer my mother's declining years' - again he hesitated, - 'I am about to return to town, assure me, that you will continue with Mrs Harley - it will soften the pain of separation.'

I struggled for more fortitude - hinted at the narrowness of my fortune - at my wish to exert my talents in some way, that should procure me a less dependent situation - spoke of my active spirit - of my abhorrence of a life of indolence and vacuity.

He insisted on my waving these subjects for the present. 'There would be time enough, in future, for their consideration. In the mean-while, I might go on improving myself, and whether present or absent, might depend upon him, for every assistance in his power.'

His soothing kindness, aided by the affectionate attentions of my friend, gradually lulled my mind into tranquillity. My bosom was agitated, only, by a slight and sweet emotion - like the gentle undulations of the ocean, when the winds, that swept over its ruffled surface, are hushed into repose.

CHAPTER XXIV

Another month passed away - every hour, I imbibed, in large draughts, the deceitful poison of hope. A few days before that appointed for the departure of Augustus, I received a visit from Mr Montague, of whose situation, during his confinement, I had made many enquiries, and it was with unaffected pleasure that I beheld him perfectly restored to health. I introduced him to my friends, who congratulated him upon his recovery, and treated him with that polite and cordial hospitality which characterized them. He was on his way to Morton Park, and was particular in his enquiries respecting the late conduct of the lady of the mansion, of which he had heard some confused reports. I could not conceal from him our final separation, but, aware of his inflammable temper, I endeavoured to soften my recital as far as was consistent with truth and justice. It was with difficulty, that our united persuasions induced him to restrain his fiery spirit, which broke out into menaces and execrations. I represented to him -

'That every thing had been already explained; that the affair had now subsided; that a reconciliation was neither probable nor desirable; that any interference, on his part, would only tend to mutual exasperation, from which I must eventually be the sufferer.'

I extorted from him a promise - that, as he was necessitated to meet Mr Morton on business, he would make no allusions to the past - I should be mortified, (I added) by having it supposed, that I stood in need of a *champion*. - Mr Morton had no doubts of the rectitude of my conduct, and it would be barbarous to involve him in a perpetual domestic warfare.

Mr Montague, at the request of Augustus, spent that day, and the next, with us. I thought, I perceived, that he regarded Mr Harley with a scrutinizing eye, and observed my respect for, and attention to, him, with jealous apprehension. Before his departure, he requested half an hour's conversation with me alone, with which request I immediately complied, and withdrew with him into an adjoining compartment. He informed me -

'That he was going to London to pursue his medical studies - that, on his return, his father had proposed to establish him in his profession - that his prospects were very favourable, and that he should esteem himself completely happy if he might, yet, hope to soften my heart in his favour, and to place me in a more assured and tranquil position.'

I breathed a heavy sigh, and sunk into a melancholy reverie.

'Speak to me, Emma,' said he, with impatience, 'and relieve the anxiety I suffer.'

'Alas! What can I say?'

'Say, that you will try to love me, that you will reward my faith and perseverance.'

'Would to God, I could' - I hesitated - my eyes filled with tears - 'Go to London,' resumed I; 'a thousand new objects will there quickly obliterate from your remembrance a romantic and ill-fated attachment, to which retirement, and the want of other impression, has given birth, and which owes its strength merely to opposition.'

'As that opposition,' retorted he, 'is the offspring of pride and insensibility - '

I looked at him with a mournful air - 'Do not reproach me, Montague, my situation is far more pitiable than yours. *I am, indeed, unhappy*,' - added I, after a pause; 'I, like you, am the victim of a raised - of, I fear - a distempered imagination.'

He eagerly entreated me to explain myself.

'I will not attempt to deceive you - I should accuse myself, were I to preserve any sentiment, however delicate its nature, that might tend to remove your present illusion. It is, I confess, with extreme reluctance - with real pain' - I trembled - my voice faultered, and I felt my colour vary - 'that I constrain myself to acknowledge a hopeless, an extravagant' - I stopped, unable to proceed.

Fire flashed from his eyes, he started from his seat, and took two or three hasty strides across the room.

'I understand you, but too well - Augustus Harley shall dispute with me a prize' -

'Stop, Sir, be not unjust - make not an ungenerous return to the confidence I have reposed in you. Respect the violence which, on your account, I have done to my own feelings. I own, that I have not been able to defend my heart against the accomplishments and high qualities of Mr Harley - I respected his virtues and attainments, and, by a too easy transition - at length - *loved his person*. But my tenderness is a secret to all the world but yourself - It has not met with' - a burning blush suffused my cheek - 'It has little hope of meeting, a return. To your honor I have confided this cherished *secret* - dare you betray my confidence? I know, you dare not!'

He seemed affected - his mind appeared torn by a variety of conflicting emotions, that struggled for victory - he walked towards me, and again to the door, several times. I approached him - I gave him my hand -

'Adieu, Montague,' said I, in a softened accent - 'Be assured of my sympathy - of my esteem - of my best wishes! When you can meet me with calmness, I shall rejoice to see you - *as a friend*. Amidst some excesses, I perceive the seeds of real worth in your character, cultivate them, they may yield a noble harvest. I shall not be forgetful of the distinction you have shewn me, *when almost a deserted orphan* - Once again - farewel, my friend, and - may God bless you!'

I precipitately withdrew my hand from his, and rushed out of the room. I retired to my chamber, and it was some hours before my spirits became sufficiently composed to allow me to rejoin my friends. On meeting them, Mrs Harley mentioned, with some surprize, the abrupt departure of Montague, who had quitted the house, without taking leave of its owners, by whom he had been so politely received.

'He is a fine young man,' added she, 'but appears to be very eccentric.'

Augustus was silent, but fixed his penetrating eyes on my face, with an expression that covered me with confusion.

CHAPTER XXV

The day fixed for the departure of Mr Harley, for London, now drew near - I had anticipated this period with the most cruel inquietude. I was going to lose, perhaps for ever, my preceptor, my friend! He, from whom my mind had acquired knowledge, and in whose presence my heart had rested satisfied. I had hitherto scarcely formed a wish beyond that of daily beholding, and listening to him - I was now to gaze on that beloved countenance, to listen to those soothing accents, no longer. He was about to mix in the gay world - to lose in the hurry of business, or of pleasure, the remembrance of those tender, rational, tranquil, moments, sacred to virtue and friendship, that had left an indelible impression on my heart. Could I, indeed, flatter myself, that the idea of the timid, affectionate, Emma, would ever recur to his mind in the tumultuous scenes of the crowded metropolis, it would doubtless quickly be effaced, and lost in the multiplicity of engagements and avocations. How should I, buried in solitude and silence, recall it to his recollection, how contrive to mingle it with his thoughts, and entangle it with his associations? Ah! did he but know my tenderness - *the desire of being beloved*, of inspiring sympathy, is congenial to the human heart - why should I hesitate to inform him of my affection - why do I blush and tremble at the mere idea? It is a false shame! It is a pernicious system of morals, which teaches us that hypocrisy can be virtue! He is well acquainted with the purity, and with the sincerity, of my heart - he will at least regard me with esteem and tender pity - and how often has 'pity melted the soul to love!' The experiment is, surely, innocent, and little hazardous. What I have to apprehend? Can I distrust, for a moment, those principles of rectitude, of honour, of goodness, which gave birth to my affection? Have I not witnessed his humanity, have I not experienced his delicacy, in a thousand instances? Though he should be obliged to wound, he is incapable of insulting, the heart that loves him; and that, loving him, believed, alas! for a long time, *that it loved only virtue*!

The morning of our separation, at last, arrived. My friend, too much indisposed to attend the breakfast table, took leave of her son in her own apartment. I awaited him, in the library, with a beating heart, and, on his departure, put into his hands a paper. -

'Read it not,' said I, in a low and almost inarticulate tone of voice, 'till arrived at the end of your journey; or, at least, till you are ten miles from hence.'

He received it in silence; but it was a silence more expressive than words.

'Suffer me,' it said, 'for a few moments, to solicit your candour and attention. You are the only man in the world, to whom I could venture to confide sentiments, that to many would be inconceivable; and by those, who are unacquainted with the human mind, and the variety of circumstances by which characters are variously impressed and formed - who are accustomed to consider mankind in masses - who have been used to bend implicitly, to custom and prescription - the deviation of a solitary individual from *rules* sanctioned by usage, by prejudice, by expediency, would be regarded as romantic. I frankly avow, while my cheeks glow with the blushe of *modesty*, not of shame, that your virtues and accomplishments have excited in my bosom an affection, as pure as the motives which gave it birth, and as animated as it is pure. - This ingenuous avowal may perhaps affect, but will scarcely (I suspect) surprise, you; for, incapable of dissimulation, the emotions of my mind are ever but too apparent in my expressions, and in my conduct, to deceive a less penetrating eye than yours - neither have I been solicitous to disguise them.

'It has been observed, that,' "the strength of an affection is generally in the same proportion, as the character of the species, in the object beloved, is lost in that of the individual,"[5] and, that individuality of character is the only fastener of the affections. It is certain, however singular it may appear, that many months before we became personally acquainted, the report of your worth and high qualities had generated in my mind, an esteem and reverence, which has gradually ripened into a tenderness, that has, at length, mixed itself with all my associations, and is become interwoven with every fibre of my heart.

'I have reflected, again and again, on the imprudence of cherishing an attachment, which a variety of circumstances combine to render so unpromising, and - What shall I say? - So peculiar is the constitution of my mind, that those very circumstances have had a tendency directly opposite to what might reasonably have been expected; and have only served to render the sentiment, I have delighted to foster, more affecting and interesting. - Yes! I am aware of the tenure upon which you retain your fortunes - of the cruel and unnatural conditions imposed on you by the capricious testator: neither can I require a sacrifice which I am unable to recompence. But while these melancholy convictions deprive me of hope, they encourage me, by proving the disinterestedness of my attachment, to relieve my heart by communication. - Mine is a whimsical pride, which dreads nothing so much as the imputation of sordid, or sinister motives. Remember, then - should we never meet again - if in future periods you should find, that the friendship of the world is - "a shade that follows wealth and fame;" - if, where you have conferred obligations, you are repaid with ingratitude - where you have placed confidence, with treachery - and where you have a claim to zeal, with coldness! Remember, *that you have once been beloved, for yourself* , by one,

5: *Wolstonecraft's* Rights of Woman.

who, in contributing to the comfort of your life, would have found the happiness of her own.

'Is it possible that a mind like yours, neither hardened by prosperity, nor debased by fashionable levity - which vice has not corrupted, nor ignorance brutalized - can be wholly insensible to the balmy sweetness, which natural, unsophisticated, affections, shed through the human heart?

> *"Shall those by heaven's own influence join'd,*
> *By feeling, sympathy, and mind,*
> *The sacred voice of truth deny,*
> *And mock the mandate of the sky?"*

'But I check my pen: - I am no longer -

> *"The hope-flush'd enterer on the stage of life."*

'The dreams of youth, chased by premature reflection, have given place to soberer, to sadder, conclusions; and while I acknowledge, that it would be inexpressibly soothing to me to believe, that in happier circumstances, my artless affection might have awakened in your mind a sympathetic tenderness: - this is the extent of my hopes! - I recollect you once told me "It was our duty to make our reason conquer the sensibility of our heart." Yet, why? Is, then, apathy the perfection of our nature - and is not that nature refined and harmonized by the gentle and social affections? The Being who gave to the mind its reason, gave also to the heart its sensibility.

'I make no apologies for, because I feel no consciousness of, weakness. An attachment sanctioned by nature, reason, and virtue, ennoble the mind capable of conceiving and cherishing it: of such an attachment a corrupt heart is utterly incapable.

'You may tell me, perhaps, "that the portrait on which my fancy has dwelt enamoured, owes all its graces, its glowing colouring - like the ideal beauty of the ancient artists - to the imagination capable of sketching the dangerous picture." - Allowing this, for a moment, *the sentiments it inspires are not the less genuine*; and without some degree of illusion, and enthusiasm, all that refines, exalts, softens, embellishes, life - genius, virtue, love itself, languishes. But, on this subject, my opinions have not been lightly formed: - it is not to the personal graces, though "the body charms, because the mind is seen," but to the virtues and talents of the individual (for without intellect, virtue is an empty name), that my heart does homage; and, were I never again to behold you - were you even the husband of another - my tenderness (a tenderness as innocent as it is lively) would never cease!

'But, methinks, I hear you say, - "Whither does all this tend, and what end does it propose?" Alas! this is a question I scarcely dare to ask myself! - Yet, allow me to request, that you will make me one promise, and resolve me one question: - ah! do not evade this enquiry; for much it imports me to have an explicit reply, lest, in indulging my own feelings, I should, unconsciously, plant a thorn in the bosom of another: - *Is your heart, at present, free*? Or should you, in future, form a tender engagement, tell me, that I shall receive the first intimation of it from yourself; and, in the assurance of your happiness, I will learn to forget my own.

'I aspire to no higher title than that of the most faithful of your friends, and the wish of becoming worthy of your esteem and confidence shall afford me a motive for improvement. I will learn of you moderation, equanimity, and self-command, and you will, perhaps, continue to afford me direction, and assistance, in the pursuit of knowledge and truth.

'I have laid down my pen, again and again, and still taken it up to add something more, from an anxiety, lest even you, of whose delicacy I have experienced repeated proofs, should misconstrue me. - "Oh! what a world is this! - into what false habits has it fallen! Can hypocrisy be virtue? Can a desire to call forth all the best affections of the heart, be misconstrued into something too degrading for expression?"[6] But I will banish these apprehensions; I am convinced they are injurious.

'Yes! - I repeat it - I relinquish my pen with reluctance. A melancholy satisfaction, from what source I can scarcely define, diffuses itself through my heart while I unfold to you its emotions. - Write to me; *be ingenuous*; I desire, I call for, truth!

'*Emma.*'

6: *Holcroft's* Anna St Ives.

CHAPTER XXVI

I had not courage to make my friend a confident of the step I had taken; so wild, and so romantic, did it appear, even to myself - a false pride, a false shame, withheld me. I brooded in silence over the sentiment, that preyed on the bosom which cherished it. Every morning dawned with expectation, and every evening closed in disappointment. I walked daily to the post-office, with precipitate steps and a throbbing heart, to enquire for letters, but in vain; and returned slow, dejected, spiritless. *Hope*, one hour, animated my bosom and flushed my cheek; the next, pale *despair* shed its torpid influence through my languid frame. Inquietude, at length, gradually gave place to despondency, and I sunk into lassitude.

My studies no longer afforded me any pleasure. I turned over my books, incapable of fixing my attention; took out my drawings, threw them aside; moved, restless and dissatisfied, from seat to seat; sought, with unconscious steps, the library, and, throwing myself on the sopha, with folded arms, fixed my eyes on the picture of Augustus, which had lately been replaced, and sunk into waking dreams of ideal perfection and visionary bliss. I gazed on the lifeless features, engraven on my heart in colours yet more true and vivid - but where was the benignant smile, the intelligent glance, the varying expression? Where the pleasant voice, whose accents had been melody in my ear; that had cheered me in sadness, dispelled the vapours of distrust and melancholy, and awakened my emulation for science and improvement? Starting from a train of poignant and distressing emotions, I fled from an apartment once so dear, presenting now but the ghosts of departed pleasures - fled into the woods, and buried myself in their deepest recesses; or, shutting myself in my chamber, avoided the sight of my friend, whose dejected countenance but the more forcibly reminded me -

'That such things were, and were most dear.'

In this state of mind, looking one day over my papers, without any known end in view, I accidentally opened a letter from Mr Francis (with whom I still continued, occasionally, to correspond), which I had recently received. I eagerly seized, and re-perused, it. My spirits were weakened; the kindness which it expressed affected me - it touched my heart - it excited my tears. I determined instantly to reply to it, and to acknowledge my sense of his goodness.

My mind was overwhelmed with the pressure of its own thoughts; a gleam of joy darted through the thick mists that pervaded it; communication would relieve the burthen. I took up my pen; and, though I dared not betray the fatal secret concealed, as a sacred treasure, in the bottom of my heart, I yet gave a loose to, I endeavoured to paint, its sensations.

74

After briefly sketching the events that had driven me from Morton Park (of which I had not hitherto judged it necessary to inform him), without hinting the name of my deliverer, or suffering myself to dwell on the services he had rendered me, I mentioned my present temporary residence at the house of a friend, and expressed an impatience at my solitary, inactive, situation.

I went on -

'To what purpose should I trouble you with a thousand wayward, contradictory, ideas and emotions, that I am, myself, unable to disentangle - which have, perhaps, floated in every mind, that has had leisure for reflection - which are distinguished by no originality, and which I may express (though not feel) without force? I sought to cultivate my understanding, and exercise my reason, that, by adding variety to my resources, I might increase the number of my enjoyments: for *happiness* is, surely, the only desirable *end* of existence! But when I ask myself, Whether I am yet nearer to the end proposed? - I dare not deceive myself - sincerity obliges me to answer in the negative. I daily perceive the gay and the frivolous, among my sex, amused with every passing trifle; gratified by the insipid *routine* of heartless, mindless, intercourse; fully occupied, alternately, by domestic employment, or the childish vanity of varying external ornaments, and "hanging drapery on a smooth block." I do not affect to despise, and I regularly practise, the necessary avocations of my sex; neither am I superior to their vanities. The habits acquired by early precept and example adhere tenaciously; and are never, perhaps, entirely eradicated. But all these are insufficient to engross, to satisfy, the active, aspiring, mind. Hemmed in on every side by the constitutions of society, and not less so, it may be, by my own prejudices - I perceive, indignantly perceive, the magic circle, without knowing how to dissolve the powerful spell. While men pursue interest, honor, pleasure, as accords with their several dispositions, women, who have too much delicacy, sense, and spirit, to degrade themselves by the vilest of all interchanges, remain insulated beings, and must be content tamely to look on, without taking any part in the great, though often absurd and tragical, drama of life. Hence the eccentricities of conduct, with which women of superior minds have been accused - the struggles, the despairing though generous struggles, of an ardent spirit, denied a scope for its exertions! The strong feelings, and strong energies, which properly directed, in a field sufficiently wide, might - ah! what might they not have aided? forced back, and pent up, ravage and destroy the mind which gave them birth!

'Yes, I confess, I am *unhappy*, unhappy in proportion as I believe myself (it may be, erringly) improved. Philosophy, it is said, should regulate the feelings, but it has added fervor to mine! What are passions, but another name for powers? The mind capable of receiving the most forcible impressions is the sublimely improveable mind! Yet, into whatever trains such minds are accidentally directed, they are prone to enthusiasm, while the vulgar stupidly wonder at the effects of powers, to them wholly inconceivable: the weak and the timid, easily discouraged, are induced, by the first failure, to relinquish their pursuits. "They make the impossibility they fear!" But the bold and the persevering, from repeated disappointment, derive only new ardor and activity. "They conquer difficulties, by daring to attempt them."

'I feel, that I am writing in a desultory manner, that I am unable to crowd my ideas into the compass of a letter, and, that could I do so, I should perhaps only weary you. There are but few persons to whom I would venture to complain, few would understand, and still fewer sympathise with me. You are in health, they would say, in the spring of life, have every thing supplied you without labour (so much the worse), nature, reason, open to you their treasures! All this is, partly, true - but, with inexpressible yearnings, my soul pants for something more, something higher! The morning rises upon me with sadness, and the evening closes with disgust - Imperfection, uncertainty, is impressed on every object, on every pursuit! I am either restless or torpid, I seek to-day, what to-morrow, wearies and offends me.

'I entered life, flushed with hope - I have proceeded but a few steps, and the parterre of roses, viewed in distant prospect, nearer seen, proves a brake of thorns. The few worthy persons I have known appear, to me, to be struggling with the same half suppressed emotions. - Whence is all this? Why is intellect and virtue so far from conferring happiness? Why is the active mind a prey to the incessant conflict between truth and error? Shall I look beyond the disorders which, *here*, appear to me so inexplicable? - shall I expect, shall I demand, from the inscrutable Being to whom I owe my existence, in future unconceived periods, the *end* of which I believe myself capable, and which capacity, like a tormenting *ignis fatuus*, has hitherto served only to torture and betray? The animal rises up to satisfy the cravings of nature, and lies down to repose, undisturbed by care - has man superior powers, only to make him pre-eminently wretched? - wretched, it seems to me, in proportion as he rises? Assist me, in disentangling my bewildered ideas - write to me - reprove me - spare me not!

'Emma.'

To this letter I quickly received a kind and consolatory reply, though not unmingled with the reproof I called for. It afforded me but a temporary relief, and I once more sunk into inanity; my faculties rusted for want of exercise, my reason grew feeble, and my imagination morbid.

CHAPTER XXVII

A pacquet of letters, at length, arrived from London - Mrs Harley, with a look that seemed to search the soul, put one into my hands - The superscription bore the well known characters - yes, it was from Augustus, and addressed to Emma - I ran, with it, into my chamber, locked myself in, tore it almost asunder with a tremulous hand, perused its contents with avidity - scarce daring to respire - I reperused it again and again.

'I had trusted my confessions' (it said) 'to one who had made the human heart his study, who could not be affected by them improperly. It spoke of the illusions of the passions - of the false and flattering medium through which they presented objects to our view. He had answered my letter earlier, had it not involved him in too many thoughts to do it with ease. There was a great part of it to which he knew not how to reply - perhaps, on some subjects, it was not necessary to be explicit. And now, it may be, he had better be silent - he was dissatisfied with what he had written, but, were he to write again, he doubted if he should please himself any better. - He was highly flattered by the favourable opinion I entertained of him, it was a grateful proof, not of his merit, but of the warmth of my friendship, &c. &c.'

This letter appeared to me vague, obscure, enigmatical. Unsatisfied, disappointed, I felt, I had little to hope - and, yet, had no *distinct* ground of fear. I brooded over it, I tortured its meaning into a hundred forms - I spake of it to my friend, but in general terms, in which she seemed to acquiesce: she appeared to have made a determination, not to enquire after what I was unwilling to disclose; she wholly confided both in my principles, and in those of her son: I was wounded by what, entangled in prejudice, I conceived to be a necessity for this reserve.

Again I addressed the man, whose image, in the absence of all other impressions, I had suffered to gain in my mind this dangerous ascendency.

To Augustus Harley.
'I, once more, take up my pen with a mind so full of thought, that I foresee I am about to trespass on your time and patience - yet, perhaps, to one who makes "the human heart his study," it may not be wholly uninteresting *to trace* a faithful delineation of the emotions and sentiments of an ingenuous, uncorrupted, mind - a mind formed by solitude, and habits of reflection, to some strength of character.

'If to have been more guarded and reserved would have been more discreet, I have already forfeited all claim to this discretion - to affect it now, would be vain, and, by pursuing a middle course, I should resign the only advantage I may ever derive from my sincerity, the advantage of expressing my thoughts and feelings with freedom.

'The conduct, which I have been led to adopt, has been the result of a combination of peculiar circumstances, *and is not what I would recommend to general imitation* - To say nothing of the hazards it might involve, I am aware, generally speaking, arguments might be adduced, to prove, that certain customs, of which I, yet, think there is reason to complain, may not have been unfounded in nature - I am led to speak thus, because I am not willing to spare myself, but would alledge all which you might have felt inclined to hint, had you not been with-held by motives of delicate consideration.

'Of what then, you may ask, do I complain? - Not of the laws of nature! But when mind has given dignity to natural affections; when reason, culture, taste, and delicacy, have combined to chasten, to refine, to exalt (shall I say) to sanctity them - Is there, then, no cause to complain of rigor and severity, that such minds must either passively submit to a vile traffic, or be content to relinquish all the endearing sympathies of life? Nature has formed woman peculiarly susceptible of the tender affections. "The voice of nature is too strong to be silenced by artificial precepts." To feel these affections in a supreme degree, a mind enriched by literature and expanded by fancy and reflection, is necessary - for it is intellect and imagination only, that can give energy and interest to -

> *"The thousand soft sensations -*
> *Which vulgar souls want faculties to taste,*
> *Who take their good and evil in the gross."*

'I wish we were in the vehicular state, and that you understood the sentient language;[7] you might then comprehend the whole of what I mean to express, but find too delicate for *words*. But I do you injustice.

'If the affections are, indeed, generated by sympathy, where the principles, pursuits, and habits, are congenial - where the *end*, sought to be attained, is -

> *"Something, than beauty dearer,"*

'You may, perhaps, agree with me, that it is almost indifferent on which side the sentiment originates. Yet, I confess, my frankness has involved me in many after thoughts and inquietudes; inquietudes, which all my reasoning is, at times, insufficient to allay. The shame of being singular, it has been justly observed,[8] requires strong principles, and much native firmness of temper, to surmount. - Those who deviate from the beaten track must expect to be entangled in the thicket,

---

7: See Light of Nature Pursued. *An entertaining philosophical work.*

8: *Aikin's Letters.*

and wounded by many a thorn - my wandering feet have already been deeply pierced.

'I should vainly attempt to describe the struggles, the solicitudes, the doubts, the apprehensions, that alternately rend my heart! I feel, that I have "put to sea upon a shattered plank, and placed my trust in miracles for safety." I dread, one moment, lest, in attempting to awaken your tenderness, I may have forfeited your respect; the next, that I have mistaken a delusive meteor for the sober light of reason. In retirement, numberless contradictory emotions revolve in my disturbed mind: - in company, I start and shudder from accidental allusions, in which no one but myself could trace any application. The end of doubt is the beginning of repose. Say, then, to me, that it is a principle in human nature, however ungenerous, to esteem lightly what may be attained without difficulty. - Tell me to make distinctions between love and friendship, of which I have, hitherto, been able to form no idea. - Say, that the former is the caprice of fancy, founded on external graces, to which I have little pretension, and that it is vain to pretend, that -

> *"Truth and good are one,*
> *And beauty dwells with them."*

'Tell me, that I have indulged too long the wild and extravagant chimeras of a romantic imagination. Let us walk together into the palace of Truth, where (it is fancifully related by an ingenious writer,[9] that) every one was compelled by an irresistible, controlling, power, to reveal his inmost sentiments! All this I will bear, and will still respect your integrity, and confide in your principles; but I can no longer sustain a suspense that preys upon my spirits. It is not the Book of Fate - it is your mind, only, I desire to read. A sickly apprehension overspreads my heart - I pause here, unable to proceed.'

'Emma.'

9: *Madame de Genlis's* Tales of the Castle.

CHAPTER XXVIII

Week after week, month after month, passed away in the anguish of vain expectation: my letter was not answered, and I again sunk into despondency. - Winter drew near. I shuddered at the approach of this dreary and desolate season, when I was roused by the receipt of a letter from one of the daughters of the maternal aunt, under whose care I had spent the happy, thoughtless, days of childhood. My cousin informed me -

'That she had married an officer in the East India service; that soon after their union he was ordered abroad, and stationed in Bengal for three years, during which period she was to remain in a commodious and pleasant house, situated in the vicinity of the metropolis. She had been informed of my removal from Morton Park, and had no doubt but I should be able to give a satisfactory account of the occasion of that removal. She purposed, during the absence of her husband, to let out a part of her house; and should I not be fixed in my present residence, would be happy to accommodate me with an apartment, on terms that should be rather dictated by friendship than interest. She also hinted, that a neighbouring lady, of respectable character, would be glad to avail herself of the occasional assistance of an accomplished woman in the education of her daughters; that she had mentioned me to her in advantageous terms, conceiving that I should have no objection, by such a means, to exercise my talents, to render myself useful, and to augment my small income.'

This intelligence filled me with delight: the idea of change, of exertion, of new scenes - shall I add, *of breathing the same air with Augustus*, rushed tumultuously through my imagination. Flying eagerly to my friend, to impart these tidings, I was not aware of the ungrateful and inconsiderate appearance which these exultations must give me in her eyes, till I perceived the starting tear. - It touched, it electrified, my heart; and, throwing myself into her arms, I caught the soft contagion, and wept aloud.

'Go, Emma - my daughter,' said this excellent woman; 'I banish the selfish regret that would prompt me to detain you. I perceive this solitude is destructive to thy ardent mind. Go, vary your impressions, and expand your sensations; gladden me only from time to time with an account of your progress and welfare.'

I had but little preparation to make. I canvassed over, with my friend, a thousand plans, and formed as many expectations and conjectures; but they all secretly tended to one point, and concentrated in one object. I gave my cousin notice that I should be with her in a few days - settled a future correspondence with my friend - embraced her, at parting, with unfeigned, and tender, sorrow - and, placing myself in a stage-coach, that passed daily through the village, took the road, once more, with a fluttering heart, to London. We travelled all night - it was cold and dreary - but my *fancy* was busied with various images, and my bosom throbbing with lively, though indistinct sensations.

The next day, at noon, I arrived, without accident, at the residence of my relation, Mrs Denbeigh. She received me with unaffected cordiality: our former amity was renewed; we spent the evening together, recalling past scenes; and, on retiring, I was shewn into a neat chamber, which had been prepared for me, with a light closet adjoining. The next day, I was introduced to the lady, mentioned to me by my kind hostess, and agreed to devote three mornings in the week to the instruction of the young ladies (her daughters), in various branches of education.

End of Volume One

VOLUME II

The perceptions of persons in retirement are very different from those of people in the great world: their passions, being differently modified, are differently expressed; their imaginations, constantly impressed by the same objects, are more violently affected. The same small number of images continually return, mix with every idea, and create those strange and false notions, so remrkable in people who spend their lives in solitude.

J. J. Rousseau

To Augustus Harley

'My friend, my son, it is for your benefit, that I have determined on reviewing the sentiments, and the incidents, of my past life. Cold declamation can avail but little towards the reformation of our errors. It is by tracing, by developing, the passions in the minds of others; tracing them, from the seeds by which they have been generated, through all their extended consequences, that we learn, the more effectually, to regulate and to subdue our own.

'I repeat, it will cost me some pain to be ingenuous in the recital which I have pledged myself to give you; even in the moment when I resume my pen, prejudice continues to struggle with principle, and I feel an inclination to retract. While unfolding a series of error and mortification, I tremble, lest, in warning you to shun the rocks and quicksands amidst which my little bark has foundered, I should forfeit your respect and esteem, the pride, and the comfort, of my declining years. But you are deeply interested in my narrative, you tell me, and you entreat me to proceed.'

CHAPTER I

Change of scene, regular employment, attention to my pupils, and the conscious pride of independence, afforded a temporary relief to my spirits. My first care, on my arrival in town, was to gladden the mind of my dear benefactress, by a minute detail of the present comforts and occupations.

She had charged me with affectionate remembrance and letters to her son. I enclosed these letters; and, after informing him (in the cover) of the change of my situation, and the incident which had occasioned it, complained of the silence he had observed towards my last letter.

-'If,' said I, 'from having observed the social and sympathetic nature of our feelings and affections, I suffered myself to yield, involuntarily, to the soothing idea, that the ingenuous avowal of an attachment so tender, so sincere, so artless, as mine, could not have been unaffecting to a mind with which my own proudly claimed kindred: - if I fondly believed, that simplicity, modesty, truth - the eye beaming with sensibility, the cheek mantling with the glow of affection, the features softened, the accents modulated, by ineffable tenderness, might, in the eyes of a virtuous man, have supplied the place of more dazzling accomplishments, and more seductive charms: if I over-rated my own merit, and my own powers - surely my mistakes were sufficiently humiliating! You should not, indeed you should not, have obliged me to arrive at the conviction through a series of deductions so full of mortification and anguish. You are too well acquainted with the human heart not to be sensible, that no certainty can equal the misery of conjecture, in a mind of ardour - the agonizing images which suspense forces upon the tender and sensible heart! You should have written, in pity to the situation of my mind. I would have thanked you for being ingenuous, even though, like Hamlet, you had *spoke daggers*. I expected it, from your character, and I had a claim to your sincerity.

'But it is past! - the vision is dissolved! The barbed arrow is not extracted with more pain, than the enchantments of hope from the ardent and sanguine spirit! But why am I to lose your friendship? My heart tells me, I have not deserved this! Do not suspect, that I have so little justice, or so little magnanimity, as to refuse you the privilege, the enviable privilege, of being master of your own affections. I am unhappy, I confess; the principal charm of my life is fled, and the hopes that should enliven future prospects are faint: melancholy too often obscures reason, and a heart, perhaps too tender, preys on itself.

'I suspect I had formed some vain and extravagant expectations. I could have loved you, had you permitted it, with no mean, nor common attachment. - My words, my looks, my actions, betrayed me, ere I suffered my feelings to dictate to my pen. Would to God, I had buried this fatal secret in the bottom of my soul! But repentance is, now, too late. Yet the sensible heart yearns to disclose itself - and to whom can it confide its sentiments, with equal propriety, as to him who will know how to pity the errors, of which he feels himself, however involuntarily, the cause? The world might think my choice in a confident singular; it has been my misfortune seldom to think with the world, and I ought, perhaps, patiently to submit to the inconveniences to which this singularity has exposed me.

'I know not how, without doing myself a painful violence, to relinquish your society; and why, let me again ask, should I? I now desire only that repose which is the end of doubt, and this, I think, I should regain by one hour's frank conversation with you; I would compose myself, listen to you, and yield to the sovereignty of reason. After such an interview, my mind - no longer harrassed by vague suspicion, by a thousand nameless apprehensions and inquietudes - should struggle to subdue itself - at least, I would not permit it to dictate to my pen, not to bewilder my conduct. I am exhausted by perturbation. I ask only certainty and rest.

'Emma.'

A few days after I had written the preceding letter, Mr Harley called on me. Mrs Denbeigh was with me on his entrance; I would have given worlds to have received him alone, but had not courage to hint this to my relation. Overwhelmed by a variety of emotions, I was unable for some time to make any reply to his friendly enquiries after my health, and congratulations on my amended prospects. My confusion and embarrassment were but too apparent; perceiving my distress, he kindly contrived to engage my hostess in discourse, that I might have time to rally my spirits. By degrees, I commanded myself sufficiently to join in the conversation - I spoke to him of his mother, expressed the lively sense I felt of her goodness, and my unaffected regret at parting with her. Animated by my subject, and encouraged by the delicacy of Augustus, I became more assured: we retraced the amusements and studies of H ...... shire, and two hours passed delightfully and insensibly away, when Mrs Denbeigh was called out of the room to speak to a person who brought her letters and intelligence from the India House. Mr Harley, rising at the same time from his seat, seemed about to depart, but hesitating, stood a few moments as if irresolute.

'You leave me,' said I, in a low and tremulous tone, 'and you leave me still in suspense?'

'Could you,' replied he, visibly affected, 'but have seen me on the receipt of your last letter, you would have perceived that my feelings were not enviable - Your affecting expostulation, added to other circumstances of a vexatious nature, oppressed my spirits with a burthen more than they were able to sustain.'

He resumed his seat, spoke of his situation, of the tenure on which he held his fortune, - 'I am neither a stoic nor a philosopher,' added he, - 'I knew not how - *I could not answer your letter*. What shall I say? - I am with-held from explaining myself further, by reasons - *by obligations* - Who can look back on every action of his past life with approbation? Mine has not been free from error! I am distressed, perplexed - *insuperable obstacles* forbid what otherwise' -

'I feel,' said I, interrupting him, 'that I am the victim of my own weakness and vanity - I feel, that I have been rushing headlong into the misery which you kindly sought to spare me - I am sensible of your delicacy - of your humanity! - And is it with the full impression of your virtues on my heart that I must teach that heart to renounce you - renounce, for ever, the man with whose pure and elevated mind my own panted to mingle? My reason has been blinded by the illusions of my self-love - and, while I severely suffer, I own my sufferings just - yet, the sentiments you inspired were worthy of you! I understand little of - I have violated common forms - seeking your tenderness, I have perhaps forfeited your esteem!'

'Far, *very far*, from it - I would, but cannot, say more.'

'Must we, then, separate for ever - will you no longer assist me in the pursuit of knowledge and truth - will you no more point out to me the books I should read, and aid me in forming a just judgment of the principles they contain - Must all your lessons be at an end - all my studies be resigned? How, without your counsel and example, shall I regain my strength of mind - to what end shall I seek to improve myself, when I dare no longer hope to be worthy of him - '

A flood of tears checked my utterance; hiding my face with my hands, I gave way to the kindly relief, but for which my heart had broken. I heard footsteps in the passage, and the voice of Mrs Denbeigh as speaking to her servant - covered with shame and grief, I dared not in this situation appear before her, but, rushing out at an opposite door, hid myself in my chamber. A train of confused recollections tortured my mind, I concluded, that Augustus had another, a prior attachment. I felt, with this conviction, that I had not the fortitude, and that perhaps I ought not, to see him again. I wrote to him under this impression; I poured out my soul in anguish, in sympathy, in fervent aspirations for his happiness. These painful and protracted conflicts affected my health, a deep and habitual depression preyed upon my spirits, and, surveying every object through the medium of a distempered imagination, I grew disgusted with life.

CHAPTER II

I began, at length, to think, that I had been too precipitate, and too severe to myself. - Why was I to sacrifice a friend, from whose conversation I had derived improvement and pleasure? I repeated this question to myself, again and again; and I blushed and repented. But I deceived myself. I had too frequently acted with precipitation, I determined, now, to be more prudent - I waited three months, fortified my mind with many reflections, and resumed my pen -

To Augustus Harley.

'Near three months have elapsed, since I last addressed you. I remind you of this, not merely to suppress, as it arises, any apprehension which you may entertain of further embarrassment or importunity: for I can no longer afflict myself with the idea, that my peace, or welfare, are indifferent to you, but will rather adopt the sentiment of Plato - who on being informed, that one of his disciples, whom he had more particularly distinguished, had spoken ill of him, replied, to the slanderer - "I do not believe you, for it is impossible that I should not be esteemed by one whom I so sincerely regard."

'My motive, for calling to your remembrance the date of my last, is, that you should consider what I am now about to say, as the result of calmer reflection, the decision of judgment after having allowed the passions leisure to subside. It is, perhaps, unnecessary to premise, that I am not urged on by pride, from an obscure consciousness of having been betrayed into indiscretion, to endeavour to explain away, or to extenuate, any part of my former expressions or conduct. To a mind like yours, such an attempt would be impertinent; from one like mine, I hope, superfluous. I am not ashamed of being a human being, nor blush to own myself liable to "the shakes and agues of his fragile nature." I have ever spoken, and acted, from the genuine dictates of a mind swayed, at the time, by its own views and propensities, nor have I hesitated, as those views and propensities have changed, to avow my further convictions - "Let not the coldly wise exult, that their heads were never led astray by their hearts." I have all along used, and shall continue to use, the unequivocal language of sincerity.

'However *romantic* (a vague term applied to every thing we do not understand, or are unwilling to intimate) my views and sentiments might appear to many, I dread not, from you, this frigid censure. "The ideas, the associations, the circumstances of each man are properly his own, and it is a pernicious system, that would lead us to require all men, however different their circumstances, to act in many of the common affairs of life, by a precise, general rule." [10] The

10: Godwin's Political Justice.

genuine effusions of the heart and mind are easily distinguished, by the penetrating eye, from the vain ostentation of sentiment, lip deep, which, causing no emotion, communicates none - Oh! how unlike the energetic sympathies of truth and feeling - darting from mind to mind, enlightening, warming, with electrical rapidity!

'My ideas have undergone, in the last three months, many fluctuations. My *affection* for you (why should I seek for vague, inexpressive phrases?) has not ceased, has not diminished, but it has, in some measure, changed its nature. It was originally generated by the report, and cemented by the knowledge, of your virtues and talents; and to virtue and talents my mind had ever paid unfeigned, enthusiastic, homage! It is somewhere said by Rousseau - "That there may exist such a suitability of moral, mental, and personal, qualifications, as should point out the propriety of an union between a prince and the daughter of an executioner." Vain girl that I was! I flattered myself that between us this sympathy really existed. I dwelt on the union between mind and mind - sentiments of nature gently insinuated themselves - my sensibility grew more tender, more affecting - and my imagination, ever lively, traced the glowing picture, and dipped the pencil in rainbow tints! Possessing one of those determined spirits, that is not easily induced to relinquish its purposes - while I conceived that I had only your pride, or your insensibility, to combat, I wildly determined to persevere. - A further recapitulation would, perhaps, be unnecessary: - my situation, alas! is now changed.

'Having then examined my heart, attentively and deliberately, I suspect that I have been unjust to myself, in supposing it incapable of a disinterested attachment. - Why am I to deprive you of a faithful friend, and myself of all the benefits I may yet derive from your conversation and kind offices? I ask, why? And I should, indeed, have cause to blush, if, after having had time for reflection, I could really think this necessary. Shall I, then, sign the unjust decree, that women are incapable of energy and fortitude? Have I exercised my understanding, without ever intending to apply my principles to practice? Do I mean always to deplore the prejudices which have, systematically, weakened the female character, without making any effort to rise above them? Is the example you have given me, of a steady adherence to honour and principle, to be merely respected, without exciting in my bosom any emulation? Dare I to answer these questions in the affirmative, and still ask your esteem - the esteem of the wise and good? - I dare not! No longer weakened by alternate hopes and fears, like the reed yielding to every breeze, I believe myself capable of acting upon firmer principles; and I request, with confidence, the restoration of your friendship! Should I afterwards find, that I have over-rated my own strength, I will frankly tell you so, and expect from your humanity those allowances, which are but a poor substitute for respect.

'Believe, then, my views and motives to be simply such as I state them; at least, such, after severely scrutinizing my heart, they appear to myself; and reply to me with similar ingenuousness. My expectations are very moderate: answer me with simplicity - my very soul sickens at evasion! You have undoubtedly, a right to judge and to determine for yourself; but it will be but just to state to me the reasons for, and the result of, that judgment; in which case, if I cannot obviate those reasons, I shall be bound, however reluctantly, to acquiesce in them. Be assured, I will never complain of any consequences which may ensue, even, from the utterance of all truth.

'Emma.'

CHAPTER III

This letter was succeeded by a renewal of our intercourse and studies. Mrs Denbeigh, my kind hostess, was usually of our parties. We read together, or conversed only on general topics, or upon subjects of literature. I was introduced by Mr Harley to several respectable families, friends of his own and of his mother's. I made many indirect enquiries of our common acquaintance, with a view to discover the supposed object of my friend's attachment, but without success. All that he had, himself, said, respecting such an engagement, had been so vague, that I began to doubt of the reality of its existence. - When, in any subsequent letters (for we continued occasionally to correspond) I ventured to allude to the subject, I was warned 'not to confound my own conceptions with real existences.' When he spoke of a susceptibility to the tender affections, it was always in the past time, - 'I have felt,' - 'I have been - 'Once he wrote - 'His situation had been rendered difficult, by a combination of peculiar circumstances; circumstances, with which but few persons were acquainted.' Sometimes he would affect to reflect upon his past conduct, and warn me against appreciating him too highly. In fine, he was a perfect enigma, and every thing which he said or wrote tended to increase the mystery.

A restless, an insatiable, curiosity, devoured me, heightened by feelings that every hour became more imperious, more uncontrollable. I proposed to myself, in the gratification of this curiosity, a satisfaction that should compensate for all the injuries I might suffer in the career. This inquietude prevented my mind from resting; and, by leaving room for conjecture, left room for the illusions of fancy, and of hope. Had I never expressed this, he might have affected ignorance of my sensations; he might have pleaded guiltless, when, in the agony of my soul, I accused him of having sacrificed my peace to his disingenuousness - but vain were all my expostulations!

'If,' said I, 'I have sought, too earnestly, to learn the state of your affections, it has been with a view to the more effectually disciplining of my own - of stifling every *ignis fatuus* of false hope, that making, even, impossibilities possible, will still, at times, continue to mislead me. Objects seen through obscurity, imperfectly discerned, allow to the fancy but too free a scope; the mind grows debilitated, by brooding over its apprehensions; and those apprehensions, whether real or imaginary, are carried with accumulated pain to the heart. I have said, on this subject, you have a right to be free; but I am, now, doubtful of this right: the health of my mind being involved in the question, has rendered it a question of *utility* - and on what other basis can morals rest?'

I frequently reiterated these reasonings, always with increased fervor and earnestness: represented - 'that every step I took in advance would be miles in return - every minute that the blow was suspended, prepared it to descend with accumulated force.' I required no particulars, but merely requested to be assured of a *present, existing, engagement*. I continued, from time to time, to urge this subject.

'Much,' said I, 'as I esteem you, and deeply as a thousand associations have fixed your idea in my heart - in true candour of soul, I, yet, feel myself your superior. - I recollect a sentiment of Richardson's *Clarissa* that always pleased me, and that may afford a test, by which each of us may judge of the integrity of our own minds - "I should be glad that you, and all the world, knew my heart; let my enemies sit in judgment upon my actions; fairly scanned, I fear not the result. Let them ask me my most secret thoughts; and, whether they make for me, or against me, I will reveal them."

'This is the principle, my friend, upon which I have acted towards you. I have said many things, I doubt not, which make against me; but I trusted them to one, who told me, that he had made the human heart his study: and it is only in compliance with the prejudices of others, if I have taken any pains to conceal all I have thought and felt on this, or on any other, subject, from the rest of the world. Had I not, in the wild career of fervent feeling, had sufficient strength of mind to stop short, and to reason calmly, how often, in the bitterness of my spirit, should I have accused you of sporting with my feelings, by involving me in a hopeless maze of conjecture - by leaving me a prey to the constant, oppressive, apprehension of hearing something, which I should not have had the fortitude to support with dignity; which, in proportion as it is delayed, still contributes to harrass, to weaken, to incapacitate, my mind from bearing its disclosure.

'I know you might reply - and more than nine-tenths of the world would justify you in this reply - "That you had already said, what ought to have been sufficient, and would have been so to any other human being; - that you had not sought the confidence I boast of having reposed in you; - and that so far from affording you any satisfaction, it has occasioned you only perplexity. If my own destiny was not equivocal, of what importance could it be to me, and what right had I to enquire after circumstances, in which, however affecting, I could have no real concern."

'You may think all this, perhaps - I will not spare myself - and it may be reasonable. *But could you say it* - and have you, indeed, studied the human heart - *have you, indeed, ever felt the affections*? - Whatever may be the event - and it is in the mind of powers only that passions are likely to become fatal - and however irreproachable every other part of your conduct may have been, I shall, *here*, always say, you were culpable!'

I changed my style. 'I know not,' said I, 'the nature of those stern duties, which oblige you to with-hold from me your tenderness; neither do I any longer enquire. I dread, only, lest I should acquire this knowledge when I am the least able to support it. Ignorant, then, of any reasons which should prevent me from giving up my heart to an attachment, now become interwoven with my existence, I yield myself up to these sweet and affecting emotions, so necessary to my disposition - to which apathy is abhorrent. "The affections (truly says Sterne) must be exercised on something; for, not to love, is to be miserable. Were I in a desert, I would find out wherewith in it to call forth my affections. If I could do no better, I would fasten them upon some sweet myrtle, or seek some melancholy cypress to connect myself to - I would court their shade, and greet them kindly for their protection. I would cut my name upon them, and swear they were the loveliest trees throughout the desert. If their leaves withered, I would teach myself to mourn; and, when they rejoiced, I would rejoice with them."

'An attachment, founded upon a full conviction of worth, must be both safe and salutary. My mind has not sufficient strength to form an abstract idea of perfection. I have ever found it stimulated, improved, advanced, by its affections. I will, then, continue to love you with fervor and purity; I will see you with joy, part from you with regret, grieve in your griefs, enter with zeal into your concerns, interest myself in your honour and welfare, and endeavour, with all my little power, to contribute to your comfort and satisfaction. - Is your heart so differently constituted from every other human heart, that an affection, thus ardent and sincere, excites in it no grateful, and soothing, emotions? Why, then, withdraw yourself from me, and by that means afflict, and sink into despondency, a mind that entrusts its peace to your keeping.

'Emma.'

We met the next day at the house of a common friend. My accents, involuntarily, were softened, my attentions pointed. - Manifestly agitated, embarrassed, even distressed, Augustus quitted the company at an early hour.

It would be endless to enumerate all the little incidents that occurred; which, however trifling they might appear in the recital, continued to operate in one direction. Many letters passed to the same purport. My curiosity was a consuming passion; but this inflexible, impenetrable, man, was still silent, or alternately evaded, and resented, my enquiries. We continued, occasionally, to meet, but generally in company.

CHAPTER IV

During the ensuing summer, Mr Harley proposed making a visit to his mother, and, calling to take his leave of me, on the evening preceding his journey, accidentally found me alone. - We entered into conversation on various subjects: twilight stole upon us unperceived. The obscure light inspired me with courage: I ventured to resume a subject, so often discussed; I complained, gently, of his reserve.

'Could I suppose,' he asked, 'that he had been without *his share* of suffering?'

I replied something, I scarce know what, adverting to his stronger mind.

'Strength!' said he, turning from me with emotion, 'rather say, weakness!'

I reiterated the important, the so often proposed, enquiry - 'Had he, or had he not, *a present, existing, engagement?*'

He endeavoured to evade my question - I repeated it - He answered, with a degree of impatience, '*I cannot tell you;* if I could, do you think I would have been silent so long?' - as once, before, he spoke of the circumstances of his past life, as being of '*a singular, a peculiar, nature.*'

At our separation, I asked, if he would write to me during his absence. 'Certainly, he would.' The next morning, having some little commissions to execute for Mrs Harley, I sent them, accompanied by a few lines, to her son.

'Why is it,' said I, 'that our sagacity, and penetration, frequently desert us on the most interesting occasions? I can read any mind with greater facility than I can read your's; and, yet, what other have I so attentively studied? This is a problem I know not how to solve. One conclusion will force itself upon me - if a mistaken one, whom have you to blame? - That an *honourable*, suitable, engagement, could have given no occasion for mystery.' I added, 'I should depend on hearing from him, according to his promise.'

Week after week, month after month, wore away, and no letter arrived. Perturbation was succeeded by anxiety and apprehension; but hearing, through my maternal friend, Mrs Harley, of the welfare of this object of our too tender cares, my solicitude subsided into despondency. The pressure of one corroding train of ideas preyed, like a canker-worm, upon my heart, and destroyed all its tranquillity.

In the beginning of the winter, this mysterious, inexplicable, being, again returned to town. I had undertaken a little business, to serve him, during his absence - I transmitted to him an account of my proceedings; subjoining a gentle reproach for his unkind silence.

'You promised you would write to me,' said I, 'during your residence in ..... shire. I therefore depended upon hearing from you; and, yet, I was disappointed. You should not, indeed you should not, make these experiments upon my mind. My sensibility, originally acute, from having been too much exercised, has become nearly morbid, and has almost unfitted me for an inhabitant of this world. I am willing to believe, that your conduct towards me has originated in good motives, nevertheless, you have made some sad mistakes - you have *deeply*, though undesignedly, wounded me: I have been harrassed, distressed, mortified. You know not, neither will I attempt to describe, all I have suffered! language would be inadequate to paint the struggles of a delicate, susceptible, mind, in some peculiar and interesting situations.

'You may suspect me of wanting resolution, but strong, persevering affections, are no mark of a weak mind. To have been the wife of a man of virtue and talents was my dearest ambition, and would have been my glory: I judged myself worthy of the confidence and affection of such a man - I felt, that I could have united in his pursuits, and shared his principles - aided the virtuous energies of his mind, and assured his domestic comforts. I earnestly sought to inspire you with tenderness, from the conviction, that I could contribute to your happiness, and to the worth of your character. And if, from innumerable associations, I at length loved your person, it was the magnanimity of your conduct, it was your virtues, that first excited my admiration and esteem. But you have rejected an attachment originating in the highest, the purest, principles - you have thrown from you a heart of exquisite sensibility, and you leave me in doubt, whether you have not sacrificed that heart to prejudice. Yet, contemned affection has excited in my mind no resentment; true tenderness is made up of gentle and amiable emotions; nothing hostile, nothing severe, can mix with it: it may gradually subside, but it will continue to soften the mind it has once subdued.

'I see much to respect in your conduct, and though, it is probable, some parts of it may have originated in mistaken principles, I trust, that their source was pure! I, also, have made many mistakes - have been guilty of many extravagances. Yet, distrust the morality, that sternly commands you to pierce the bosom that most reveres you, and then to call it virtue - Yes! distrust and suspect its origin!' I concluded with expressing a wish to see him - 'merely as a friend' - requesting a line in reply.

He wrote not, but came, unexpectedly came, the next evening. I expressed, in lively terms, the pleasure I felt in seeing him. We conversed on various subjects, he spoke affectionately of his mother, and of the tender interest she had expressed for my welfare. He enquired after my pursuits and acquirements during his absence, commending the progress I had made. Just before he quitted me, he adverted to the reproach I had made him, for not having written to me, according to his engagement.

'Recollect,' said he, 'in the last letter I received from you, before I left London, you hinted some suspicions -' I looked at him, 'and what,' added he, 'could I reply?'

I was disconcerted, I changed colour, and had no power to pursue the subject.

CHAPTER V

From this period, he continued to visit me (I confess at my solicitation) more frequently. We occasionally resumed our scientific pursuits, read together, or entered into discussion on various topics. At length he grew captious, disputatious, gloomy, and imperious - the more I studied to please him, the less I succeeded. He disapproved my conduct, my opinions, my sentiments; my frankness offended him. This change considerably affected me. In company, his manners were studiously cold and distant; in private capricious, yet reserved and guarded. He seemed to overlook all my efforts to please, and, with a severe and penetrating eye, to search only for my errors - errors, into which I was but too easily betrayed, by the painful, and delicate, situation, in which I had placed myself.

We, one day, accompanied Mrs Denbeigh on a visit of congratulation to her brother (eldest son of my deceased uncle Mr Melmoth), who had, when a youth, been placed by his father in a commercial house in the West Indies, and who had just returned to his native country with an ample fortune. His sister and myself anticipated the pleasure of renewing our early, fraternal, affection and intimacy, while I felt a secret pride in introducing to his acquaintance a man so accomplished and respectable as Mr Harley. We were little aware of the changes which time and different situations produce on the character, and, with hearts and minds full of the frank, lively, affectionate, youth, from whom we had parted, seven years since, with mutual tears and embraces, shrunk spontaneously, on our arrival at Mr Melmoth's elegant house in Bedford square, from the cold salutation, of the haughty, opulent, purse-proud, Planter, surrounded by ostentatious luxuries, and evidently valuing himself upon the consequence which he imagined they must give him in our eyes.

Mr Harley received the formal compliments of this favourite of fortune with the easy politeness which distinguishes the gentleman and the man of letters, and the dignified composure which the consciousness of worth and talents seldom fails to inspire. Mr Melmoth, by his awkward and embarrassed manner, tacitly acknowledged the impotence of wealth and the real superiority of his guest. We were introduced by our stately relation to his wife, the lady of the mansion, a young woman whom he had accidentally met with in a party of pleasure at Jamaica, whither she had attended a family in the humble office of companion or chief attendant to the lady. Fascinated by her beauty and lively manner, our trader had overlooked an empty mind, a low education, and a doubtful character, and, after a very few interviews, tendered to her acceptance his hand and fortune; which, though not without some affectation of doubt and delay, were in a short time joyfully accepted.

A gentleman joined our party in the dining-room, whom the servant announced by the name of Pemberton, in whom I presently recognized, notwithstanding some years had elapsed since our former meeting, the man of fashion and gallantry who had been the antagonist of Mr Francis, at the table of my father. He had lately (we were informed by our host) been to Jamaica, to take possession of an estate bequeathed to him, and had returned to England in the same vessel with Mr and Mrs Melmoth. After an elegant dinner of several courses had been served up and removed for the desert, a desultory conversation took place.

Mr Pemberton, it appeared, held a commission in the militia, and earnestly solicited Mrs Melmoth, on whom he lavished a profusion of compliments, to grace their encampment, which was to be stationed in the ensuing season near one of the fashionable watering places, with her presence.

This request the lady readily promised to comply with, expressing, in tones of affected softness, her admiration of military men, and of the

'Pride, pomp and circumstance of glorious war!'

'Do you not think, Miss Courtney,' said she, turning to me, 'that soldiers are the most agreeable and charming men in the world?'

'Indeed I do not, Madam; their trade is *murder*, and their trappings, in my eyes, appear but as the gaudy pomp of sacrifice.'

'*Murder*, indeed! What a harsh word - I declare you are a shocking creature - There have always been wars in the world, and there always must be: but surely you would not confound the brave fellows, who fight to protect their King and Country, and *the ladies*, with common ruffians and housebreakers!'

'All the difference between them is, that the one, rendered desperate by passion, poverty, or injustice, endeavours by *wrong* means to do himself *right,* and through this terrible and pitiable mistake destroys the life or the property of a fellow being - The others, wantonly and in cold blood, cut down millions of their species, ravage whole towns and cities, and carry devastation through a country.'

'What *odd notions*! Dear, Mr Pemberton, did you ever hear a lady talk so strangely?'

Thus called upon, Mr Pemberton thought it incumbent upon him to interfere - '*Courtney*, I think, Madam, your name is! The daughter of an old friend of mine, if I am not mistaken, and who, I remember, was, when a very young lady, a great admirer of Roman virtues.'

'Not of *Roman virtues*, I believe, Sir; they had in them too much of the destructive spirit which Mrs Melmoth thinks so admirable.'

'Indeed, I said nothing about *Roman virtues*, nor do I trouble myself with such subjects - I merely admired the soldiers because they are so brave and so polite; besides, the military dress is so elegant and becoming - Dear, Mr Pemberton, how charmingly you must look in your regimentals!'

Mr Pemberton, bowing in return to the compliment, made an animated eulogium on the taste and beauty of the speaker.

'Pray, Sir,' resumed she, addressing herself to Mr Harley, whose inattention seemed to pique her, and whose notice she was determined to attract, 'are you of Miss Courtney's opinion - do you think it right to call soldiers *murderers*?'

'Upon my word, Madam,' with an air of irony, 'you must excuse me from entering into such *nice distinctions* - when *ladies* differ, who shall presume to decide?'

Mr Melmoth interposed, by wishing, 'that they had some thousands more of these *murderers* in the West Indies, to keep the slaves in subordination, who, since absurd notions of liberty had been put into their heads, were grown very troublesome and refractory, and, in a short time, he supposed, would become as insolent as the English servants.'

'Would you believe it, Mrs Denbeigh,' said the Planter's lady, addressing the sister of her husband, 'Mr Melmoth and I have been in England but a month, and have been obliged three times to change our whole suit of servants?'

'This is a land of freedom, my dear sister; servants, here, will not submit to be treated like the slaves of Jamaica.'

'Well, I am sure it is very provoking to have one's will disputed by such low, ignorant, creatures. How should they know what is right? It is enough for them to obey the orders of their superiors.'

'But suppose,' replied Mrs Denbeigh, 'they should happen to think their superiors unreasonable!'

'*Think*! sister,' said the lordly Mr Melmoth, with an exulting laugh, 'what have servants, or women, to do with thinking?'

'Nay, now,' interrupted Mr Pemberton, 'you are too severe upon the ladies - how would the elegant and tasteful arrangement of Mrs Melmoth's ornaments have been produced without thinking?'

'Oh, you flatterer!' said the lady.

'Let them think only about their dress, and I have no objection, but don't let them plague us with *sermonizing*.'

'Mrs Melmoth,' said I, coolly, 'does not often, I dare say, offend in this way. That some of the gentlemen, present, should object to a woman's exercising her discriminating powers, is not wonderful, since it might operate greatly to their disadvantage.'

'A blow on the right cheek, from so fair a hand,' replied Mr Pemberton, affectedly bending his body, 'would almost induce one to adopt the christian maxim, and turn the left, also. What say you, Mr Harley?'

'Mr Harley, I believe, Sir, does not feel himself included in the reflection.'

'He is a happy man then.'

'No, Sir, merely a *rational one*!'

'You are pleased to be severe; of all things I dread a female wit.'

'It is an instinctive feeling of self-preservation - nature provides weak animals with timidity as a guard.'

Mr Pemberton reddened, and, affecting a careless air, hummed a tune. Mr Melmoth again reverted to the subject of English servants, which gave rise to a discussion on the Slave Trade. Mr Harley pleaded the cause of freedom and humanity with a bold and manly eloquence, expatiating warmly on the iniquity as well as impolicy of so accursed a traffic. Melmoth was awed into silence. Mr Pemberton advanced some trite arguments in opposition, respecting the temporary mischiefs which might ensue, in case of an abolition, to the planters, landholders, traders, &c. Augustus explained, by contending only for the gradual emancipation, after their minds had been previously prepared, of the oppressed Africans. The conversation grew interesting. Pemberton was not devoid of talents when he laid aside his affectation; the subject was examined both in a moral and a political point of view. I listened with delight, while Augustus exposed and confuted the specious reasoning and sophistry of his antagonist: exulting in the triumph of truth and justice, I secretly gloried - '*with more than self vanity*' - in the virtues and abilities of my friend. Though driven from all his resources, Mr Pemberton was too much the courtier to be easily disconcerted, but complimenting his adversary on his eloquence, declared he should be happy to hear of his having a seat in Parliament.

Mrs Melmoth, who had yawned and betrayed various symptoms of weariness during the discussion, now proposed the adjournment of the ladies into the drawing-room, whither I was compelled, by a barbarous and odious custom, reluctantly to follow, and to submit to be entertained with a torrent of folly and impertinence.

'I was ill-natured,' she told me. - 'How could I be so severe upon the charming and elegant Mr Pemberton?'

It was in vain I laboured to convince her, that to be treated like idiots was no real compliment, and that the men who condescend to flatter our foibles, despised the weak beings they helped to form.

My remonstrances were as fatiguing, and as little to be comprehended by this *fine lady*, as the arguments respecting the Slave Trade: - she sought refuge from them in interrogating Mrs Denbeigh respecting the last new fashions, and in consulting her taste on the important question - whether blue or violet colour was the most becoming to a brunette complexion? The gentlemen joined us, to our great relief, at the tea-table: - other company dropped in, and the evening was beguiled with cards and the chess-board; - at the latter Mr Melmoth and Mr Harley were antagonists; - the former was no match for Augustus. I amused myself by observing their moves, and overlooking the game.

During our return from this visit, some conversation occurred between Mr Harley, my cousin, and myself, respecting the company we had quitted. I expressed my disappointment, disgust, and contempt, in terms, it may be, a little too strong.

'I was *fastidious*,' Augustus told me, 'I wanted a world made on purpose for me, and beings formed after one model. It was both amusing, and instructive, to contemplate varieties of character. I was a romantic enthusiast - and should endeavour to become more like an inhabitant of the world.'

Piqued at these remarks, and at the tone and manner in which they were uttered, I felt my temper rising, and replied with warmth; but it was the glow of a moment; for, to say truth, vexation and disappointment, rather than reason, had broken and subdued my spirit. Mrs Denbeigh, perceiving I was pained, kindly endeavoured to give a turn to the conversation; yet she could not help expressing her regret, on observing the folly, levity, and extravagance, of the woman whom her brother had chosen for a wife.

'No doubt,' said Augustus, a little peevishly, 'he is fond of her - she is a fine woman - there is no accounting for the caprices of the affections.'

I sighed, and my eyes filled with tears - 'Is, then, affection so *capricious* a sentiment - is it possible to love what we despise?'

'I cannot tell,' retorted Mr Harley, with quickness. 'Triflers can give no *serious* occasion for uneasiness: - the humours of superior women are sometimes still less tolerable.'

'Ah! how unjust. If gentleness be not *the perfection of reason*, it is a quality which I have never, yet, properly understood.'

He made no reply, but sunk into silence, reserve, and reverie. On our arrival at my apartments. I ventured (my cousin having left us) to expostulate with him on his unkind behaviour; but was answered with severity. Some retrospection ensued, which gradually led to the subject ever present to my thoughts. - Again I expressed a solicitude to be informed of the real state of his heart, of the nature of those mysterious obstacles, to which, when clearly ascertained, I was ready to submit. - 'Had he, or had he not, an attachment, that looked to, as its *end*, a serious and legal engagement?' He appeared ruffled and discomposed. - 'I ought not to be so urgent - he had already sufficiently explained himself.' He then repeated to me some particulars, apparently adverse to such a supposition - asking me, in his turn, 'If these circumstances bespoke his having any such event in view?'

CHAPTER VI

For some time after this he absented himself from me; and, when he returned, his manners were still more unequal; even his sentiments, and principles, at times, appeared to me equivocal, and his character seemed wholly changed. I tried, in vain, to accommodate myself to a disposition so various. My affection, my sensibility, my fear of offending - a thousand conflicting, torturing, emotions, threw a constraint over my behaviour. - My situation became absolutely intolerable - time was murdered, activity vain, virtue inefficient: yet, a secret hope inspired me, that *indifference* could not have produced the irritations, the inequalities, that thus harrassed me. I thought, I observed a conflict in his mind; his fits of absence, and reflection, were unusual, deep, and frequent: I watched them with anxiety, with terror, with breathless expectation. My health became affected, and my mind disordered. I perceived that it was impossible to proceed, in the manner we had hitherto done, much longer - I felt that it would, inevitably, destroy me.

I reflected, meditated, reasoned, with myself - 'That one channel, into which my thoughts were incessantly impelled, was destructive of all order, of all connection.' New projects occurred to me, which I had never before ventured to encourage - I revolved them in my mind, examined them in every point of view, weighed their advantages and disadvantages, in a moral, in a prudential, scale. - Threatening evils appeared on all sides - I endeavoured, at once, to free my mind from prejudice, and from passion; and, in the critical and singular circumstances in which I had placed myself, coolly to survey the several arguments of the case, and nicely to calculate their force and importance.

'If, as we are taught to believe, the benevolent Author of nature be, indeed, benevolent,' said I, to myself, 'he surely must have intended the *happiness* of his creatures. Our morality cannot extend to him, but must consist in the knowledge, and practice, of those duties which we owe to ourselves and to each other. - Individual happiness constitutes the general good: - *happiness* is the only true end of existence; - all notions of morals, founded on any other principle, involve in themselves a contradiction, and must be erroneous. Man does right, when pursuing interest and pleasure - it argues no depravity - this is the fable of superstition: he ought to only be careful, that, in seeking his own good, he does not render it incompatible with the good of others - that he does not consider himself as standing alone in the universe. The infraction of established rules may, it is possible, in some cases, be productive of mischief; yet, it is difficult to state any *rule* so precise and determinate, as to be alike applicable to every situation: what, in one instance, might be a *vice*, in another may possibly become a *virtue*: - a thousand imperceptible, evanescent, shadings, modify every thought, every motive, every action, of our lives - no one can estimate the sensations of, can form an exact judgment for, another.

'I have sometimes suspected, that all mankind are pursuing phantoms, however dignified by different appellations. - The healing operations of time, had I patience to wait the experiment, might, perhaps, recover my mind from its present distempered state; but, in the meanwhile, the bloom of youth is fading, and the vigour of life running to waste. - Should I, at length, awake from a delusive vision, it would be only to find myself a comfortless, solitary, shivering, wanderer, in the dreary wilderness of human society. I feel in myself the capacities for increasing the happiness, and the improvement, of a few individuals - and this circle, spreading wider and wider, would operate towards the grand end of life - *general utility*.'

Again I repeated to myself - 'Ascetic virtues are equally barbarous as vain: - the only just morals, are those which have a tendency to increase the bulk of enjoyment. My plan tends to this. The good which I seek does not appear to me to involve injury to any one - it is of a nature, adapted to the disposition of my mind, for which every event of my life, the education both of design and accident, have fitted me. If I am now put out, I may, perhaps, do mischief: - the placid stream, forced from its channel, lays waste the meadow. I seem to stand as upon a wide plain, bounded on all sides by the horizon: - among the objects which I perceive within these limits, some are so lofty, my eyes ache to look up to them; others so low, I disdain to stoop for them. *One*, only, seems fitted to my powers, and to my wishes - *one, alone*, engages my attention! Is not its possession worthy an arduous effort: *Perseverance* can turn the course of rivers, and level mountains! Shall I, then, relinquish my efforts, when, perhaps, on the very verge of success?

'The mind must have an object: - should I desist from my present pursuit, after all it has cost me, for what can I change it? I feel, that I am neither a philosopher, nor a heroine - but a *woman, to whom education has given a sexual character.* It is true, I have risen superior to the generality of my *oppressed* sex; yet, I have neither the talents for a legislator, nor for a reformer, of the world. I have still many female foibles, and shrinking delicacies, that unfit me for rising to arduous heights. Ambition cannot stimulate me, and to accumulate wealth, I am still less fitted. Should I, then, do violence to my heart, and compel it to resign its hopes and expectations, what can preserve me from sinking into, the most abhorred of all states, *languor and inanity*? - Alas! that tender and faithful heart refuses to change its object - it can never love another. Like Rousseau's Julia, my strong individual attachment has annihilated every man in the creation: - him I love appears, in my eyes, something more - every other, something less.

'I have laboured to improve myself, that I might be worthy of the situation I have chosen. I would unite myself to a man of worth - I would have our mingled virtues and talents perpetuated in our offspring - I would experience those sweet sensations, of which nature has formed my heart so exquisitely susceptible. My ardent sensibilities incite me to love - to seek to inspire sympathy - to be beloved! My heart obstinately refuses to renounce the man, to whose mind my own seems akin! From the centre of private affections, it will at length embrace - like spreading circles on the peaceful bosom of the smooth and expanded lake - the whole sensitive and rational creation. Is it virtue, then, to combat, or to yield to, my passions?'

I considered, and reconsidered, these reasonings, so specious, so flattering, to which passion lent its force. One moment, my mind seemed firmly made up on the part I had to act; - I persuaded myself, that I had gone too far to recede, and that there remained for me no alternative: - the next instant, I shrunk, gasping, from my own resolves, and shuddered at the important consequences which they involved. Amidst a variety of perturbations, of conflicting emotions, I, at length, once more, took up my pen.

CHAPTER VII

To Augustus Harley.

'I blush, when I reflect what a weak, wavering, inconsistent being, I must lately have appeared to you. I write to you on important subjects - I forbid you to answer me on paper; and, when you seem inclined to put that period to the present, painful, high-wrought, and trying, state of my feelings, which is now become so necessary, I appear neither to hear, nor to comprehend you. I fly from the subject, and thicken the cloud of mystery, of which I have so often, and, I still think, so justly complained. - These are some of the effects of the contradictory systems, that have so long bewildered our principles and conduct. A combination of causes, added to the conflict between a thousand delicate and nameless emotions, have lately conspired to confuse, to weaken, my spirits. You can conceive, that these acute, mental, sensations, must have had a temporary effect on the state of my health. To say truth (and, had I not said it, my countenance would have betrayed me), I have not, for some time past, been so thoroughly disordered.

'Once more, I have determined to rally my strength; for I feel, that a much longer continuance in the situation, in which my mind has been lately involved, would be insupportable: - and I call upon you, now, with a resolution to summon all my fortitude to bear the result, for the *written* state of your mind, on the topic become so important to my future welfare and usefulness.

'You may suppose, that a mind like mine must have, repeatedly, set itself to examine, on every side, all that could possibly have a relation to a subject affecting it so materially. You have hinted at *mysterious* obstacles to the wish, in which every faculty of my soul has been so long absorbed - the wish of forming with you, a connection, nearer, *and more tender,* than that of friendship. This mystery, by leaving room for conjecture (and how frequently have I warned you of this!), left room for the illusions of imagination, and of hope - left room for the suspicion, that you might, possibly, be sacrificing *your own feelings* as well as mine, to a mistaken principle. Is it possible that you were not aware of this - you, who are not unacquainted with the nature of the mind! Still less were you ignorant of the nature of my mind - which I had so explicitly, so unreservedly, laid open! I had a double claim upon your confidence - a confidence, that I was utterly incapable of abusing, or betraying - a confidence, which must have stopped my mind in its career - which would have saved me the bitter, agonizing, pangs I have sustained. Mine were not common feelings - it is *obscurity* and *mystery* which has wrought them up to frenzy - *truth* and *certainty* would, long ere this, have caused them temporarily to subside into their accustomed channels. You understand little of the human heart, if you cannot conceive this - "Where the imagination is vivid, the feelings strong, the views and desires not bounded by common rules; - in such minds, passions, if not subdued, become ungovernable and fatal: where there is much warmth, much enthusiasm, there is much danger. - My mind is no less ardent than yours, though education and habit may have given it a different turn - it glows with equal zeal to attain its end."[11] Yes, I must continue to repeat, there has been in your conduct *one grand mistake*; and the train of consequences which may, yet, ensue, are uncertain, and threatening. - But, I mean no reproach - we are all liable to errors; and my own, I feel, are many, and various. But to return -

'You may suppose I have revolved, in my thoughts, every possible difficulty on the subject alluded to; balancing their degrees of probability and force: - and, I will frankly confess, such is the sanguine ardour of my temper, that I can conceive but one obstacle, that would be *absolutely invincible*; which is, supposing that you have already contracted a *legal, irrecoverable*, engagement. Yet, this I do not suppose. I will arrange, under five heads, (on all occasions, I love to class and methodize) every other possible species of objection, and subjoin all the reasonings which have occurred to me on the subjects.

'And, first, I will imagine, as the most serious and threatening difficulty, that you love another. I would, then, ask - Is she capable of estimating your worth - does she love you - has she the magnanimity to tell you so - would she sacrifice to that affection every meaner consideration - has she the merit to secure, as well as accomplishments to attract, your regard? - You are too well acquainted with the human heart, not to be aware, that what is commonly called love is of a fleeting nature, kept alive only by hopes and fears, if the qualities upon which it is founded afford no basis for its subsiding into tender confidence, and rational esteem. Beauty may inspire a transient desire, vivacity amuse, for a time, by its sportive graces; but the first will quickly fade and grow familiar - the last degenerate into impertinence and insipidity. Interrogate your own heart - Would you not, when the ardour of the passions, and the fervor of the imagination, subsided, wish to find the sensible, intelligent, friend, to take place of the engaging mistress? - Would you not expect the economical manager of your affairs, the rational and judicious mother to your offspring, the faithful sharer of your cares, the firm friend to your interest, the tender consoler of your sorrows, the companion in whom you could wholly confide, the discerning participator of your nobler pursuits, the friend of your virtues, your talents, your reputation - who could understand you, who was formed to pass the ordeal of honour, virtue,

11: Holcraft's Anna St Ives.

friendship? - Ask yourself these questions - ask them closely, without sophistry, and without evasion. You are not, now, an infatuated boy! Supposing, then, that you are, at present, entangled in an engagement which answers not this description - Is it virtue to fulfil, or to renounce, it? Contrast it with my affection, with its probable consequences, and weigh our different claims! *Would you have been the selected choice, of this woman, from all mankind* - would no other be capable of making her equally happy - would nothing compensate to her for your loss - are you the only object that she beholds in creation - might not another engagement suit her equally well, or better - is her whole soul absorbed but by one sentiment, that of fervent love for you - is her future usefulness, as well as peace, at stake - does she understand your high qualities better than myself - will she emulate them more? - Does the engagement promise a favourable issue, or does it threaten to wear away the best period of life in protracted and uncertain feeling - *the most pernicious, and destructive, of all states of mind*? Remember, also, that the summer of life will quickly fade; and that he who has reached the summit of the hill, has no time to lose - if he seize not the present moment, age is approaching, and life melting fast away. - I quit this, to state my second hypothesis -

'That you esteem and respect me, but that your heart has hitherto refused the sympathies I have sought to awaken in it. If this be the case, it remains to search for the reason; and, I own, I am at a loss to find it, either in moral, or physical, causes. Our principles are in unison, our tastes and habits not dissimilar, our knowledge of, and confidence in, each other's virtues is reciprocal, tried, and established - our ages, personal accomplishments, and mental acquirements do not materially differ. From such an union, I conceive, mutual advantages would result. I have found myself distinguished, esteemed, beloved by, others, where I have not sought for this distinction. How, then, can I believe it compatible with the nature of mind, that so many strong efforts, and reiterated impressions, can have produced no effect upon yours? Is your heart constituted differently from every other human heart? - I have lately observed an inequality in your behaviour, that has whispered something flattering to my heart. Examine yourself - Have you felt no peculiar interest in what concerns me - would the idea of our separation affect you with no more than a slight and common emotion? - One more question propose to yourself, as a test - Could you see me form a new, and more fortunate, attachment, with indifference? If you cannot, without hesitation, answer these questions, I have still a powerful pleader in your bosom, though unconscious of it yourself, that will, ultimately, prevail. If I have, yet, failed of producing an unequivocal effect, it must arise from having mistaken the means proper to produce the desired *end*. My own sensibility, and my imperfect knowledge of your character may, here, have combined to mislead me. The first, by its suffocating and depressing powers, clouding my vivacity, incapacitating me from appearing to you with my natural advantages - these effects would diminish as assurance took the place of doubt. The last, every day would contribute to correct. Permit me, then, *to hope for*, as well as to seek your affections, and if I do not, at length, gain and secure them, it will be a phenomenon in the history of mind!

'But to proceed to my third supposition - The peculiar, pecuniary, embarrassments of your situation - Good God! did this barbarous, insidious, relation, allow himself to consider the pernicious consequences of his absurd bequest? - threatening to undermine every manly principle, to blast every social virtue? Oh! that I had the eloquence to rouse you from this tame and unworthy acquiescence - to stimulate you to exercise your talents, to trust to the independent energies of your mind, to exert yourself to procure the honest rewards of virtuous industry. In proportion as we lean for support on foreign aid, we lose the dignity of our nature, and palsey those powers which constitute that nature's worth. Yet, I will allow, from my knowledge of your habits and associations, this obstacle its full force. But there remains one method of obviating, even this! I will frankly confess, that could I hope to gain the interest in your heart, which I have so long and so earnestly sought - my confidence in your honour and integrity, my tenderness for you, added to the wish of contributing to your happiness, would effect, what no lesser considerations could have effected - would triumph, not over my principles, (*for the individuality of an affection constitutes its chastity*) but over my prudence. I repeat, I am willing to sacrifice every inferior consideration - retain your legacy, so capriciously bequeathed - retain your present situation, and I will retain mine. This proposition, though not a violation of modesty, certainly involves in it very serious hazards - *It is, wholly, the triumph of affection*! You cannot suppose, that a transient engagement would satisfy a mind like mine; I should require a reciprocal faith plighted and returned - an after separation, otherwise than by mutual consent, would be my destruction - I should not survive your desertion. My existence, then, would be in your hands. Yet, having once confided, your affection should be my recompence - my sacrifice should be a cheerful and a voluntary one; I would determine not to harrass you with doubts nor jealousies, I would neither reflect upon the past, nor distrust the future: I would rest upon you, I would confide in you fearlessly and entirely! but, though I would not enquire after the past, my delicacy would require the assurance of your present, undivided, affection.

'The fourth idea that has occurred to me, is the probability of your having formed a plan of seeking some agreeable woman of fortune, who should be willing to reward a man of merit for the injustice of society. Whether you may already have experienced some disappointments of this nature, I will not pretend to determine. I can conceive, that, by many women, a coxcomb might be preferred to you - however this may be, the plan is not unattended with risque, nor with some possible degrading circumstances - and you may succeed, and yet be miserable: happiness depends not upon the abundance of our possessions.

'The last case which I shall state, and on which I shall lay little comparative stress, is the possibility of an engagement of a very inferior nature - a mere affair of the senses. The arguments which might here be adduced are too obvious to be repeated. Besides, I think highly of your refinement and delicacy - Having therefore just hinted, I leave it with you.

'And now to conclude - After considering all I have urged, you may, perhaps, reply - That the subject is too nice and too subtle for reasoning, and that the heart is not to be compelled. These, I think, are mistakes. There is no subject, in fact, that may not be subjected to the laws of investigation and reasoning. What is it that we desire - *pleasure* - *happiness*? I allow, pleasure is the supreme good: but it may be analyzed - it must have a stable foundation - to this analysis I now call you! This is the critical moment, upon which hangs a long chain of events - This moment may decide your future destiny and mine - it may, even, affect that of unborn myriads! My spirit is pervaded with these important ideas - my heart flutters - I breathe with difficulty - *My friend* - *I would give myself to you* - the gift is not worthless. Pause a moment, ere you rudely throw from you an affection so tried, so respectable, so worthy of you! The heart may be compelled - compelled by the touching sympathies which bind, with sacred, indissoluble ties, mind to mind! Do not prepare for yourself future remorse - when lost, you may recollect my worth, and my affection, and remember them with regret - Yet mistake me not, I have no intention to intimidate - I think it my duty to live, while I may possibly be useful to others, however bitter and oppressive may be that existence. I will live *for duty*, though peace and enjoyment should be for ever fled. You may rob me of my happiness, you may rob me of my strength, but, even, you cannot destroy my principles. And, if no other motive with-held me from rash determinations, my tenderness for you (it is not a selfish tenderness), would prevent me from adding, to the anxieties I have already given you, the cruel pang, of feeling yourself the occasion, however unintentionally, of the destruction of a fellow creature.

'While I await your answer, I summon to my heart all its remaining strength and spirits. Say to me, in clear and decisive terms, that the obstacles which oppose my affection *are absolutely, and altogether, insuperable* - Or that there is a possibility of their removal, but that time and patience are, yet, necessary to determine their force. In this case, I will not disturb the future operations of your mind, assuring myself, that you will continue my suspence no longer than is proper and requisite - or frankly accept, and return, the faith of her to whom you are infinitely dearer than life itself!

'Early to-morrow morning, a messenger shall call for the paper, which is to decide the colour of my future destiny. Every moment, that the blow has been suspended, it has acquired additional force - since it must, at length, descend, it would be weakness still to desire its protraction - We have, already, refined too much - *I promise to live - more, alas! I cannot promise.*

'*Farewell*! dearest and most beloved of men - whatever may be my fate - *be happiness yours*! Once more, my lingering, foreboding heart, repeats *farewell*!

'*Emma.*'

It would be unnecessary to paint my feelings during the interval in which I waited a reply to this letter - I struggled to repress hope, and to prepare my mind for the dissolution of a thousand air-built fabrics. The day wore tediously away in strong emotion, and strong exertion. On the subsequent morning, I sat, waiting the return of my messenger, in a state of mind, difficult even to be conceived - I heard him enter - breathless, I flew to meet him - I held out my hand - I could not speak.

'Mr Harley desired me to tell you, *he had not had time to write.*'

Gracious God! I shudder, even now, to recall the convulsive sensation! I sunk into a chair - I sat for some time motionless, every faculty seemed suspended. At length, returning to recollection, I wrote a short incoherent note, entreating -

'To be spared another day, another night, like the preceding - I asked only *one single line*! In the morning I had made up my mind to fortitude - it was now sinking - another day, I could not answer for the consequences.'

Again an interval of suspense - again my messenger returned with a verbal reply - '*He would write to-morrow.*' Unconsciously, I exclaimed - '*Barbarous, unfeeling, unpitying, man*!' A burst of tears relieved - no - i*t did not relieve me.* The day passed - I know not how - I dare not recollect.

The next morning, I arose, somewhat refreshed; my exhausted strength and spirits had procured me a few hours of profound slumber. A degree of resentment gave a temporary firmness to my nerves. 'What happiness (I repeated to myself) could I have expected with a man, thus regardless of my feelings?' I composed my spirits - *hope was at an end* - into a sort of sullen resignation to my fate - a half stupor!

At noon the letter arrived, coldly, confusedly written; methought there appeared even a degree of irritation in it.

'*Another, a prior attachment* - His behaviour had been such, as necessarily resulted from such an engagement - unavoidable circumstances had prevented an earlier reply.' My swollen heart - but it is enough - ' He blamed my impatience - he would, in future, perhaps, when my mind had attained more composure, make some remarks on my letter.'

CHAPTER VIII

To write had always afforded a temporary relief to my spirits - The next day I resumed my pen.

To Augustus Harley.

'If, after reflecting upon, and comparing, many parts of your past conduct, you can acquit yourself, at the sacred bar of humanity - it is well! How often have I called for - urged, with all the energy of truth and feeling - but in vain - such a letter as you have at length written - and, *even now*, though somewhat late, I thank you for it. Yet, what could have been easier, than to repeat so plain and so simple a tale? The vague hints, you had before given, I had repeatedly declared to be insufficient. Remember, all my earnestness, and all my simplicity, and learn *the value of sincerity*! "Oh! with what difficulty is an active mind, once forced into any particular train, persuaded to desert it as hopeless!"[12]

'This recital, then, was not to be confirmed, till the whole moral conformation of my mind was effected - till the barbed arrow had fixed, and rankled in, and poisoned, with its envenomed point, every vein, every fibre, of my heart. This, I confess, is now the case - Reason and self-respect sustain me - but the wound you have inflicted is *indelible* - it will continue to be the corroding canker at the root of my peace. My youth has been worn in anguish - and the summer of life will probably be overshadowed by a still thicker and darker cloud. But I mean not to reproach you - it is not given me to contribute to your happiness - the dearest and most ardent wish of my soul - I would not then inflict unnecessary pain - yet, I would fix upon your mind, the value of *unequivocal sincerity*.

'Had the happiness of any human being, the meanest, the vilest, depended as much upon me, as mine has done on you, I would have sacrificed, for their relief, the dearest secret of my heart - the secret, even upon which my very existence had depended. It is true, you did not directly deceive me - but is that enough for the delicacy of humanity? May the past be an affecting lesson to us both - it is written upon my mind in characters of blood. I feel, and acknowledge, my own errors, in yielding to the illusion of vague, visionary, expectation; but my faults have originated in a generous source - they have been the wild, ardent, fervent, excesses, of a vigorous and an exalted mind!

'I checked my tears, as they flowed, and they are already dried - uncalled, unwished, for - why do they, thus, struggle to force their way? my mind has, I hope, too much energy, utterly to sink - I know what it is to suffer, and to combat

---

12: *Godwin's* Caleb Williams.

with, if not to subdue, my feelings - and *certainty,* itself, is some relief. I am, also, supported by the retrospect of my conduct; with all its mistakes, and all its extravagances, it has been that of a virtuous, ingenuous, uncorrupted, mind. You have contemned a heart of no common value, you have sported with its exquisite sensibilities - but it will, still, know how to separate your virtues from your errors.

'You reprove, perhaps justly, my impatience - I can only say, that circumstanced as you were, I should have stolen an hour from rest, from company, from business, however, important, to have relieved and soothed a fellow-creature in a situation, so full of pain and peril. Every thought, during a day scarcely to be recollected without agony, *was a two-edged sword* - but some hours of profound and refreshing slumber recruited my exhausted spirits, and enabled me, yesterday, to receive my fate, with a fortitude but little hoped for.

'You would oblige me exceedingly by the remarks you allow me to hope for, on my letter of the .... th. You know, I will not shrink from reproof - that letter afforded you the last proof of my affection, and I repent not of it. I loved you, first, for what, I conceived, high qualities of mind - from nature and association, my tenderness became personal - till at length, I loved you, not only rationally and tenderly - but *passionately* - it became a pervading and a devouring fire! And, yet, I do not blush - my affection was modest, if intemperate, *for it was individual* - it annihilated in my eyes every other man in the creation. I regret these natural sensations and affections, their forcible suppression injures the mind - it converts the mild current of gentle, and genial sympathies, into a destructive torrent. This, I have the courage to avow it, has been one of the miserable mistakes in morals, and, like all other partial remedies, has increased the evil, it was intended to correct. From monastic institutions and principles have flowed, as from a polluted source, streams, that have at once spread through society a mingled contagion of dissoluteness and hypocrisy.

'You have suddenly arrested my affections in their full career - in all their glowing effervescence - you have taken

> *"The rose*
> *From the fair forehead of an innocent love,*
> *And placed a blister there."*

'And, yet, I survive the shock, and determine to live, not for future enjoyment - that is now, for ever, past - *but for future usefulness* - Is not this virtue?

'I am sorry your attachment has been and I fear is likely to be, protracted - I know, too well, the misery of these situations, and I should, now, feel a melancholy satisfaction in hearing of its completion - In that completion, may you experience no disappointment! I do not wish you to be beloved, as I have loved you; this, perhaps, is unnecessary; such an affection, infallibly, enslaves the heart that cherishes it; and slavery is the tomb of virtue and of peace.

'I believe it would not be proper for us to meet again - at least at present - should I hear of sickness, or calamity, befalling you, I shall, I suspect, be impelled, by an irresistible impulse to seek you - but I will no more interrupt your repose - Though you have contemned my affection, my friendship will still follow you.

'If you really *love*, I think you ought to make some sacrifices, and not render yourself, and the happy object of your tenderness, the victims of factitious notions. - Remember - youth and life will quickly fade. Relinquish, call upon her to relinquish, her prejudices - should she refuse, she is unworthy of you, and you will regret, too late, the tender, faithful, ingenuous heart, that you have pierced through and through - that you have almost broken! Should she make you happy, I will esteem, though I may never have an opportunity of thanking, her - Were she informed of my conduct, she might rejoice in the trial of your affection - though I should not.

'The spirits, that had crowded round my heart, are already subsiding - a flood of softness, a tide of overwhelming affection, gushes upon it - and I feel myself sinking into helpless, infantine, distress! Hasten to me your promised remarks - they will rouse, they will strengthen, me - *Truth* I will never call indelicate or inhuman - it is only the virtuous mind can dare to practise, to challenge, it: - simplicity is true refinement.

'Let us reap from the past all the good we can - a close, and searching, knowledge of the secret springs and foldings of our hearts. Methinks, I could wish you justified, even at my own expense. - I ask, unshrinkingly, a frank return.

'A heart-rending sigh accompanies my *farewell* - the last struggles of expiring nature will be far less painful - but my philosophy, now, sternly calls upon me to put its precepts in practice - trembling - shuddering - I obey!

'Farewell!

'Emma.'

Perhaps it cost me some effort to make the preceding letter so moderate - yet, every victory gained over ourselves is attended with advantages. But this apparent calm was the lethargy of despair - it was succeeded by severer conflicts, by keener anguish. A week passed, and near a second - I received no answer.

CHAPTER IX

A letter from the country made it necessary for me, again, to address Mr Harley, to make some enquiries which respected business of his mother's. It may be, that I felt a mixture of other motives; - it is certain, that when I wrote, I spoke of more than business.

'I had hoped,' I told him, 'ere this, to have received the promised letter - Yet, I do not take up my pen,' said I, 'either to complain of, or to importune, you. If I have already expressed myself with bitterness, let the harrassed state of my mind be my excuse. My own conduct has been too erroneous, too eccentric, to enable me to judge impartially of your's. Forgive me, if by placing you in an embarrassing situation, I have exposed you to consequent mistake or uneasiness. I feel, that whatever errors we may either of us have committed, originated only with myself, and I am content to suffer all the consequences. It is true, had you reposed in me an early, generous, confidence, much misery would have been avoided - I had not been wounded

"There, where the human heart most exquisitely feels!"

'You had been still my friend, and I had been comparatively happy. Every passion is, in a great measure, the growth of indulgence: all our desires are, in their commencement, easily suppressed, when there appears no probability of attaining their object; but when strengthened, by time and reflection, into habit, in endeavouring to eradicate them, we tear away part of the mind. In my attachments there is a kind of savage tenacity - they are of an elastic nature, and, being forced back, return with additional violence.

'My affection for you has not been, altogether, irrational or selfish. While I felt that I loved you, as no other woman, I was convinced, would love you - I conceived, could I once engage your heart, I could satisfy, and even, purify it. While I loved your virtues, I thought I saw, and I lamented, the foibles which sullied them. I suspected you, perhaps erroneously, of pride, ambition, the love of distinction; yet your ambition could not, I thought, be of an ignoble nature - I feared that the gratifications you sought, if, indeed, attainable, were factitious - I even fancied I perceived you, against your better judgment, labouring to seduce yourself!' "He is under a delusion," said I, to myself; - "reason may be stunned, or blinded, for awhile; but it will revive in the heart, and do its office, when sophistry will be of no avail." I saw you struggling with vexations, that I was assured might be meliorated by tender confidence - I longed to pour its balms into your bosom. My sensibility disquieted you, and myself, only because it was constrained. I thought I perceived a conflict in your mind - I watched its progress with attention and solicitude. A thousand times has my fluttering heart yearned to break the cruel chains that fettered it, and to chase the cloud, which stole over your brow, by the tender, yet chaste, caresses and endearments of ineffable affection! My feelings became too highly wrought, and altogether insupportable. Sympathy for your situation, zeal for your virtues, love for your mind, tenderness for your person - a complication of generous, affecting, exquisite, emotions, impelled me to make one great effort. - "[13] The world might call my plans absurd, my views romantic, my pretensions extravagant - Was I, or was I not, guilty of any crime, when, in the very acme of the passions, I so totally disregarded the customs of the world?" Ah! what were my sensations - what did I not suffer, in the interval? - and you prolonged that cruel interval - and still you suffer me to doubt, whether, at the moment in my life when I was actuated by the highest, the most fervent, the most magnanimous, principles - whether, at that moment, when I most deserved your respect, I did not for ever forfeit it.

'I seek not to extenuate any part of my conduct - I confess that it has been wild, extravagant, romantic - I confess, that, even for your errors, I am justly blameable - and yet I am unable to bear, because I feel they would be unjust, your hatred and contempt. I cherish no resentment - my spirit is subdued and broken - your unkindness sinks into my soul.

'Emma.'

Another fortnight wore away in fruitless expectation - the morning rose, the evening closed, upon me, in sadness. I could not, yet, think the mystery developed: on a concentrated view of the circumstances, they appeared to me contradictory, and irreconcileable. A solitary enthusiast, a child in the drama of the world, I had yet to learn, that those who have courage to act upon advanced principles, must be content to suffer moral martyrdom.[14] In subduing our own prejudices, we have done little, while assailed on every side by the prejudices of others. My own heart acquitted me; but I dreaded that distortion of mind, that should wrest guilt out of the most sublime of its emanations.

I ruminated in gloomy silence, on my forlorn, and hopeless, situation. 'If there be not a future state of being,' said I to myself, 'what is this! - Tortured in every stage of it, "Man cometh forth like a flower, and is cut down - he fleeth, as a shadow, and continueth not!" - I looked backward on my past life, and my heart sickened - its confidence in humanity was shaken - I looked forward, and all was cheerless. I had certainly committed many errors! - Who has not - who,

---

13: *Holcroft's* Anna St Ives.

14: *This sentiment may be just in some particular cases, but it is by no means of general application, and must be understood with great limitations.*

with a fancy as lively, feelings as acute, and a character as sanguine, as mine? "What, in fact," says a philosophic writer,[15] "is character? - the production of a lively and constant affection, and consequently, of a strong passion:" - eradicate that passion, that ferment, that leaven, that exuberance, which raises and makes the mind what it is, and what remains? Yet, let us beware how we wantonly expend this divine, this invigorating, power. Every grand error, in a mind of energy, in its operations and consequences, carries us years forward - *precious years, never to be recalled!'* I could find no substitute for the sentiments I regretted - for that sentiment formed my character; and, but for the obstacles which gave it force, though I might have suffered less misery, I should, I suspect, have gained less improvement; still adversity *is a real evil*; and I foreboded that this improvement had been purchased too dear.

15: Helvetius.

CHAPTER X

Weeks elapsed ere the promised letter arrived - a letter still colder, and more severe, than the former. I wept over it, bitter tears! It accused me 'of adding to the vexations of a situation, before sufficiency oppressive.' - Alas! had I known the nature of those vexations, could I have merited such a reproof? The Augustus, I had so long and so tenderly loved, no longer seemed to exist. Some one had, surely, usurped his signature, and imitated those characters, I had been accustomed to trace with delight. He tore himself from me, *nor would he deign to soften the pangs of separation.* Anguish overwhelmed me - my heart was pierced. Reclining my head on my folded arms, I yielded myself up to silent grief. Alone, sad, desolate, no one heeded my sorrows - no eye pitied me - no friendly voice cheered my wounded spirit! The social propensities of a mind forbidden to expand itself, forced back, preyed incessantly upon that mind, secretly consuming its powers.

I was one day roused from these melancholy reflections by the entrance of my cousin, Mrs Denbeigh. She held in her hand a letter, from my only remaining friend, Mrs Harley. I snatched it hastily; my heart, lacerated by the seeming unkindness of him in whom it had confided, yearned to imbibe the consolation, which the gentle tenderness of this dear, maternal, friend, had never failed to administer. The first paragraph informed me -

'That she had, a few days since, received a letter from the person to whom the legacy of her son devolved, should he fail in observing the prescribed conditions of the testator: that this letter gave her notice, that those conditions had already been infringed, Mr Harley having contracted a marriage, three years before, with a foreigner, with whom he had become acquainted during his travels; that this marriage had been kept a secret, and, but very lately, by an accidental concurrence of circumstances, revealed to the person most concerned in the detection. Undoubted proofs of the truth of this information could be produced; it would therefore be most prudent in her son to resign his claims, without putting himself, and the legal heir, to unnecessary expense and litigation. Ignorant of the residence of Mr Harley, the writer troubled his mother to convey to him these particulars.'

The paper dropped from my hand, the colour forsook my lips and cheeks; - yet I neither wept, nor fainted. Mrs Denbeigh took my hands - they were frozen - the blood seemed congealed in my veins - and I sat motionless - my faculties suspended, stunned, locked up! My friend spake to me - embraced, shed tears over, me - but she could not excite mine; - my mind was pervaded by a sense of confused misery. I remained many days in this situation - it was a state, of which I have but a feeble remembrance; and I, at length, awoke from it, as from a troublesome dream.

With returning reason, the tide of recollection also returned. Oh! how complicated appeared to me the guilt of Augustus! Ignorant of his situation, I had been unconsciously, and perseveringly, exerting myself to seduce the affections of a *husband* from his *wife*. He had made me almost criminal in my own eyes - he had risqued, at once, by a disingenuous and cruel reserve, the virtue and the happiness of three beings. What is virtue, but a calculation of *the consequences of our actions*? Did we allow ourselves to reason on this principle, to reflect on its truth and importance, we should be compelled to shudder at many parts of our conduct, which, *taken unconnectedly*, we have habituated ourselves to consider as almost indifferent. Virtue can exist only in a mind capable of taking comprehensive views. How criminal, then, is ignorance!

During this sickness of the soul, Mr Francis, who had occasionally visited me since my residence in town, called, repeatedly, to enquire after my welfare; expressing a friendly concern for my indisposition. I saw him not - I was incapable of seeing any one - but, informed by my kind hostess of his humane attentions, soothed by the idea of having yet a friend who seemed to interest himself in my concerns, I once more had recourse to my pen (Mrs Denbeigh having officiously placed the implements of writing in my way), and addressed him in the wild and incoherent language of despair.

To Mr Francis.

'You once told me, that I was incapable of heroism; and you were right - yet, I am called to great exertions! a blow that has been suspended over my head, days, weeks, months, years, has at length fallen - still I live! My tears flow - I struggle, in vain, to suppress them, but they are not tears of blood! - My heart, though pierced through and through, is not broken!

'My friend, come and teach me how to acquire fortitude - I am wearied with misery - All nature is to me a blank - an envenomed shaft rankles in my bosom - philosophy will not heal the festering wound - I am exquisitely wretched!

'Do not chide me till I get more strength - I speak to you of my sorrows, for your kindness, while I was yet a stranger to you, inspired me with confidence, and my desolate heart looks round for support.

'I am indebted to you - how shall I repay your goodness? Do you, indeed, interest yourself in my fate? Call upon me, then, for the few incidents of my life - I will relate them simply, and without disguise. There is nothing uncommon in them, but the effect which they have produced upon my mind - yet, that mind they formed.

'After all, my friend, what a wretched farce is life! Why cannot I sleep, and, close my eyes upon it for ever? But something whispers, "this would be wrong." - How shall I tear from my heart all its darling, close twisted, associations? - And must I live - *live for what*? God only knows! Yet, how am I sure that there is a God - is he wise - is he powerful - is he benevolent? If he be, can he sport himself in the miseries of poor, feeble, impotent, beings, forced into existence, without their choice - impelled, by the iron hand of necessity, through mistake, into calamity? - Ah! my friend, who will condemn the poor solitary wanderer, whose feet are pierced with many a thorn, should he turn suddenly out of the rugged path, seek an obscure shade to shrowd his wounds, his sorrows, and his indignation, from the scorn of a pitiless world, and accelerate the hour of repose.[16] Who would be born if they could help it? You would perhaps - you may *do good* - But on me, the sun shines only to mock my woes - Oh! that I had never seen the light.

'Torn by conflicting passions - wasted in anguish - life is melting fast away - A burthen to myself, a grief to those who love me, and worthless to every one. Weakened by long suspence - preyed upon, by a combination of imperious feelings - I fear, I greatly fear, *the irrecoverable blow is struck!* But I blame no one - I have been entangled in error - *who is faultless*?

'While pouring itself out on paper, my tortured mind has experienced a momentary relief: If your heart be inaccessible to tender sympathies, I have only been adding one more to my numberless mistakes!

'Emma.'

Mr Francis visited me, and evinced for my situation the most humane and delicate consideration. He reminded me of the offer I had made him, and requested the performance of my engagement. In compliance with this request, and to beguile my melancholy thoughts, I drew up a sketch of the events of my past life, and unfolded a history of the sentiments of my mind (from which I have extracted the preceding materials) reserving only any circumstance which might lead to a detection of the name and family of the man with whom they were so intimately blended.

16: *This is the reasoning of a mind distorted by passion. Even in the moment of disappointment, our heroine judged better.*

CHAPTER XI

After having perused my manuscript, Mr Francis returned it, at my desire, accompanied by the following letter.

To Emma Courtney.

'Your narrative leaves me full of admiration for your qualities, and compassion for your insanity.

'I entreat however your attention to the following passage, extracted from your papers. "After considering all I have urged, you may perhaps reply, that the subject is too nice, and too subtle, for reasoning, and that the heart is not to be compelled. This, I think, is a mistake. There is no topic, in fact, that may not be subjected to the laws of investigation and reasoning. What is it we desire? pleasure, happiness. What! the pleasure of an instant, only; or that which is more solid and permanent? I allow, pleasure is the supreme good! but it may be analysed. To this analysis I now call you."

'Could I, if I had studied for years, invent a comment on your story, more salutary to your sorrows, more immoveable in its foundation, more clearly expressed, or more irresistibly convincing to every rational mind?

'How few real, substantial, misfortunes there are in the world! how few calamities, the sting of which does not depend upon our cherishing the viper in our bosom, and applying the aspic to our veins! The general pursuit of all men, we are frequently told, is happiness. I have often been tempted to think, on the contrary, that the general pursuit is misery. It is true, men do not recognize it by its genuine appellation; they content themselves with the pitiful expedient of assigning it a new denomination. But, if their professed purpose were misery, could they be more skilful and ingenious in the pursuit?

'Look through your whole life. To speak from your own description, was there ever a life, in its present period, less chequered with substantial *bona fide* misfortune? The whole force of every thing which looks like a misfortune was assiduously, unintermittedly, provided by yourself. You nursed in yourself a passion, which, taken in the degree in which you experienced it, is the unnatural and odious invention of a distempered civilization, and which in almost all instances generates an immense overbalance of excruciating misery. Your conduct will scarcely admit of any other denomination than moon-struck madness, hunting after torture. You addressed a man impenetrable as a rock, and the smallest glimpse of sober reflection, and common sense, would have taught you instantly to have given up the pursuit.

'I know you will tell me, and you will tell yourself, a great deal about constitution, early association, and the indissoluble chain of habits and sentiments. But I answer with small fear of being erroneous, "It is a mistake to suppose, that the heart is not to be compelled. There is no topic, in fact, that may not be subjected to the laws of investigation and reasoning. Pleasure, happiness, is the supreme good; and happiness is susceptible of being analysed." I grant, that the state of a human mind cannot be changed at once; but, had you worshipped at the altar of reason but half as assiduously as you have sacrificed at the shrine of illusion, your present happiness would have been as enviable, as your present distress is worthy of compassion. If men would but take the trouble to ask themselves, once every day, Why should I be miserable? how many, to whom life is a burthen, would become chearful and contented.

'Make a catalogue of all the real evils of human life; bodily pain, compulsory solitude, severe corporal labour, in a word, all those causes which deprive us of health, or the means of spending our time in animated, various, and rational pursuits. Aye, these are real evils! But I should be ashamed of putting disappointed love into my enumeration. Evils of this sort are the brood of folly begotten upon fastidious indolence. They shrink into non-entity, when touched by the wand of truth.

'The first lesson of enlightened reason, the great fountain of heroism and virtue, the principle by which alone man can become what man is capable of being, is *independence*. May every power that is favourable to integrity, to honour, defend me from leaning upon another for support! I will use the word, I will use my fellow men, but I will not abuse these invaluable benefits of the system of nature. I will not be weak and criminal enough, to make my peace depend upon the precarious thread of another's life or another's pleasure. I will judge for myself; I will draw my support from myself - the support of my existence and the support of my happiness. The system of nature has perhaps made me dependent for the means of existence and happiness upon my fellow men taken collectively; but nothing but my own folly can make me dependent upon individuals. Will these principles prevent me from admiring, esteeming, and loving such as are worthy to excite these emotions? Can I not have a mind to understand, and a heart to feel excellence, without first parting with the fairest attribute of my nature?

'You boast of your sincerity and frankness. You have doubtless some reason for your boast - Yet all your misfortunes seem to have arisen from concealment. You brooded over your emotions, and considered them as a sacred deposit - You have written to me, I have seen you frequently, during the whole of this transaction, without ever having received the slightest hint of it, yet, if I be a fit counsellor now, I was a fit counsellor then; your folly was so gross, that, if it had been exposed to the light of day, it could not have subsisted for a moment. Even now you suppress the name of your hero: yet, unless I know how much of a hero and a model of excellence he would appear in my eyes, I can be but a very imperfect judge of the affair.

'- *Francis.*'

CHAPTER XII

To the remonstrance of my friend, which roused me from the languor into which I was sinking, I immediately replied -

To Mr Francis.

'You retort upon me my own arguments, and you have cause. I felt a ray of conviction dart upon my mind, even, while I wrote them. But what then? - I seemed to be in a state, in which reason had no power; I felt as if I could coolly survey the several arguments of the case - perceive, that they had prudence, truth, and common sense on their side - And then answer - I am under the guidance of a director more energetic than you!"[17] I am affected by your kindness - I am affected by your letter. I could weep over it, bitter tears of conviction and remorse. But argue with the wretch infected with the plague - will it stop the tide of blood, that is rapidly carrying its contagion to the heart? I blush! I shed burning tears! But I am still desolate and wretched! And how am I to stop it? The force which you impute to my reasoning was the powerful frenzy of a high delirium.

'What does it signify whether, abstractedly considered, a misfortune be worthy of the names real and substantial, if the consequences produced are the same? That which embitters all my life, that which stops the genial current of health and peace is, whatever be its nature, a real calamity to me. There is no end to this reasoning - what individual can limit the desires of another? The necessaries of the civilized man are whimsical superfluities in the eye of the savage. Are we, or are we not (as you have taught me) the creatures of sensation and circumstance?

'I agree with you - and the more I look into society, the deeper I feel the soul-sickening conviction - "The general pursuit is misery" - necessarily - excruciating misery, from the source to which you justly ascribe it - "*The unnatural and odious inventions of a distempered civilization.*" I am content, you may perceive, to recognize things by their genuine appellation. I am, at least, a reasoning maniac: perhaps the most dangerous species of insanity. But while the source continues troubled, why expect the streams to run pure?

'You know I will tell you - "about the indissoluble chains of association and habit:" and you attack me again with my own weapons! Alas! while I confess their impotence, with what consistency do I accuse the flinty, impenetrable, heart, I so earnestly sought, in vain, to move? What materials does this stubborn mechanism of the mind offer to the wise and benevolent legislator!

17: Godwin's Caleb Williams.

'Had I, you tell me, "worshipped at the altar of reason, but half as assiduously as I have sacrificed at the shrine of illusion, my happiness might have been enviable." But do you not perceive, that my reason was the auxiliary of my passion, or rather my passion the generative principle of my reason? Had not these contradictions, these oppositions, roused the energy of my mind, I might have domesticated, tamely, in the lap of indolence and apathy.

'I do ask myself, every day - "Why should I be miserable?" - and I answer, "Because the strong, predominant, sentiment of my soul, close twisted with all its cherished associations, has been rudely torn away, and the blood flows from the lacerated wound. You would be ashamed of placing disappointed love in your enumeration of evils! Gray was not ashamed of this -

> *'And pining love shall waste their youth,*
> *And jealousy, with rankling tooth,*
> *That inly gnaws the secret heart!'*
>
> ....
>
> *'These shall the stings of falsehood try,*
> *And hard unkindness' alter'd eye,*
> *That mocks the tear it forc'd to flow.'"*

'Is it possible that you can be insensible of all the mighty mischiefs which have been caused by this passion - of the great events and changes of society, to which it has operated as a powerful, though secret, spring? That Jupiter shrouded his glories beneath a mortal form; that he descended yet lower, and crawled as a reptile - that Hercules took the distaff, and Sampson was shorn of his strength, are in their spirit, no fables. Yet, these were the legends of ages less degenerate than this, and states of society less corrupt. Ask your own heart - whether some of its most exquisite sensations have not arisen from sources, which, to nine-tenths of the world, would be equally inconceivable: Mine, I believe, is a solitary madness in the eighteenth century: it is not on the altars of love, but of gold, that men, now, come to pay their offerings.

'Why call woman, miserable, oppressed, and impotent, woman - crushed, and then insulted - why call her to independence - which not nature, but the barbarous and accursed laws of society, have denied her? *This is mockery*! Even you, wise and benevolent as you are, can mock the child of slavery and sorrow! "Excluded, as it were, by the pride, luxury, and caprice, of the world, from expanding my sensations, and wedding my soul to society, I was constrained to bestow the strong affections, that glowed consciously within me, upon a few."[18]

18: Godwin's Caleb Williams.

Love, in minds of any elevation, cannot be generated but upon a real, or fancied, foundation of excellence. But what would be a miracle in architecture, is true in morals - the fabric can exist when the foundation has mouldered away. *Habit* daily produces this wonderful effect upon every feeling, and every principle. Is not this the theory which you have taught me?

'Am I not sufficiently ingenuous? - I will give you a new proof of my frankness (though not the proof you require). - From the miserable consequences of wretched moral distinctions, from chastity having been considered as a sexual virtue, all these calamities have flowed. Men are thus rendered sordid and dissolute in their pleasures; their affections vitiated, and their feelings petrified; the simplicity of modest tenderness loses its charm; they become incapable of satisfying the heart of a woman of sensibility and virtue. - Half the sex, then, are the wretched, degraded, victims of brutal instinct: the remainder, if they sink not into mere frivolity and insipidity, are sublimed into a sort of - [what shall I call them?] - refined, romantic, factitious, unfortunate, beings; who, for the sake of the present moment, dare not expose themselves to complicated, inevitable, evils; evils, that will infallibly overwhelm them with misery and regret! Woe be, more especially, to those who, possessing the dangerous gifts of fancy and feeling, find it as difficult to discover a substitute for the object as for the sentiment! You, who are a philosopher, will you still controvert the principles founded in truth and nature? "Gross as is my folly," (and I do not deny it) "you may perceive I was not wholly wandering in darkness. But while the wintry sun of hope illumined the fairy frost-work with a single, slanting ray - dazzled by the transient brightness, I dreaded the meridian fervors that should dissolve the glittering charm." Yes! it was madness - but it was the pleasurable madness which none but madmen know.

'I cannot answer your question - Pain me not by its repetition; neither seek to ensnare me to the disclosure. Unkindly, severely, as I have been treated, I will not risque, even, the possibility of injuring the man, whom I have so tenderly loved, in the esteem of any one. Were I to name him, you know him not; you could not judge of his qualities. He is not "a model of excellence." I perceive it, with pain - and if obliged to retract my judgment on some parts of his character - I retract it with agonizing reluctance! But I could trace the sources of his errors, and candour and self-abasement imperiously compel me to a mild judgment, to stifle the petulant suggestions of a wounded spirit.

'Ought not our principles, my friend, to soften the asperity of our censures? - Could I have won him to my arms, I thought I could soften, and even elevate, his mind - a mind, in which I still perceive a great proportion of good. I weep for him, as well as for myself. He will, one day, know my value, and feel my loss. Still, I am sensible, that, by my extravagance, I have given a great deal of vexation (possibly some degradation), to a being, whom I had no right to persecute, or to compel to chuse happiness through a medium of my creation. I cannot exactly tell the extent of the injury I may have done him. A long train of consequences succeed, even, our most indifferent actions. - Strong energies, though they answer not the end proposed, must yet produce correspondent effects. Morals and mechanics are here analogous. No longer, then, distress me by the repetition of a question I ought not to answer. I am content to be the victim - Oh! may I be the only victim - of my folly!

'One more observation allow me to make, before I conclude. That we can "admire, esteem, and love," an individual - (for love in the abstract, loving mankind collectively, conveys to me no idea) - which must be, in fact, depending upon that individual for a large share of our felicity, and not lament his loss, in proportion to our apprehension of his worth, appears to me a proposition, involving in itself an absurdity; therefore demonstrably false.

'Let me, my friend, see you ere long - your remonstrance has affected me - save me from myself!'

To The Same [In continuation.]

'My letter having been delayed a few days, through a mistake - I resume my pen; for, running my eye over what I had written, I perceive (confounded by the force of your expressions) I have granted you too much. My conduct was not, altogether, so insane as I have been willing to allow. It is certain, that could I have attained the end proposed, my happiness had been encreased. "It is necessary for me to love and admire, or I sink into sadness." The behaviour of the man, whom I sought to move, appeared to me too inconsistent to be the result of *indifference.* To be roused and stimulated by obstacles - obstacles admitting hope, because obscurely seen - is no mark of weakness. Could I have subdued, what I, then, conceived to be the *prejudices* of a worthy man, I could have increased both his happiness and my own. I deeply reasoned, and philosophized, upon the subject. Perseverance, with little ability, has effected wonders; - with perseverance, I felt, that, I had the power of uniting ability - confiding in that power, I was the dupe of my own reason. No other man, perhaps, could have acted the part which this man has acted: - how, then, was I to take such a part into my calculations?

'Do not misconceive me - it is no miracle that I did not inspire affection. On this subject, the mortification I have suffered has humbled me, it may be, even, unduly in my own eyes - but to the emotions of my pride, I would disdain to give words. Whatever may have been my feelings, I am too proud to express the rage of slighted love! - Yet, I am sensible to all the powers of those charming lines of Pope -

> *"Unequal talk, a passion to resign,*
> *For hearts so touch'd, so pierc'd, so lost, as mine!*

Ere such a soul regains its peaceful state,
How often must it love, how often hate;
How often hope, despair, resent, regret,
Conceal, disdain, do all things but forget!"

'But to return. I pursued, comparatively, (as I thought) a certain good; and when, at times, discouraged, I have repeated to myself - What! after all these pains, shall I relinquish my efforts, when, perhaps, on the very verge of success? - To say nothing of the difficulty of forcing an active mind out of its trains - if I desisted, what was to be the result? The sensations I now feel - apathy, stagnation, abhorred vacuity!

'You cannot resist the force of my reasoning - you, who are acquainted with, who know how to paint, in colours true to nature, the human heart - you, who admire, as a proof of power, the destructive courage of an Alexander, even the fanatic fury of a Ravaillac - you, who honour the pernicious ambition of an Augustus Cæsar, as bespeaking the potent, energetic, mind! - why should you affect to be intolerant to a passion, though differing in nature, generated on the same principles, and by a parallel process. The capacity of perception, or of receiving sensation, is (or generates) the power; into what channel that power shall be directed, depends not on ourselves. Are we not the creatures of outward impressions? Without such impressions, should we be any thing? Are not passions and powers synonymous - or can the latter be produced without the lively interest that constitutes the former? Do you dream of annihilating the one - and will not the other be extinguished? With the apostle, Paul, permit me to say - "I am not mad, but speak the words of truth and soberness."

'To what purpose did you read my confessions, but to trace in them a character formed, like every other human character, by the result of unavoidable impressions, and the chain of necessary events. I feel, that my arguments are incontrovertible: - I suspect that, by affecting to deny their force, you will endeavour to deceive either me or yourself. - I have acquired the power of reasoning on this subject at a dear rate - at the expense of inconceivable suffering. Attempt not to deny me the miserable, expensive, victory. I am ready to say - (ungrateful that I am) - Why did you put me upon calling forth my strong reasons?

'I perceive there is no cure for me - (apathy is, not the restoration to health, but, the morbid lethargy of the soul) but by a new train of impressions, of whatever nature, equally forcible with the past. - You will tell me, It remains with myself whether I will predetermine to resist such impressions. Is this true? Is it philosophical? Ask yourself. What! - can even you shrink from the consequences of your own principles?

'One word more - You accuse me of brooding in silence over my sensations -

of considering them as a "sacred deposit." Concealment is particularly repugnant to my disposition - yet a thousand delicacies - a thousand nameless solicitudes, and apprehensions, sealed my lips! - He who inspired them was, alone, the depositary of my most secret thoughts! - my heart was unreservedly open before him - I covered my paper with its emotions, and transmitted it to him - like him who whispered his secret into the earth, to relieve the burden of uncommunicated thought. My secret was equally safe, and received in equal silence! Alas! he was not then ignorant of the effects it was likely to produce!

'Emma.'

Mr Francis continued his humane and friendly attentions; and, while he opposed my sentiments, as conceiving them destructive of my tranquillity, mingled with his opposition a gentle and delicate consideration for my feelings, that sensibly affected me, and excited my grateful attachment. He judged right, that, by stimulating my mind into action, the sensations, which so heavily oppressed it, might be, in some measure, mitigated - by diverting the course of my ideas into different channels, and by that means abating their force. His kindness soothed and flattered me, and communications relieved my thoughts.

CHAPTER XIII

The period which succeeded these events, though tedious in wearing away, marked by no vicissitude, has left little impression behind. The tenor of my days resembled the still surface of a stagnant lake, embosomed in a deep cavern, over which the refreshing breezes never sweep. Sad, vacant, inactive - the faculties both of mind and body seemed almost suspended. I became weak, languid, enervated - my disorder was a lethargy of soul. This was gradually succeeded by disease of body: - an inactivity, so contrary to all the habits of my past life, generated morbid humours, and brought on a slow, remitting, fever. I recovered, by degrees, from this attack, but remained for some time in a debilitated, though convalescent, state. A few weeks after my disorder returned, lasted longer, and left me still more weakened and depressed. A third time it assailed me, at a shorter interval; and, though less violent, was more protracted, and more exhausting.

Mrs Denbeigh, alarmed by my situation, wrote to Mrs Harley, expressing the apprehensions which she entertained. From this dear friend, who was herself in a declining state of health, I received a pressing invitation to visit, once more, the village of F ...... ; and to seek, from change of air, change of scene, and the cordial endearments of friendship, a restoration for my debilitated frame, and a balm for my wounded mind.

My relation, at this period, had letters from her husband, informing her, that the term of his residence in India was prolonged; pressing her to join him there, and to come over in the next ship. To this request she joyfully acceded; and, hearing that a packet was about to sail for Bengal, secured her passage, and began immediately to make preparations for her departure. I no longer hesitated to comply with the entreaties of my friend; besides the tie of strong affection, which drew me to her, I had, at present, little other resource.

After affectionately embracing Mrs Denbeigh, wishing a happy issue to her voyage, thanking her for all her kindness, and leaving a letter of grateful acknowledgement for Mr Francis, I quitted the metropolis, with an aching heart, and a wasted frame. My cousin accompanied me to the inn, from whence the vehicle set out that was to convey me to Mrs Harley. We parted in silence - a crowd of retrospective ideas of the past, and solicitudes respecting the future, occupied our thoughts - our sensations were too affecting for words.

The carriage quitted London at the close of the evening, and travelled all night: - it was towards the end of the year. At midnight we passed over Hounslow and Bagshot heaths. 'The moon,' to adopt the language of Ossian, 'looked through broken clouds, and brightened their dark-brown sides.' A loud November blast howled over the heath, and whistled through the fern. - There was a melancholy desolation in the scene, that was in unison with my feelings, and which overwhelmed my spirits with a tide of tender recollections. I recalled to my imagination a thousand interesting images - I indulged in all the wild enthusiasm of my character. My fellow-travellers slept tranquilly, while my soul was awake to agonizing sorrow. I adopted the language of the tender Eloisa - 'Why,' said I, 'am I indebted for life to his care, whose cruelty has rendered it insupportable? Inhuman, as he is, let him fly from me for ever, and deny himself the savage pleasure of being an eye-witness to my sorrows! - But why do I rave thus? - He is not to be blamed - *I, alone, am guilty* - I, alone, am the author of my own misfortunes, and should, therefore, be the only object of anger and resentment.'[19]

Weakened by my late indisposition, fatigued by the rough motion of the carriage, and exhausted by strong emotion, when arrived at the end of my journey, I was obliged to be lifted from the coach, and carried into the cottage of my friend. The servant led the way to the library - the door opened - Mrs Harley advanced, to receive me, with tottering steps. The ravages of grief, and the traces of sickness, were visible in her dear, affectionate, countenance. I clasped my hands, and, lifting up my eyes, beheld the portrait of Augustus - beheld again the resemblance of those features so deeply engraven on my heart! My imagination was raised - methought the lively colours of the complexion had faded, the benignant smile had vanished, and an expression of perplexity and sternness usurped its place. I uttered a faint shriek, and fell lifeless into the arms of my friend. It was some time before I returned to sense and recollection, when I found myself on the bed, in the little chamber which had formerly been appropriated to my use. My friend sat beside me, holding my hand in her's, which she bathed with her tears. 'Thank God!' she exclaimed, in a rapturous accent, (as, with a deep sigh, I raised my languid eyes, and turned them mournfully towards her) - 'she lives! - My Emma! - child of my affections!' - sobs suppressed her utterance. I drew the hand, which held mine, towards me - I pressed it to my bosom - '*My mother*!' - I would have said; but the tender appellation died away upon my lips, in inarticulate murmurs.

These severe struggles were followed by a return of my disorder. Mrs Harley would scarcely be persuaded to quit my chamber for a moment - her tenderness seemed to afford her new strength; - but these exertions accelerated the progress of an internal malady, which had for some time past been gaining ground, and gradually undermining her health.

Youth, and a good constitution, aided by the kind solicitudes of friendship, restored me, in a few weeks, to a state of convalescence. I observed the declining

19: Rousseau.

strength of my friend with terror - I accused myself of having, though involuntarily, added to these alarming symptoms, by the new fatigues and anxieties which I had occasioned her. Affection inspired me with those energies, that reason had vainly dictated. I struggled to subdue myself - I stifled the impetuous suggestions of my feelings, in exerting myself to fulfil the duties of humanity. My mind assumed a firmer tone - I became, once more, the cheerful companion, the tender consoler, the attentive nurse, of this excellent woman, to whose kindness I was so much indebted - and, if I stole a few moments in the day, while my friend reposed, to gaze on the resemblance of Augustus, to weep over the testimonies of his former respect and friendship, I quickly chased from my bosom, and my countenance, every trace of sadness, when summoned to attend my friend.

CHAPTER XIV

The winter came on severe and cold. Mrs Harley was forbidden to expose herself to the frosty air, which seemed to invigorate my languid frame. I was constituted her almoner, to distribute to the neighbouring poor the scanty portion, which she was enabled, by a rigid œconomy, to spare from her little income: yet the value of this distribution had been more than redoubled, by the gentler charities of kind accents, tender sympathy, and wholesome counsels. To these indigent, but industrious, cottagers, I studied to be the worthy representative of their amiable benefactress, and found my reward in their grateful attachment, and the approving smiles of my friend.

By degrees, she ventured to converse with me on the subject nearest her heart - the situation of her son. He had been obliged to yield to the proofs produced of his marriage, which he had, at first, seemed desirous of evading. He had written, with reserve, upon the subject to his mother; but, from the enquiries of a common friend, she had reason to apprehend, that his engagement had been of an imprudent nature. Two children, were, already the fruits of it: the mother, with a feminine helplessness of character, had a feeble constitution. The small fortune, which Augustus had originally shared with his family, was greatly reduced. His education and habits had unfitted him for those exertions which the support of an encreasing family necessarily required: - his spirits (her friend had informed her) seemed broken, and his temper soured. Some efforts had been made to serve him, which his lofty spirit had repelled with disdain.

This narration deeply affected my heart - I had resigned myself to his loss - but the idea of his suffering, I felt, was an evil infinitely severer. It was this conviction that preyed incessantly on the peace and health of his mother. My fortitude failed, when I would have tried to sustain her; and I could only afford the melancholy satisfaction of mingling my sorrows with her's.

The disorder of my friend rapidly increased - her mind became weakened, and her feelings wayward and irritable. I watched her incessantly - I strove, by every alleviating care, to soften her pains. Towards the approach of spring the symptoms grew more threatening; and it was judged, by her physician, necessary to apprize her family of her immediate danger. What a trial for my exhausted heart! I traced, with a trembling hand, a line to this melancholy purpose - addressed it to Mr Harley, and through him to his younger brothers and sisters.

In a few days they arrived in the village - sending from the inn a servant, to prepare their mother for their approach. I gently intimated to her the visitants we might expect. The previous evening, a change had taken place, which indicated approaching dissolution; and her mind (not uncommon in similar cases) seemed, almost instantaneously, to have recovered a portion of its original strength. She sighed deeply, while her eyes, which were fixed wistfully on my face, were lighted with a bright, but transient, lustre.

'My dear Emma,' said she, 'this is a trying moment for us both. I shall soon close my eyes, for ever, upon all worldly cares. - Still cherish, in your pure and ingenuous mind, a friendship for my Augustus - the darling of my soul! He may, in future, stand in need of consolation. I had formed hopes - vain hopes! - in which you and he were equally concerned. In the happiness of this partially-favoured child - this idol of my affections - all mine was concentrated. He has disappointed me, and I have lost the desire of living - Yet, he has noble qualities! - Who, alas! is perfect? Summon your fortitude, collect your powers, my child, for this interview!'

She sunk on her pillow - I answered her only with my tears. A servant entered - but spoke not - her look announced her tidings - It caught the eye of Mrs Harley -

'Let them enter,' said she; and she raised herself, to receive them, and assumed an aspect of composure.

I covered my face with my handkerchief - I heard the sound of footsteps approaching the bed - I heard the murmurs of filial sorrow - The voice of Augustus, in low and interrupted accents, struck upon my ear - it thrilled through my nerves - I shuddered, involuntarily - What a moment! My friend spoke a few words, in a faint tone.

'My children,' she added, 'repay to this dear girl,' laying her hand upon mine, 'the debt of kindness I owe her - she has smoothed the pillow of death - she is an orphan - she is tender and unfortunate.'

I ventured to remove for a moment the handkerchief from my eyes - they met those of Augustus - he was kneeling by the bed-side - his countenance was wan, and every feature sunk in dejection; a shivering crept through my veins, and chilled my heart with a sensation of icy coldness - he removed his eyes, fixing them on his dying mother.

'My son,' she resumed, in still fainter accents, 'behold in Emma, your sister - *your friend*! - confide in her - she is worthy of your confidence!' - 'Will you not love him, my child,' - (gazing upon me,) - 'with a sisterly affection?'

I hid my face upon the pillow of my friend - I threw my arms around her - 'Your request is superfluous, my friend, my more than parent, *ah, how superfluous*!'

'Forgive me, I know the tenderness of your nature - yielding, in these parting moments, to the predominant affection of my heart - I fear, I have wounded that tender nature.' 'Farewell, my children! Love and assist each other - Augustus, where is your hand? - my sight fails me - God bless you and your little ones - *God bless you all*! - My last sigh - my last prayer - is yours.'

Exhausted by these efforts, she fainted - Augustus uttered a deep groan, and raised her in his arms - but life was fled.

At the remembrance of these scenes, even at this period, my heart is melted within me.

What is there of mournful magic in the emotions of virtuous sorrow, that in retracing, in dwelling upon them, mingles with our tears a sad and sublime rapture? Nature, that has infused so much misery into the cup of human life, has kindly mixed this strange and mysterious ingredient to qualify the bitter draught.

CHAPTER XV

After the performance of the last melancholy duties, this afflicted family prepared to separate. I received from them, individually, friendly offers of service, and expressions of acknowledgment, for my tender attentions to their deceased parent. I declined, for the present, their invitations, and profferred kindness, though uncertain how to dispose of myself, or which way to direct my course. Augustus behaved towards me with distant, cold, respect. I observed in his features, under a constrained appearance of composure, marks of deep and strong emotion. I recalled to my mind the injunctions of my deceased friend - I yearned to pour into his bosom the balm of sympathy, but, with an aspect bordering on severity, he repressed the expression of those ingenuous feelings which formed my character, and shunned the confidence I so earnestly sought. Unfortunate love had, in my subdued and softened mind, laid the foundation of a fervent and durable friendship - But my love, my friendship, were equally contemned! I relinquished my efforts - I shut myself in my chamber - and, in secret, indulged my sorrows.

The house of my deceased friend was sold, and the effects disposed of. On the day previous to their removal, and the departure of the family for London, I stole into the library, at the close of the evening, to view, *for the last time*, the scene of so many delightful, so many afflicting emotions. A mysterious and sacred enchantment is spread over every circumstance, even every inanimate object, connected with the affections. To those who are strangers to these delicate, yet powerful sympathies, this may appear ridiculous - but the sensations are not the less genuine, nor the less in nature. I will not attempt to analyse them, it is a subject upon which the language of philosophy would appear frigid, and on which I feel myself every moment on the verge of fanaticism. Yet, affections like these are not so much weakness, as strength perhaps badly exerted. Rousseau was, right, when he asserted, that, 'Common men know nothing of violent sorrows, nor do great passions ever break out in weak minds. Energy of sentiment is the characteristic of a noble soul.'

I gazed from the windows on the shrubbery, where I had so often wandered with my friends - where I had fondly cherished so many flattering, so many visionary, prospects. Every spot, every tree, was associated with some past pleasure, some tender recollection. The last rays of the setting sun, struggling from beneath a louring cloud, streamed through its dark bosom, illumined its edges, played on the window in which I was standing, and gilding the opposite side of the wainscot, against which the picture of Augustus still hung, shed a soft and mellow lustre over the features. I turned almost unconsciously, and contemplated it with a long and deep regard. It seemed to smile benignly - it wore no traces of the cold austerity, the gloomy and inflexible reserve, which now clouded the aspect of the original. I called to my remembrance a thousand interesting conversations - when

'Tuned to happy unison of soul, a fairer world of which the vulgar never had a glimpse, displayed, its charms.'

Absorbed in thought, the crimson reflection from the western clouds gradually faded, while the deep shades of the evening, thickened by the appearance of a gathering tempest, involved in obscurity the object on which, without distinctly perceiving it, I still continued to gaze.

I was roused from this reverie by the sudden opening of the door. Some person, whom the uncertain light prevented me from distinguishing, walked across the room, with a slow and solemn pace, and, after taking several turns backwards and forwards, reclined on the sopha, remaining for some time perfectly still. A tremor shook my nerves - unable either to speak, or to move, I continued silent and trembling - my heart felt oppressed, almost to suffocation - at length, a deep, convulsive sigh, forced its way.

'My God!' exclaimed the person, whose meditations I had interrupted, 'what is that?'

It was the voice of Mr Harley, he spoke in a stern tone, though with some degree of trepidation, and advanced hastily towards the window against which I leaned.

The clouds had for some hours been gathering dark and gloomy. Just as Augustus had reached the place where I stood, a flash of lightning, pale, yet vivid, glanced suddenly across my startled sight, and discovered to him the object which had alarmed him.

'Emma,' said he, in a softened accent, taking my trembling and almost lifeless hand, 'how came you here, which way did you enter?'

I answered not - Another flash of lightning, still brighter, blue and sulphurous, illuminated the room, succeeded by a loud and long peal of thunder. Again the heavens seemed to rend asunder and discover a sheet of livid flame - a crash of thunder, sudden, loud, short, immediately followed, bespeaking the tempest near. I started with a kind of convulsive terror. Augustus led me from the window, and endeavoured, in vain, to find the door of the library - the temporary flashes, and total darkness by which they were succeeded, dazzled and confounded the sight. I stumbled over some furniture, which stood in the middle of the room, and unable to recover my feet, which refused any longer to sustain me, sunk into the arms of Augustus, suffering him to lift me to the sopha. He seated himself beside me, the storm continued; the clouds, every moment parting with a horrible noise, discovered an abyss of fire, while the rain descended in a deluge. We silently contemplated this sublime and terrible scene. Augustus supported me with one arm, while my trembling hand remained in his. The tempest soon exhausted itself by its violence - the lightning became less fierce, gleaming at intervals - the thunder rolled off to a distance - its protracted sound, lengthened by the echoes, faintly died away; while the rain continued to fall in a still, though copious, shower.

My spirits grew calmer, I gently withdrew my hand from that of Mr Harley. He once more enquired, but in a tone of greater reserve, how I had entered the room without his knowledge? I explained, briefly and frankly, my situation, and the tender motives by which I had been influenced.

'It was not possible,' added I, 'to take leave of this house *for ever*, without recalling a variety of affecting and melancholy ideas - I feel, that I have lost *my only friend.*'

'This world,' said he, 'may not unaptly be compared to the rapids on the American rivers - We are hurried, in a frail bark, down the stream - It is in vain to resist its course - happy are those whose voyage is ended!'

'My friend,' replied I in a faultering voice, 'I could teach my heart to bear your loss - though, God knows, the lesson has been sufficiently severe - but I know not how, with fortitude, to see you suffer.'

'Suffering is the common lot of humanity - but, pardon me, when I say, your conduct has not tended to lessen my vexations!'

'My errors have been the errors of *affection* - Do they deserve this rigor?'

'Their source is not important, their consequences have been the same - you make not the allowances you claim.'

'Dear, and severe, friend! - Be not unjust - the confidence which I sought, and merited, would have been obviated' -

'I know what you would alledge - that confidence, you had reason to judge, was of a painful nature - it ought not to have been extorted.'

'If I have been wrong, my faults have been severely expiated - if the error has been only mine, surely my sufferings have been in proportion; seduced by the fervor of my feelings; ignorant of your situation, if I wildly sought to oblige you to chuse happiness through a medium of my creation - yet, to have assured yours, was I not willing to risque all my own? I perceive my extravagance, my views were equally false and romantic - dare I to say - they were the ardent excesses of a generous mind? Yes! my wildest mistakes had in them a dignified mixture of virtue. While the institutions of society war against nature and happiness, the mind of energy, struggling to emancipate itself, will entangle itself in error' -

'Permit me to ask you,' interrupted Augustus, 'whether, absorbed in your own sensations, you allowed yourself to remember, and to respect, the feelings of others?'

I could no longer restrain my tears, I wept for some moments in silence - Augustus breathed a half-suppressed sigh, and turned from me his face.

'The pangs which have rent my heart,' resumed I, in low and broken accents, 'have, I confess, been but too poignant! That lacerated heart still bleeds - we have neither of us been guiltless - *Alas! who is*? Yet in my bosom, severe feelings are not more painful than transient - already have I lost sight of your unkindness, (God knows how little I merited it!) in stronger sympathy for your sorrows - whatever be their nature! We have both erred - why should we not exchange mutual forgiveness? Why should we afflict each other? Friendship, like charity, should suffer all things and be kind!'

'My mind,' replied he coldly, 'is differently constituted.'

'Unpitying man! It would be hard for us, if we were all to be judged at so severe a tribunal - you have been a lover,' added I, in a softer tone, 'and can you not forgive the faults of love?'

He arose, visibly agitated - I also stood up - my bosom deeply wounded, and, unknowing what I did, took his hand, and pressed it to my lips.

'You have rudely thrown from you a heart of exquisite sensibility - you have contemned my love, and you disdain my friendship - is it brave, is it manly,' added I wildly - almost unconscious of what I said - forgetting at the moment his situation and my own - 'thus to triumph over a spirit, subdued by its affections into unresisting meekness?'

He broke from me, and precipitately quitted the room.

I threw myself upon the floor, and, resting my head on the seat which Augustus had so lately occupied, passed the night in cruel conflict - a tempest more terrible than that which had recently spent its force, shook my soul! The morning dawned, ere I had power to remove myself from the fatal spot, where the measure of my afflictions seemed filled up. - Virtue may conquer weakness, but who can bear to be despised by those they love. The sun darted its beams full upon me, but its splendour appeared mockery - hope and joy were for ever excluded from my benighted spirit. The contempt of the world, the scoffs of ignorance, the contumely of the proud, I could have borne without shrinking - but to find myself rejected, contemned, scorned, by him with whom, of all mankind, my heart claimed kindred; by him for whom my youth, my health, my powers, were consuming in silent anguish - who, instead of pouring balm into the wound he had inflicted, administered only corrosives! - *It was too painful*! I felt, that I had been a lavish prodigal - that I had become a wretched bankrupt; that there was but *one way* to make me happy and a *thousand* to make me miserable! Enfeebled and exhausted, I crawled to my apartment, and, throwing myself on the bed, gave a loose to the agony of my soul.

CHAPTER XVI

Under pretence of indisposition, I refused to meet the family. I heard them depart. Too proud to accept of obligation, I had not confided to them my plans, if plans they could be called, where no distinct end was in view.

A few hours after their departure, I once more seated myself in a stage coach, in which I had previously secured a place, and took the road to London. I perceived, on entering the carriage, only one passenger, who had placed himself in the opposite corner, and in whom, to my great surprize, I immediately recognized Mr Montague. We had not met since the visit he had paid me at Mrs Harley's, the result of which I have already related: since that period, it had been reported in the village, that he addressed Sarah Morton, and that they were about to be united. Montague manifested equal surprize at our meeting: the intelligence of my friend's death (at which he expressed real concern) had not reached him, neither was he acquainted with my being in that part of the country. He had not lately been at Mr Morton's, he informed me, but had just left his father's, and was going to London to complete his medical studies.

After these explanations, absorbed in painful contemplation, I for some time made little other return to his repeated civilities, than by cold monosyllables: till at length, his cordial sympathy, his gentle accents, and humane attentions, awakened me from my reverie. Ever accessible to the soothings of kindness, I endeavoured to exert myself, to prove the sense I felt of his humanity. Gratified by having succeeded in attracting my attention, he redoubled his efforts to cheer and amuse me. My dejected and languid appearance had touched his feelings, and, towards the end of our journey, his unaffected zeal to alleviate the anxiety under which I evidently appeared to labour, soothed my mind and inspired me with confidence.

He respectfully requested to know in what part of the town I resided, and hoped to be permitted to pay his respects to me, and to enquire after my welfare? This question awakened in my bosom so many complicated and painful sensations, that, after remaining silent for a few minutes, I burst into a flood of tears.

'I have no home;' said I, in a voice choaked with sobs - 'I am an alien in the world - and alone in the universe.'

His eyes glistened, his countenance expressed the most lively, and tender, commiseration, while, in a timid and respectful voice, he made me offers of service, and entreated me to permit him to be useful to me.

'I then mentioned, in brief, my present unprotected situation, and hinted, that as my fortune was small, I could wish to procure a humble, but decent, apartment in a reputable fami_y, till I had consulted one friend, who, I yet flattered myself, was interested in my concerns, or till I could fix on a more eligible method of providing for myself.'

He informed me - 'That he had a distant relation in town, a decent, careful, woman, who kept a boarding house, and whose terms were very reasonable. He was assured, would I permit him to introduce me to her, she would be happy, should her accommodation suit me, to pay me every attention in her power.'

In my forlorn situation, I confided, without hesitation, in his recommendation, and gratefully acceded to the proposal.

Mr Montague introduced me to this lady in the most flattering terms, she received me with civility, but, I fancied, not without a slight mixture of distrust. I agreed with her for a neat chamber, with a sitting room adjoining, on the second floor, and settled for the terms of my board, more than the whole amount of the interest of my little fortune.

CHAPTER XVII

I took an early opportunity of addressing a few lines to Mr Francis, informing him of my situation, and entreating his counsel. I waited a week, impatiently, for his reply, but in vain: well acquainted with his punctuality, and alarmed by this silence, I mentioned the step I had taken, and my apprehensions, to Montague, who immediately repaired, himself, to the house of Mr Francis; and, finding it shut up, was informed by the neighbours, that Mr Francis had quitted England, a short time before, in company with a friend, intending to make a continental tour.

This intelligence was a new shock to me. I called on some of my former acquaintance, mentioning to them my wish of procuring pupils, or of engaging in any other occupation fitted to my talents. I was received by some with civility, by others with coldness, but every one appeared too much engrossed by his own affairs to give himself the trouble of making any great exertion for others.

I returned dispirited - I walked through the crowded city, and observed the anxious and busy faces of all around me. In the midst of my fellow beings, occupied in various pursuits, I seemed, as if in an immense desert, a solitary outcast from society. Active, industrious, willing to employ my faculties in any way, by which I might procure an honest independence, I beheld no path open to me, but that to which my spirit could not submit - the degradation of servitude. Hapless woman! - crushed by the iron hand of barbarous despotism, pampered into weakness, and trained the slave of meretricious folly! - what wonder, that, shrinking from the chill blasts of penury (which the pernicious habits of thy education have little fitted thy tender frame to encounter) thou listenest to the honied accents of the spoiler; and, to escape the galling chain of servile dependence, rushest into the career of infamy, from whence the false and cruel morality of the world forbids thy return, and perpetuates thy disgrace and misery! When will mankind be aware of the uniformity, of the importance, of truth? When will they cease to confound, by sexual, by political, by theological, distinctions, those immutable principles, which form the true basis of virtue and happiness? The paltry expedients of combating error with error, and prejudice with prejudice, in one invariable and melancholy circle, have already been sufficiently tried, have already been demonstrated futile: - they have armed man against man, and filled the world with crimes, and with blood. - How has the benign and gentle nature of Reform been mistated! 'One false idea,' justly says an acute and philosophic writer, [20] 'united with others, produces such as are

20: *Helvetius.*

necessarily false; which, combining again with all those the memory retains, give to all a tinge of falsehood. One error, alone, is sufficient to infect the whole mass of the mind, and produce an infinity of capricious, monstrous, notions. - Every vice is the error of the understanding; crimes and prejudices are brothers; truth and virtue sisters. These things, known to the wise, are hid from fools!'

Without a sufficiently interesting pursuit, a fatal torpor stole over my spirits - my blood circulated languidly through my veins. Montague, in the intervals from business and amusement, continued to visit me. He brought me books, read to me, chatted with me, pressed me to accompany him to places of public entertainment, which (determined to incur no pecuniary obligation) I invariably refused.

I received his civilities with the less scruple, from the information I had received of his engagement with Miss Morton; which, with his knowledge of my unhappy attachment, I thought, precluded every idea of a renewal of those sentiments he had formerly professed for me.

In return for his friendship, I tried to smile, and exerted my spirits, to prove my grateful sensibility of his kindness: but, while he appeared to take a lively interest in my sorrows, he carefully avoided a repetition of the language in which he had once addressed me; yet, at times, his tender concern seemed sliding into a sentiment still softer, which obliged me to practise more reserve: he was not insensible of this, and was frequently betrayed into transient bursts of passion and resentment, which, on my repelling with firmness, he would struggle to repress, and afterwards absent himself for a time.

Unable to devise any method of increasing my income, and experiencing the pressure of some daily wants and inconveniencies, I determined, at length, on selling the sum invested, in my name, in the funds, and purchasing a life annuity.

Recollecting the name of a banker, with whom my uncle, the friend of my infancy, had formerly kept cash, I learned his residence, and, waiting upon him, made myself known as the niece of an old and worthy friend; at the same time acquainting him with my intentions. - He offered to transact the affair for me immediately, the funds being, then, in a very favourable position; and to preserve the money in his hands till an opportunity should offer of laying it out to advantage. I gave him proper credentials for the accomplishing of this business, and returned to my apartment with a heart somewhat lightened. This scheme had never before occurred to me. The banker, who was a man of commercial reputation, had assured me, that my fortune might now be sold out with little loss; and that, by purchasing an annuity, on proper security, at seven or eight per cent, I might, with œconomy, be enabled to support myself decently, with comfort and independence.

CHAPTER XVIII

Some weeks elapsed, and I heard no more from my banker. A slight indisposition confined me to the house. One evening, Mr Montague, coming to my apartment to enquire after my health, brought with him a newspaper (as was his frequent custom), and, finding me unwell, and dispirited, began to read some parts from it aloud, in the hope of amusing me. Among the articles of home intelligence, a paragraph stated - 'The failure of a considerable mercantile house, which had created an alarm upon the Exchange, as, it was apprehended, some important consequences would follow in the commercial world. A great banking-house, it was hinted, not many miles from ......, was likely to be affected, by some rumours, in connection with this business, which had occasioned a considerable run upon it for the last two or three days.'

My attention was roused - I eagerly held out my hand for the paper, and perused this alarming paragraph again and again, without observing the surprize expressed in the countenance of Montague, who was at a loss to conceive why this intelligence should be affecting to me. - I sat, for some minutes, involved in thought, till a question from my companion, several times repeated, occasioned me to start. I immediately recollected myself, and tried to reason away my fears, as vague and groundless. I was about to explain the nature of them to my friend - secretly accusing myself for not having done so sooner, and availed myself of his advice, when a servant, entering, put a letter into his hand.

Looking upon the seal and superscription, he changed colour, and opened it hastily. Strong emotion was painted in his features while he perused it. I regarded him with anxiety. He rose from his seat, walked up and down the room with a disordered pace - opened the door, as if with an intention of going out - shut it - returned back again - threw himself into a chair - covered his face with his handkerchief - appeared in great agitation - and burst into tears. I arose, went to him, and took his hand - '*My friend*!' said I - I would have added something more - but, unable to proceed, I sunk into a seat beside him, and wept in sympathy. He pressed my hand to his lips - folded me wildly in his arms, and attempted to speak - but his voice was lost in convulsive sobs. I gently withdrew myself, and waited, in silence, till the violence of his emotions should subside. He held out to me the letter he had received. I perused it. It contained an account of the sudden death of his father, and a summons for his immediate return to the country, to settle the affairs, and to take upon him his father's professional employment.

'You leave me, then!' said I - 'I lose my only remaining friend!'

'*Never*!' - he replied, emphatically.

I blushed for having uttered so improper, so selfish, a remark; and endeavoured to atone for it by forgetting the perils of my own situation, in attention to that of this ardent, but affectionate, young man. - His sufferings were acute and violent for some days, during which he quitted me only at the hours of repose - I devoted myself to sooth and console him. I felt, that I had been greatly indebted to his friendship and kindness, and I endeavoured to repay the obligation. He appeared fully sensible of my cares, and, mingled with his acknowledgments expressions of a tenderness, so lively, and unequivocal, as obliged me, once more, to be more guarded in my behaviour.

In consideration for the situation of Mr Montague - I had forgotten the paragraph in the paper, till an accidental intelligence of the bankruptcy of the house, in which my little fortune was entrusted, confirmed to me the certainty of this terrible blow. Montague was sitting with me when I received the unwelcome news.

'Gracious God!' I exclaimed, clasping my hands, and raising my eyes to heaven - 'What is to become of me now? - The measure of my sorrows is filled up!'

It was some time before I had power to explain the circumstances to my companion.

'Do not distress yourself, my lovely Emma,' said he; 'I will be your friend - your guardian - ' (and he added, in a low, yet fervent, accent) - 'your husband!'

'No - no - no!' answered I, shaking my head, 'that must not, cannot, be! I would perish, rather than take advantage of a generosity like yours. I will go to service - I will work for my bread - and, if I cannot procure a wretched sustenance - *I can but die*! Life, to me, has long been worthless!'

My countenance, my voice, my manner, but too forcibly expressed the keen anguish of my soul. I seemed to be marked out for the victim of a merciless destiny - *for the child of sorrow*! The susceptible temper of Montague, softened by his own affliction, was moved by my distress. He repeated, and enforced, his proposal, with all the ardour of a youthful, a warm, an uncorrupted, mind.

'You add to my distress,' replied I. 'I have not a heart to bestow - I lavished mine upon one, who scorned and contemned it. Its sensibility is now exhausted. Shall I reward a faithful and generous tenderness, like yours, with a cold, a worthless, an alienated, mind? No, no! - Seek an object more worthy of you, and leave me to my fate.'

At that moment, I had forgotten the report of his engagement with Miss Morton; but, on his persisting, vehemently, to urge his suit, I recollected, and immediately mentioned, it, to him.

He confessed -

'That, stung by my rejection, and preference of Mr Harley, he had, at one period, entertained a thought of that nature; but that he had fallen out with the family, in adjusting the settlements. Mrs Morton had persuaded her husband to make, what he conceived to be, ungenerous requisitions. Miss Morton had discovered much artifice, but little sensibility, on the occasion. Disgusted with the apathy of the father, the insolence of the mother and the low cunning of the daughter, he had abruptly quitted them, and broken off all intercourse with the family.'

It is not necessary to enlarge on this part of my narrative. Suffice it to say, that, after a long contest, my desolate situation, added to the persevering affection of this enthusiastic young man, prevailed over my objections. His happiness, he told me, entirely depended on my decision. I would not deceive him: - I related to him, with simplicity and truth, all the circumstances of my past conduct towards Mr Harley. He listened to me with evident emotion - interrupted me, at times, with execrations; and, once or twice, vowing vengeance on Augustus, appeared on the verge of outrage. But I at length reasoned him into greater moderation, and obliged him to do justice to the merit and honour of Mr Harley. He acquiesced reluctantly, and with an ill grace, yet, with a lover-like partiality, attributed his conduct to causes, of which I had discerned no traces. He assured himself that the affections of a heart, tender as mine, would be secured by kindness and assiduity - and I at last yielded to his importunity. We were united in a short time, and I accompanied my husband to the town of ...... , in the county of ...... , the residence of his late father.

CHAPTER XIX

Mr Montague presented me to his relations and friends, by whom I was received with a flattering distinction. My wearied spirits began now to find repose. My husband was much occupied in the duties of his profession. We had a respectable circle of acquaintance: In the intervals of social engagement, and domestic employment, ever thirsting after knowledge, I occasionally applied myself to the study of physic, anatomy, and surgery, with the various branches of science connected with them; by which means I frequently rendered myself essentially serviceable to my friend; and, by exercising my understanding and humanity, strengthened my mind, and stilled the importunate suggestions of a heart too exquisitely sensible.

The manners of Mr Montague were kind and affectionate, though subject, at times, to inequalities and starts of passion; he confided in me, as his best and truest friend - and I deserved his confidence: - yet, I frequently observed the restlessness and impetuosity of his disposition with apprehension.

I felt for my husband a rational esteem, and a grateful affection: - but those romantic, high-wrought, frenzied, emotions, that had rent my heart during its first attachment - that enthusiasm, that fanaticism, to which opposition had given force, the bare recollection of which still shook my soul with anguish, no longer existed. Montague was but too sensible of this difference, which naturally resulted from the change of circumstances, and was unreasonable enough to complain of what secured our tranquillity. If a cloud, sometimes, hung over my brow - if I relapsed, for a short period, into a too habitual melancholy, he would grow captious, and complain.

'You esteem me, Emma: I confide in your principles, and I glory in your friendship - but, you have never *loved* me!'

'Why will you be so unjust, both to me, and to yourself?'

'Tell me, then, sincerely - I know you will not deceive me - Have you ever felt for me those sentiments with which Augustus Harley inspired you?'

'Certainly not - I do not pretend to it - neither ought you to wish it. My first attachment was the morbid excess of a distempered imagination. Liberty, reason, virtue, usefulness, were the offerings I carried to its shrine. It preyed incessantly upon my heart, I drank up its vital spirit, it became a vice from its excess - it was a pernicious, though a sublime, enthusiasm - its ravages are scarcely to be remembered without shuddering - all the strength, the dignity, the powers, of my mind, melted before it! Do you wish again to see me the slave of my passions - do you regret, that I am restored to reason? To you I owe every thing - life, and its comforts, rational enjoyments, and the opportunity of usefulness. I feel for you all the affection that a reasonable and a virtuous mind ought to feel - that affection which is compatible with the fulfilling of other duties. We are guilty of vice and selfishness when we yield ourselves up to unbounded desires, and suffer our hearts to be wholly absorbed by one object, however meritorious that object may be.'

'Ah! how calmly you reason, - while I listen to you I cannot help loving and admiring you, but I must ever hate that accursed Harley - No! *I am not satisfied* - and I sometimes regret that I ever beheld you.'

Many months glided away with but little interruptions to our tranquillity. - A remembrance of the past would at times obtrude itself, like the broken recollections of a feverish vision. To banish these painful retrospections, I hastened to employ myself; every hour was devoted to active usefulness, or to social and rational recreation.

I became a mother; in performing the duties of a nurse, my affections were awakened to new and sweet emotions. - The father of my child appeared more respectable in my eyes, became more dear to me: the engaging smiles of my little Emma repayed me for every pain and every anxiety. While I beheld my husband caress his infant, I tasted a pure, a chaste, an ineffable pleasure.

CHAPTER XX

About six weeks after my recovery from childbed, some affairs of importance called Mr Montague to London. Three days after he had quitted me, as, bending over the cradle of my babe, I contemplated in silence its tranquil slumbers, I was alarmed by an uncommon confusion in the lower part of the house. Hastening down stairs, to enquire into the cause, I was informed - that a gentleman, in passing through the town, had been thrown from his horse, that he was taken up senseless, and, as was customary in cases of accident, had been brought into our house, that he might receive assistance.

Mr Montague was from home, a young gentleman who resided with us, and assisted my husband in his profession, was also absent, visiting a patient. Having myself acquired some knowledge of surgery, I went immediately into the hall to give the necessary directions on the occasion. The gentleman was lying on the floor, without any signs of life. I desired the people to withdraw, who, crowding round with sincere, but useless sympathy, obstructed the circulation of air. Approaching the unfortunate man, I instantly recognised the well-known features, though much altered, wan and sunk, of *Augustus Harley*. Staggering a few paces backward - a death-like sickness overspread my heart - a crowd of confused and terrible emotions rushed through my mind. - But a momentary reflection recalled my scattered thoughts. Once before, I had saved from death an object so fatal to my repose. I exerted all my powers, his hair was clotted, and his face disfigured with blood; I ordered the servants to raise and carry him to an adjoining apartment, wherein was a large, low sopha, on which they laid him. Carefully washing the blood from the wound, I found he had received a dangerous contusion in his head, but that the scull, as I had at first apprehended, was not fractured. I cut the hair from the wounded part, and applied a proper bandage. I did more - no other assistance being at hand, I ventured to open a vein: the blood presently flowed freely, and he began to revive. I bathed his temples, and sprinkled the room with vinegar, opened the windows to let the air pass freely through, raised his head with the pillows of the sopha, and sprinkled his face and breast with cold water. I held his hand in mine - I felt the languid and wavering pulse quicken - I fixed my eyes upon his face - at that moment every thing else was forgotten, and my nerves seemed firmly braced by my exertions.

He at length opened his eyes, gazed upon me with a vacant look, and vainly attempted, for some time, to speak. At last, he uttered a few incoherent words, but I perceived his senses were wandering, and I conjectured, too truly, that his brain had received a concussion. He made an effort to rise, but sunk down again.

'Where am I,' said he, 'every object appears to me double.'

He shut his eyes, and remained silent. I mixed for him a cordial and composing medicine, and entreating him to take it, he once more raised himself, and looked up. - Our eyes met, his were wild and unsettled.

'That voice,' - said he, in a low tone, 'that countenance - Oh God! where am I?'

A strong, but transient, emotion passed over his features. With a trembling hand he seized and swallowed the medicine I had offered, and again relapsed into a kind of lethargic stupor. I then gave orders for a bed to be prepared, into which I had him conveyed. I darkened the room, and desired, that he might be kept perfectly quiet.

I retired to my apartment, my confinement was yet but recent, and I had not perfectly recovered my strength. Exhausted by the strong efforts I had made, and the stronger agitation of my mind, I sunk into a fainting fit, (to which I was by no means subject) and remained for some time in a state of perfect insensibility. On my recovery, I learnt that Mr Lucas, the assistant of my husband, had returned, and was in the chamber of the stranger; I sent for him on his quitting the apartment, and eagerly interrogated him respecting the state of the patient. He shook his head - I related to him the methods I had taken, and enquired whether I had erred? He smiled -

'You are an excellent surgeon,' said he, 'you acted very properly, but,' observing my pallid looks, 'I wish your little nursery may not suffer from your humanity' -

'I lay no claim,' replied I with emotion - 'to extraordinary humanity - I would have done the same for the poorest of my fellow creatures - but this gentleman is an old acquaintance, *a friend*, whom, in the early periods of my life, I greatly respected.'

'I am sorry for it, for I dare not conceal from you, that I think him in a dangerous condition.'

I changed countenance - 'There is no fracture, no bones are broken.' -

'No, but the brain has received an alarming concussion - he is also, otherwise, much bruised, and, I fear, has suffered some internal injury.'

'You distress and terrify me,' said I, gasping for breath - 'What is to be done - shall we call in further advice?'

'I think so; in the mean time, if you are acquainted with his friends, you would do well to apprize them of what has happened.'

'I know little of them, I know not where to address them - Oh! save him,' continued I, clasping my hands with encreased emotion, unconscious of what I did, 'for God's sake save him, if you would preserve me from dis - '

A look penetrating and curious from Lucas, recalled me to reason. Commending his patient to my care, he quitted me, and rode to the next town to procure the aid of a skilful and experienced Physician. I walked up and down the room for some time in a state of distraction.

'He will die' - exclaimed I - 'die in my house - fatal accident! Oh, Augustus! *too tenderly beloved*, thou wert fated to be the ruin of my peace! But, whatever may be the consequences, I will perform, for thee, the last tender offices. - I will not desert my duty!'

The nurse brought to me my infant, it smiled in my face - I pressed it to my bosom - I wept over it. - How could I, from that agitated bosom, give it a pernicious sustenance?

CHAPTER XXI

In the evening, I repaired to the chamber of Mr Harley, I sat by his bed-side, I gazed mournfully on his flushed, but vacant countenance - I took his hand - it was dry and burning - the pulse beat rapidly, but irregularly, beneath my trembling fingers. His lips moved, he seemed to speak, though inarticulately - but sometimes raising his voice, I could distinguish a few incoherent sentences. In casting my eyes round the room, I observed the scattered articles of his dress, his cloaths were black, and in his hat, which lay on the ground, I discovered a crape hatband. I continued to hold his burning hand in mine.

'She died,' - said he - 'and my unkindness killed her - unhappy Emma - thy heart was too tender!' - I shuddered - 'No, no,' - continued he, after a few minutes pause, 'she is not married - she dared not give her hand without her heart, *and that heart was only mine*!' he added something more, in a lower tone, which I was unable to distinguish.

Overcome by a variety of sensations, I sunk into a chair, and, throwing my handkerchief over my face, indulged my tears.

Sometimes he mentioned his wife, sometimes his mother. - At length, speaking rapidly, in a raised voice - 'My son,' - said he, 'thou hast no mother - but Emma will be a mother to thee - she will love thee - *she loved thy father* - her heart was the residence of gentle affections - yet, I pierced that heart!'

I suspected, that a confused recollection of having seen me on recovering from the state of insensibility, in which he had been brought, after the accident, into our house, had probably recalled the associations formerly connected with this idea. The scene became too affecting: I rushed from the apartment. All the past impressions seemed to revive in my mind - my thoughts, with fatal mechanism, ran back into their old and accustomed channels. - For a moment, conjugal, maternal, duties, every consideration *but for one object* faded from before me!

In a few hours, Mr Lucas returned with the physician; - I attended them to the chamber, heedfully watching their looks. The fever still continued very high, accompanied with a labouring, unsteady pulse, a difficult respiration, and strong palpitations of the heart. The doctor said little, but I discovered his apprehensions in his countenance. The patient appeared particularly restless and uneasy, and the delirium still continued. On quitting the apartment, I earnestly conjured the gentlemen to tell me their opinion of the case. They both expressed an apprehension of internal injury.

'But a short time,' they added, 'would determine it; in the mean while he must be kept perfectly still.'

I turned from them, and walked to the window - I raised my eyes to heaven - I breathed an involuntary ejaculation - I felt that the crisis of my fate was approaching, and I endeavoured to steel my nerves - to prepare my mind for the arduous duties which awaited me.

Mr Lucas approached me, the physician having quitted the room. '*Mrs Montague*,' said he, in an emphatic tone - 'in your sympathy for a *stranger*, do not forget other relations.'

'I do not need, sir, to be reminded by you of my duties; were not the sufferings of a fellow being a sufficient claim upon our humanity, this gentleman has *more affecting claims* - I am neither a stranger to him, nor to his virtues.'

'So I perceive, madam,' said he, with an air a little sarcastic, 'I wish, Mr Montague were here to participate your cares.'

'I wish he were, sir, his generous nature would not disallow them.' I spoke haughtily, and abruptly left him.

I took a turn in the garden, endeavouring to compose my spirits, and, after visiting the nursery, returned to the chamber of Mr Harley. I there found Mr Lucas, and in a steady tone, declared my intention of watching his patient through the night.

'As you please, madam,' said he coldly.

I seated myself in an easy chair, reclining my head on my hand. The bed curtains were undrawn on the side next me. Augustus frequently started, as from broken slumbers; his respiration grew, every moment, more difficult and laborious, and, sometimes, he groaned heavily, as if in great pain. Once he suddenly raised himself in the bed, and, gazing wildly round the room, exclaimed in a distinct, but hurried tone -

'Why dost thou persecute me with thy ill-fated tenderness? A fathomless gulf separates us! - Emma!' added he, in a plaintive voice, '*dost thou, indeed, still love me*?' and, heaving a convulsive sigh, sunk again on his pillow.

Mr Lucas, who stood at the feet of the bed, turned his eye on me. I met his glance with the steady aspect of conscious rectitude. About midnight, our patient grew worse, and, after strong agonies, was seized with a vomiting of blood. The fears of the physician were but too well verified, he had again ruptured the blood-vessel, once before broken.

Mr Lucas had but just retired, I ordered him to be instantly recalled, and, stifling every feeling, that might incapacitate me for active exertion, I rendered him all the assistance in my power - I neither trembled, nor shed a tear - I banished the woman from my heart - I acquitted myself with a firmness that would not have disgraced the most experienced, and veteran surgeon. My services were materially useful, my solicitude vanquished every shrinking sensibility, *affection had converted me into a heroine*! The hæmorrhage continued, at intervals, all the next day: I passed once or twice from the chamber to the nursery, and immediately returned. We called in a consultation, but little hope was afforded.

The next night, Mr Lucas and myself continued to watch - towards morning our exhausted patient sunk into an apparently tranquil slumber. Mr Lucas intreated me to retire, and take some repose, on my refusal, he availed himself of the opportunity, and went to his apartment, desiring to be called if any change should take place. The nurse slept soundly in her chair, I alone remained watching - I felt neither fatigue nor languor - my strength seemed preserved as by a miracle, so omnipotent is the operation of moral causes!

Silence reigned throughout the house; I hung over the object of my tender cares - his features were serene - but his cheeks and lips were pale and bloodless. From time to time I took his lifeless hand - a low, fluttering, pulse, sometimes seeming to stop, and then to vibrate with a tremulous motion, but too plainly justified my fears - his breath, though less laborious, was quick and short - a cold dew hung upon his temples - I gently wiped them with my handkerchief, and pressed my lips to his forehead. Yet, at that moment, that solemn moment - while I beheld the object of my virgin affections - whom I had loved with a tenderness, 'passing the love of woman' - expiring before my eyes - I forgot not that I was a wife and a mother. - The purity of my feelings sanctified their enthusiasm!

The day had far advanced, though the house still remained quiet, when Augustus, after a deep drawn sigh, opened his eyes. The loss of blood had calmed the delirium, and though he regarded me attentively, and with evident surprize, the wildness of his eyes and countenance had given place to their accustomed steady expression. He spoke in a faint voice.

'Where am I, how came I here?'

I drew nearer to him - 'An unfortunate accident has thrown you into the care of kind friends - you have been very ill - it is not proper that you should exert yourself - rely on those to whom your safety is precious.'

He looked at me as I spoke - his eyes glistened - he breathed a half smothered sigh, but attempted not to reply. He continued to doze at intervals throughout the day, but evidently grew weaker every hour - I quitted him not for a moment, even my nursery was forgotten. I sat, or knelt, at the bed's head, and, between his short and broken slumbers, administered cordial medicines. He seemed to take them with pleasure from my hand, and a mournful tenderness at times beamed in his eyes. I neither spake nor wept - my strength appeared equal to every trial.

In the evening, starting from a troubled sleep, he fell into convulsions - I kept my station - our efforts were successful - he again revived. I supported the pillows on which his head reclined, sprinkled the bed cloaths, and bathed his temples, with hungary water, while I wiped from them the damps of death. A few tears at length forced their way, they fell upon his hand, which rested on the pillow - he kissed them off, and raised to mine his languid eyes, in which death was already painted.

The blood forsaking the extremities, rushed wildly to my heart, a strong palpitation seized it, my fortitude had well nigh forsaken me. But I had been habituated to subdue my feelings, and should I suffer them to disturb the last moments of him, *who had taught me this painful lesson*? He made a sign for a cordial, an attendant offering one - he waved his hand and turned from her his face - I took it - held it to his lips, and he instantly drank it. Another strong emotion shook my nerves - once more I struggled and gained the victory. He spoke in feeble and interrupted periods - kneeling down, scarce daring to breathe, I listened.

'I have a son,' said he, - 'I am dying - he will have no longer a parent - transfer to him a portion of - '

'I comprehend you - say no more - *he is mine* - I adopt him - where shall I find - ?'

He pointed to his cloaths; - 'a pocket book' - said he, in accents still fainter.

'Enough! - I swear, in this awful moment, never to forsake him.'

He raised my hand to his lips - a tender smile illumined his countenance - 'Surely,' said he, 'I have sufficiently fulfilled the dictates of a rigid honour! - In these last moments - when every earthly tie is dissolving - when human institutions fade before my sight - I may, without a crime, tell you - *that I have loved you.* - Your tenderness early penetrated my heart - aware of its weakness - I sought to shun you - I imposed on myself those severe laws of which you causelessly complained. - Had my conduct been less rigid, I had been lost - I had been unjust to the bonds which I had voluntarily contracted; and which, therefore, had on me indispensible claims. I acted from good motives, but no doubt, was guilty of some errors - yet, my conflicts were, even, more cruel than yours - I had not only to contend against my own sensibility, but against yours also. - The fire which is pent up burns the fiercest!' -

He ceased to speak - a transient glow, which had lighted up his countenance, faded - exhausted, by the strong effort he had made, he sunk back - his eyes grew dim - they closed - *their last light beamed on me*! - I caught him in my arms - and - *he awoke no more.* The spirits, that had hitherto supported me, suddenly subsided. I uttered a piercing shriek, and sunk upon the body.

CHAPTER XXII

Many weeks passed of which I have no remembrance, they were a blank in my life - a long life of sorrow! When restored to recollection, I found myself in my own chamber, my husband attending me. It was a long time before I could clearly retrace the images of the past. I learned -

'That I had been seized with a nervous fever, in consequence of having exerted myself beyond my strength; that my head had been disordered; that Mr Montague on his return, finding me in this situation, of which Mr Lucas had explained the causes, had been absorbed in deep affliction; that, inattentive to every other concern, he had scarcely quitted my apartment; that my child had been sent out to nurse; and that my recovery had been despaired of.'

My constitution was impaired by these repeated shocks. I continued several months in a low and debilitated state. - With returning reason, I recalled to my remembrance the charge which Augustus had consigned to me in his last moments. I enquired earnestly for the pocket-book he had mentioned, and was informed, that, after his decease, it had been found, and its contents examined, which were a bank note of fifty pounds, some letters, and memorandums. Among the letters was one from his brother, by which means they had learned his address, and had been enabled to transmit to him an account of the melancholy catastrophe, and to request his orders respecting the disposal of the body. On the receipt of this intelligence, the younger Mr Harley had come immediately into ...... shire, had received his brother's effects, and had his remains decently and respectfully interred in the town where the fatal accident had taken place, through which he was passing in his way to visit a friend.

As soon as I had strength to hold a pen, I wrote to this gentleman, mentioning the tender office which had been consigned to me; and requesting that the child, or children, of Mr Augustus Harley, might be consigned to my care. To this letter I received an answer, in a few days, hinting -

'That the marriage of my deceased friend had not been more imprudent than unfortunate; that he had struggled with great difficulties and many sorrows; that his wife had been dead near a twelve-month; that he had lost two of his children, about the same period, with the small-pox, one only surviving, the younger, a son, a year and a half old; that it was, at present, at nurse, under his (his brother's) protection; that his respect for me, and knowledge of my friendship for their family, added to his wish of complying with every request of his deceased brother, prevented him from hesitating a moment respecting the propriety of yielding the child to my care; that it should be delivered to any person whom I should commission for the purpose; and that I might draw upon him for the necessary charges towards the support and education of his nephew.'

I mentioned to Mr Montague these particulars, with a desire of availing myself of his counsel and assistance on the occasion.

'You are free, madam,' he replied, with a cold and distant air, 'to act as you shall think proper; but you must excuse me from making myself responsible in this affair.'

I sighed deeply. I perceived, but too plainly, that *a mortal blow was given to my tranquillity*; but I determined to persevere in what I considered to be my duty. On the retrospect of my conduct, my heart acquitted me; and I endeavoured to submit, without repining, to my fate.

I was, at this period, informed by a faithful servant, who attended me during my illness, of what I had before but too truly conjectured - That in my delirium I had incessantly called upon the name of Augustus Harley, and repeated, at intervals, in broken language, the circumstances of our last tender and fatal interview: this, with some particulars related by Mr Lucas to Mr Montague on his return, had, it seems, at the time, inflamed the irascible passions of my husband, almost to madness. His transports had subsided, by degrees, into gloomy reserve: he had watched me, till my recovery, with unremitting attention; since which his confidence and affection became, every day, more visibly alienated. Self-respect suppressed my complaints - conscious of deserving, even more than ever, his esteem, I bore his caprice with patience, trusting that time, and my conduct, would restore him to reason, and awaken in his heart a sense of justice.

I sent for my babe from the house of the nurse, to whose care it had been confided during my illness, and placed the little Augustus in its stead. 'It is unnecessary, my friend, to say, that you were that lovely and interesting child. - Oh! with what emotion did I receive, and press, you to my care-worn bosom; retracing in your smiling countenance the features of your unfortunate father! Adopting you for my own, I divided my affection between you and my Emma. Scarce a day passed that I did not visit the cottage of your nurse. I taught you to call me by the endearing name of *mother*! I delighted to see you caress my infant with fraternal tenderness - I endeavoured to cherish this growing affection, and found a sweet relief from my sorrows in these tender, maternal, cares.'

CHAPTER XXIII

My health being considerably injured, I had taken a young woman into my house, to assist me in the nursery, and in other domestic offices. She was in her eighteenth year - simple, modest, and innocent. This girl had resided with me for some months. I had been kind to her, and she seemed attached to me. One morning, going suddenly into Mr Montague's dressing-room, I surprised Rachel sitting on a sopha with her master: - he held her hand in his, while his arm was thrown round her waist; and they appeared to be engaged in earnest conversation. They both started, on my entrance: - Unwilling to encrease their confusion, I quitted the room.

Montague, on our meeting at dinner, affected an air of unconcern; but there was an apparent constraint in his behaviour. I preserved towards him my accustomed manner, till the servants had withdrawn. I then mildly expostulated with him on the impropriety of his behaviour. His replies were not more unkind than ungenerous - they pierced my heart.

'It is well, sir, I am inured to suffering; but it is not of *myself* that I would speak. I have not deserved to lose your confidence - this is my consolation; - yet, I submit to it: - but I cannot see you act in a manner, that will probably involve you in vexation, and intail upon you remorse, without warning you of your danger. Should you corrupt the innocence of this girl, she is emphatically *ruined*. It is the strong mind only, that, firmly resting on its own powers, can sustain and recover itself amidst the world's scorn and injustice. The morality of an uncultivated understanding, is that of custom, not of reason: break down the feeble barrier, and there is nothing to supply its place - you open the flood-gates of infamy and wretchedness. Who can say where the evil may stop?'

'You are at liberty to discharge your servant, when you please, madam.'

'I think it my duty to do so, Mr Montague - not on my own, but on *her*, account. If I have no claim upon your affection and principles, I would disdain to watch your conduct. But I feel myself attached to this young woman, and would wish to preserve her from destruction!'

'You are very generous, but as you thought fit to bestow on me your *hand*, when your *heart* was devoted to another - '

'It is enough, sir! - To your justice, only, in your cooler moments, would I appeal!'

I procured for Rachel a reputable place, in a distant part of the county. - Before she quitted me, I seriously, and affectionately, remonstrated with her on the consequences of her behaviour. She answered me only with tears and blushes.

In vain I tried to rectify the principles, and subdue the cruel prejudices, of my husband. I endeavoured to shew him every mark of affection and confidence. I frequently expostulated with him, upon his conduct, with tears - urged him to respect himself and me - strove to convince him of the false principles upon which he acted - of the senseless and barbarous manner in which he was sacrificing my peace, and his own, to a romantic chimera. Sometimes he would appear, for a moment, melted with my tender and fervent entreaties.

'Would to God ' he would say, with emotion, 'the last six months of my life could be obliterated for ever from my remembrance!'

He was no longer active, and chearful: he would sit, for hours, involved in deep and gloomy silence. When I brought the little Emma, to soften, by her engaging caresses, the anxieties by which his spirits appeared to be overwhelmed, he would gaze wildly upon her - snatch her to his breast - and then, suddenly throwing her from him, rush out of the house; and, inattentive to the duties of his profession, absent himself for days and nights together: - his temper grew, every hour, more furious and unequal.

He by accident, one evening, met the little Augustus, as his nurse was carrying him from my apartment; and, breaking rudely into the room, overwhelmed me with a torrent of abuse and reproaches. I submitted to his injustice with silent grief - my spirits were utterly broken. At times, he would seem to be sensible of the impropriety of his conduct - would execrate himself and entreat my forgiveness; - but quickly relapsed into his accustomed paroxysms, which, from having been indulged, were now become habitual, and uncontrollable . These agitations seemed daily to encrease - all my efforts to regain his confidence - my patient, unremitted, attentions - were fruitless. He shunned me - he appeared, even, to regard me with horror. I wept in silence. The hours which I passed with my children afforded me my only consolation - they became painfully dear to me. Attending to their little sports, and innocent gambols, I forgot, for a moment, my griefs.

CHAPTER XXIV

Some months thus passed away, with little variation in my situation. Returning home one morning, early, from the nurse's, where I had left my Emma with Augustus (whom I never, now, permitted to be brought to my own house) as I entered, Mr Montague shot suddenly by me, and rushed up stairs towards his apartment. I saw him but transiently, as he passed; but his haggard countenance, and furious gestures, filled me with dismay. He had been from home the preceding night; but to these absences I had lately been too much accustomed to regard them as any thing extraordinary. I hesitated a few moments, whether I should follow him. I feared, lest I might exasperate him by so doing; yet, the unusual disorder of his appearance gave me a thousand terrible and nameless apprehensions. I crept toward the door of his apartment - listened attentively, and heard him walking up and down the room, with hasty steps - sometimes he appeared to stop, and groaned heavily: - once I heard him throw up the sash, and shut it again with violence.

I attempted to open the door, but, finding it locked, my terror increased. - I knocked gently, but could not attract his attention. At length I recollected another door, that led to this apartment, through my own chamber, which was fastened on the outside, and seldom opened. With trembling steps I hurried round, and, on entering the room, beheld him sitting at a table, a pen in his hand, and paper before him. On the table lay his pistols - his hair was dishevelled - his dress disordered - his features distorted with emotion - while in his countenance was painted the extreme of horror and despair.

I uttered a faint shriek, and sunk into a chair. He started from his seat, and, advancing towards me with hurried and tremulous steps, sternly demanded, Why I intruded on his retirement? I threw myself at his feet, - I folded my arms round him - I wept - I deprecated his anger - I entreated to be heard - I said all that humanity, all that the most tender and lively sympathy could suggest, to inspire him with confidence - to induce him to relieve, by communication, the burthen which oppressed his heart. - He struggled to free himself from me - my apprehensions gave me strength - I held him with a strenuous grasp - he raved - he stamped - he tore his hair - his passion became frenzy! At length, forcibly bursting from him, I fell on the floor, and the blood gushed from my nose and lips. He shuddered convulsively - stood a few moments, as if irresolute - and, then, throwing himself beside me, raised me from the ground; and, clasping me to his heart, which throbbed tumultuously, burst into a flood of tears.

'I will not be thy *murderer*, Emma!' said he, in a voice of agony, interrupted by heart-rending sobs - 'I have had enough of blood!'

I tried to sooth him - I assured him I was not hurt - I besought him to confide his sorrows to the faithful bosom of his wife! He appeared softened - his tears flowed without controul.

'Unhappy woman! - you know not what you ask! To be ingenuous, belongs to purity like yours! - Guilt, black as hell! - conscious, aggravated, damnable, guilt! - *Your fatal attachment* - my accursed jealousy! - Ah! Emma! I have injured you - but you are, indeed, revenged!'

Every feature seemed to work - seemed pregnant with dreadful meaning - he was relapsing into frenzy.

'Be calm, my friend - be not unjust to yourself - you can have committed no injury that I shall not willingly forgive - you are incapable of persisting in guilt. The ingenuous mind, that avows, has already made half the reparation. Suffer me to learn the source of your inquietude! I may find much to extenuate - I may be able to convince you, that you are too severe to yourself.'

'Never, never, never! - nothing can extenuate - *the expiation must be made*! - Excellent, admirable, woman! - Remember, without hating, the wretch who has been unworthy of you - who could not conceive, who knew not how to estimate, your virtues! - Oh! - do not - do not' - straining me to his bosom - 'curse my memory!'

He started from the ground, and, in a moment, was out of sight.

I raised myself with difficulty - faint, tottering, gasping for breath, I attempted to descend the stairs. I had scarcely reached the landing-place, when a violent knocking at the door shook my whole frame. I stood still, clinging to the balustrade, unable to proceed. I heard a chaise draw up - a servant opening the door - a plain-looking countryman alighted, and desired instantly to speak to the lady of the house - his business was, he said, of life and death! I advanced towards him, pale and trembling!

'What is the matter, my friend - whence came you?'

'I cannot stop, lady, to explain myself - you must come with me - I will tell you more as we go along.'

'Do you come,' enquired I, in a voice scarcely articulate, 'from my husband?'

'No - no - I come from a person who is dying, who has somewhat of consequence to impart to you - Hasten, lady - there is no time to lose!'

'Lead, then, I follow you.'

He helped me into the chaise, and we drove off with the rapidity of lightning.

CHAPTER XXV

I asked no more questions on the road, but attempted to fortify my mind for the scenes which, I foreboded, were approaching. After about an hour's ride, we stopped at a small, neat, cottage, embosomed in trees, standing alone, at a considerable distance from the high-road. A decent-looking, elderly, woman, came to the door, at the sound of the carriage, and assisted me to alight. In her countenance were evident marks of perturbation and horror. I asked for a glass of water; and, having drank it, followed the woman, at her request, up stairs. She seemed inclined to talk, but I gave her no encouragement - I knew not what awaited me, nor what exertions might be requisite - I determined not to exhaust my spirits unnecessarily.

On entering a small chamber, I observed a bed, with the curtains closely drawn. I advanced towards it, and, unfolding them, beheld the unhappy Rachel lying in a state of apparent insensibility.

'She is dying,' whispered the woman, 'she has been in strong convulsions; but she could not die in peace without seeing Madam Montague, and obtaining her forgiveness.'

I approached the unfortunate girl, and took her lifeless hand. - A feeble pulse still trembled - I gazed upon her, for some moments, in silence. - She heaved a deep sigh - her lips moved, inarticulately. She, at length, opened her eyes, and, fixing them upon me, the blood seemed to rush through her languid frame - reanimating it. She sprung up in the bed, and, clasping her hands together, uttered a few incoherent words.

'Be pacified, my dear - I am not angry with you - I feel only pity.'

She looked wildly. 'Ah! my dear lady, I am a wicked girl - but not - Oh, no! - *not a murderer*! I did not - indeed, I did not - murder my child!'

A cold tremor seized me - I turned heart-sick - a sensation of horror thrilled through my veins!

'My dear, my kind mistress,' resumed the wretched girl, 'can you forgive me? - Oh! that cruel, barbarous, man! - It was *he* who did it - indeed, it was *he* who did it!' Distraction glared in her eyes.

'I do forgive you,' said I, in broken accents. 'I will take care of you - but you must be calm.'

'I will - I will' - replied she, in a rapid tone of voice - 'but do not send me to prison - *I did not murder it*! - Oh! my child, my child!' continued she, in a screaming tone of frantic violence, and was again seized with strong convulsions.

We administered all the assistance in our power. I endeavoured, with success, to stifle my emotions in the active duties of humanity. Rachel once more revived.

After earnestly commending her to the care of the good woman of the house, and promising to send medicines and nourishment proper for her situation, and to reward their attentions - desiring that she might be kept perfectly still, and not be suffered to talk on subjects that agitated her - I quitted the place, presaging but too much, and not having, at that time, the courage to make further enquiries.

CHAPTER XXVI

On entering my own house my heart misgave me. I enquired, with trepidation, for my husband, and was informed - 'That he had returned soon after my departure, and had shut himself in his apartment; that, on being followed by Mr Lucas, he had turned fiercely upon him, commanding him, in an imperious tone, instantly to leave him; adding, he had affairs of importance to transact; and should any one dare to intrude on him, it would be at the peril of their lives.' All the family appeared in consternation, but no one had presumed to disobey the orders of their master. - They expressed their satisfaction at my return - Alas! I was impotent to relieve the apprehensions which, I too plainly perceived, had taken possession of their minds.

I retired to my chamber, and, with a trembling hand, traced, and addressed to my husband, a few incoherent lines - briefly hinting my suspicions respecting the late transactions - exhorting him to provide for his safety, and offering to be the companion of his flight. I added - 'Let us reap wisdom from these tragical consequences of *indulged passion*! It is not to atone for the past error, by cutting off the prospect of future usefulness - Repentance for what can never be recalled, is absurd and vain, but as it affords a lesson for the time to come - do not let us wilfully forfeit the fruits of our dear-bought experience! I will never reproach you! Virtuous resolution, and time, may yet heal these aggravated wounds. Dear Montague, be no longer the slave of error; inflict not on my tortured mind new, and more insupportable, terrors! I await your directions - let us fly - let us summon our fortitude - let us, at length, bravely stem the tide of passion - let us beware of the criminal pusillanimity of despair!'

With faultering steps, I sought the apartment of my husband. I listened a moment at the door - and hearing him in motion, while profound sighs burst every instant from his bosom, I slid my paper under the door, unfolded, that it might be the more likely to attract his attention. Presently, I had the satisfaction of hearing him take it up. After some minutes, a slip of paper was returned, by the same method which I had adopted, in which was written, in characters blotted, and scarcely legible, the following words -

'Leave me, one half hour, to my reflections: at the end of that period, be assured, I will see, or write, to you.'

I knew him to be incapable of falsehood - my heart palpitated with hope. I went to my chamber, and passed the interval in a thousand cruel reflections, and vague plans for our sudden departure. Near an hour had elapsed, when the bell rang. I started, breathless, from my seat. A servant passed my door, to take his master's orders. He returned instantly, and, meeting me in the passage, delivered to me a letter. I heard Montague again lock the door. - Disappointed, I re-entered my chamber. In my haste to get at the contents of the paper, I almost tore it in pieces - the words swam before my sight. I held it for some moments in my hand, incapable of decyphering the fatal characters. I breathed with difficulty - all the powers of life seemed suspended - when the report of a pistol roused me to a sense of confused horror. - Rushing forward, I burst, with preternatural strength, into the apartment of my husband - What a spectacle! - Assistance was vain! - Montague - the impetuous, ill-fated, Montague - *was no more - was a mangled corpse*! - Rash, unfortunate, young, man!

But, why should I harrow up your susceptible mind, by dwelling on these cruel scenes? *Ah! suffer me to spread a veil over this fearful catastrophe*! Some time elapsed ere I had fortitude to examine the paper addressed to me by my unfortunate husband. Its contents, which were as follows, affected me with deep and mingled emotions.

To Mrs Montague.

'Amidst the reflections which press, by turns, upon my burning brain, an obscure consciousness of the prejudices upon which my character has been formed, is not the least torturing - because I feel the *inveterate force of habit* - I feel, that my convictions come too late!

'I have destroyed myself, and you, dearest, most generous, and most unfortunate, of women! I am a monster! - I have seduced innocence, and embrued my hands in blood! - Oh, God! - Oh, God! - *'Tis there distraction lies*! - I would, circumstantially, retrace my errors; but my disordered mind, and quivering hand, refuse the cruel task - yet, it is necessary that I should attempt a brief sketch.

'After the cruel accident, which destroyed our tranquillity, I nourished my senseless jealousies (the sources of which I need not, now, recapitulate), till I persuaded myself - injurious wretch that I was! - that I had been perfidiously and ungenerously treated. Stung by false pride, I tried to harden my heart, and foolishly thirsted for revenge. Your meekness, and magnanimity, disappointed me. - I would willingly have seen you, not only suffer the pangs, but express the *rage*, of a slighted wife. The simple victim of my baseness, by the artless affection she expressed for me, gained an ascendency over my mind; and, when you removed her from your house, we still contrived, at times, to meet. The consequences of our intercourse could not long be concealed. It was, then, that I first began to open my eyes on my conduct, and to be seized with remorse! - Rachel, now, wept incessantly. Her father, she told me, was a stern and severe man; and should he hear of her misconduct, would, she was certain, be her destruction. I procured for her an obscure retreat, to which I removed the unhappy girl [Oh, how degrading is vice!], under false pretences. I exhorted her to conceal her situation - to pretend, that her health was in a declining state - and I visited her, from time to time, as in my profession.

'This poor young creature continued to bewail the disgrace she anticipated - her lamentations pierced my soul! I recalled to my remembrance your emphatic caution. I foresaw that, with the loss of her character, this simple girl's misfortune and degradation would be irretrievable; and I could, now, plainly distinguish the morality of *rule* from that of *principle*. Pursuing this train of reasoning, I entangled myself, for my views were not yet sufficiently clear and comprehensible! Bewildered, amidst contending principles - distracted by a variety of emotions - in seeking a remedy for one vice, I plunged (as is but too common), into others of a more scarlet dye. With shame and horror, I confess, I repeatedly tried, by medical drugs, to procure an abortive birth: the strength and vigour of Rachel's constitution defeated this diabolical purpose. Foiled in these attempts, I became hardened, desperate, and barbarous!

'Six weeks before the allotted period, the infant saw the light - for a moment - to close its eyes on it for ever! I, only, was with the unhappy mother. I had formed no deliberate purpose - I had not yet arrived at the acme of guilt - but, perceiving, from the babe's premature birth, and the consequences of the pernicious potions which had been administered to the mother, that the vital flame played but feebly - that life was but as a quivering, uncertain, spark - a sudden and terrible thought darted through my mind. I know not whether my emotion betrayed me to the ear of Rachel - but, suddenly throwing back the curtain of the bed, she beheld me grasp - with savage ferocity - *with murderous hands*! - Springing from the bed, and throwing herself upon me - her piercing shrieks -

'*I can no more* - of the rest you seem, from whatever means, but too well informed!

I need not say - protect, if she survive, the miserable mother! - To you, whose heavenly goodness I have so ill requited, it would be injurious as unnecessary! I read, too late, the heart I have insulted!

'I have settled the disposal of my effects - I have commanded my feelings to give you this last, sad, proof of my confidence. - *Kneeling*, I entreat your forgiveness for the sufferings I have caused you! I found your heart wounded - and into those festering wounds I infused a deadly venom - curse not my memory - *We meet no more.*

'Farewell! first, and last, and only, beloved of women! - a long - a long farewell

    '*Montague.*'

These are the consequences of confused systems of morals - and thus it is, that minds of the highest hope, and fairest prospect, are blasted!

CHAPTER XXVII

The unhappy Rachel recovered her health by slow degrees. I had determined, when my affairs were settled, to leave a spot, that had been the scene of so many tragical events. I proposed to the poor girl to take her again into my family, to which she acceded with rapture. She has never since quitted me, and her faithful services, and humble, grateful attachment, have repaid my protection an hundred fold.

Mr Montague left ten thousand pounds, the half of which was settled on his daughter, the remainder left to my disposal. This determined me to adopt you wholly for my son. I wrote to your uncle to that purport, taking upon myself the entire charge of your education, and entreating, that you might never know, unless informed by myself, to whom you owed your birth. That you should continue to think me *your mother*, flattered my tenderness, nor was my Emma, herself, more dear to me.

I retired in a few months to my present residence, sharing my heart and my attentions between my children, who grew up under my fostering care, lovely and beloved.

> *While every day, soft as it roll'd along,*
> *Shew'd some new charm.'*

I observed your affection for each other with a flattering presage. With the features of your father, you inherited his intrepidity, and manly virtues - even, at times, I thought I perceived the seeds of his inflexible spirit; but the caresses of my Emma, more fortunate than her mother - yet, with all her mother's sensibility - could, in an instant, soften you to tenderness, and melt you into infantine sweetness.

I endeavoured to form your young minds to every active virtue, to every generous sentiment. - You received, from the same masters, the same lessons, till you attained your twelfth year; and my Emma emulated, and sometimes outstripped your progress. I observed, with a mixture of hope and solicitude, her lively capacity - her enthusiastic affections; while I laboured to moderate and regulate them.

It now became necessary that your educations should take a somewhat different direction; I wished to fit you for a commercial line of life; but the ardor you discovered for science and literature occasioned me some perplexity, as I feared it might unfit you for application to trade, in the pursuit of which so many talents are swallowed up, and powers wasted. Yet, as to the professions my objections were still more serious. - The study of law, is the study of chicanery. - The church, the school of hypocrisy and usurpation! You could only enter the universities by a moral degradation, that must check the freedom, and contaminate the purity, of the mind, and, entangling it in an inexplicable maze of error and contradiction, *poison virtue at its source*, and lay the foundation for a duplicity of character and a perversion of reason, destructive of every manly principle of integrity. For the science of physic you expressed a disinclination. A neighbouring gentleman, a surveyor, a man high in his profession, and of liberal manners, to whose friendship I was indebted, offered to take you. You were delighted with this proposal, (to which I had no particular objection) as you had a taste for drawing and architecture.

Our separation, though you were to reside in the same town, cost us many tears - I loved you with more than a mother's fondness - and my Emma clung round the neck of her beloved brother, her Augustus, her playfellow, and sobbed on his bosom. It was with difficulty that you could disentangle yourself from our embraces. Every moment of leisure you flew to us - my Emma learned from you to draw plans, and to study the laws of proportion. Every little exuberance in your disposition, which, generated by a noble pride, sometimes wore the features of asperity, was soothed into peace by her gentleness and affection: while she delighted to emulate your fortitude, and to rise superior to the feebleness fostered in her sex, under the specious name of delicacy. Your mutual attachment encreased with your years, I renewed my existence in my children, and anticipated their more perfect union.

Ah! my son, need I proceed? Must I continually blot the page with the tale of sorrow? Can I tear open again, can I cause to bleed afresh, in your heart and my own, wounds scarcely closed? In her fourteenth year, in the spring of life, your Emma and mine, lovely and fragile blossom, was blighted by a killing frost - After a few days illness, she drooped, faded, languished, and died!

It was now that I felt - 'That no agonies were like the agonies of a mother.' My broken spirits, from these repeated sorrows, sunk into habitual, hopeless, dejection. Prospects, that I had meditated with ineffable delight, were for ever veiled in darkness. Every earthly tie was broken, except that which bound you to my desolated heart with a still stronger cord of affection. You wept, in my arms, the loss of her whom you, yet, fondly believed your sister. - I cherished the illusion lest, by dissolving it, I should weaken your confidence in my maternal love, weaken that tenderness which was now my only consolation.

To Augustus Harley.

My Augustus, *my more than son*, around whom my spirit, longing for dissolution, still continues to flutter! I have unfolded the errors of my past life - I have traced them to their source - I have laid bare my mind before you, that the experiments which have been made upon it may be beneficial to yours! It has been a painful, and a humiliating recital - the retrospection has been marked with anguish. As the enthusiasm - as the passions of my youth - have passed in review before me, long forgotten emotions have been revived in my lacerated heart - it has been again torn with *the pangs of contemned love* - the disappointment of rational plans of usefulness - the dissolution of the darling hopes of maternal pride and fondness. The frost of a premature age sheds its snows upon my temples, the ravages of a sickly mind shake my tottering frame. The morning dawns, the evening closes upon me, the seasons revolve, without hope; the sun shines, the spring returns, but, to me, it is mockery.

And is this all of human life - this, that passes like a tale that is told? Alas! it is a tragical tale! Friendship was the star, whose cheering influence I courted to beam upon my benighted course. The social affections were necessary to my existence, but they have been only inlets to sorrow - *yet, still, I bind them to my heart!*

Hitherto there seems to have been something strangely wrong in the constitutions of society - a lurking poison that spreads its contagion far and wide - a canker at the root of private virtue and private happiness - a principle of deception, that sanctifies error - a Circean cup that lulls into a fatal intoxication. But men begin to think and reason; reformation dawns, though the advance is tardy. Moral martyrdom may possibly be the fate of those who press forward, yet, their generous efforts will not be lost. - Posterity will plant the olive and the laurel, and consecrate their mingled branches to the memory of such, who, daring to trace, to their springs, errors the most hoary, and prejudices the most venerated, emancipate the human mind from the trammels of superstition, and teach it, *that its true dignity and virtue, consist in being free.*

Ere I sink into the grave, let me behold *the son of my affections*, the living image of him, whose destiny involved mine, who gave an early, but a mortal blow, to all my worldly expectations - let me behold my Augustus, escaped from the tyranny of the passions, restored to reason, to the vigor of his mind, to self control, to the dignity of active, intrepid virtue!

The dawn of my life glowed with the promise of a fair and bright day; before its noon, thick clouds gathered; its mid-day was gloomy and tempestuous. - It remains with thee, my friend, to gild with a mild radiance the closing evening; before the scene shuts, and veils the prospect in impenetrable darkness.

finis

AZILOTH ||| BOOKS

Aziloth Books publishes a wide range of titles ranging from hard-to-find esoteric books - Parchment Books - to classic works on fiction, politics and philosophy - Cathedral Classics. Our newest venture is Aziloth Books Children's Classics, with vibrant new covers and Black-and-White/Colour illustrations to complement some of the world's very best children's tales. All our imprints are offered to the reader at a competitive price and through as many mediums and outlets as possible.

We are committed to excellent book production and strive, whenever possible, to add value to our titles with original images, maps and author introductions. With the premium on space in most modern dwellings, we also endeavour - within the limits of good book design - to make our products as slender as possible, allowing more books to be fitted into a given bookshelf area.

We are a small, approachable company and would love to hear any of your comments and suggestions on our plans, products, or indeed on absolutely anything.

Aziloth Books is also interested in hearing from aspiring authors whom we might publish. We look forward to meeting you.

Contact us at: info@azilothbooks.com.

Cathedral Classics hosts an array of classic literature, from erudite ancient tomes to avant-garde, twentieth-century masterpieces, all of which deserve a place in your home.   All the world's great novelists are here, Jane Austen, Dickens, Conrad, Arthur Machen and Henry James, brushing shoulders with such disparate luminaries as Sun Tzu, Marcus Aurelius, Kipling, Friedrich Nietzsche, Machiavelli, and Omar Khayam. A small selection is detailed below:

The Prophet	Kahlil Gibran
Herland	Charlotte Perkins Gilman
With Her in Ourland	Charlotte Perkins Gilman
Frankenstein	Mary Shelley
The Time Machine; The Invisible Man	H. G. Wells
The Prince	Niccolo Machiavelli
The Rubaiyat of Omar Khayyam	Omar Khayyam
Heart of Darkness; The Secret Agent	Joseph Conrad
Persuasion; Northanger Abbey	Jane Austen
The Picture of Dorian Gray	Oscar Wilde
Candide	Voltaire
The Coming Race	Bulwer Lytton
The Adventures of Sherlock Holmes	Arthur Conan Doyle
The Thirty-Nine Steps	John Buchan
Beyond Good and Evil	Friedrich Nietzsche
Washington Square	Henry James
The Red Badge of Courage	Stephen Crane
Self-Reliance, & Other Essays (series1&2)	Ralph W. Emmerson
The Art of War	Sun Tzu
A Christmas Carol	Charles Dickens
The Gambler; The Double	Fyodor Dostoyevsky
To the Lighthouse; Mrs Dalloway	Virginia Woolf
The Sorrows of Young Werther	Johann W. Goethe
Leaves of Grass - 1855 edition	Walt Whitman
Analects	Confucius
Beowulf	Anonymous
Agnes Grey	Anne Bronte
Utopia	Thomas More
The Rights of Man	Thomas Paine

Obtainable at all good online and local bookstores.
View Aziloth Books' full list at: www.azilothbooks.com

Parchment Books enshrines the concept of the oneness of all true religious traditions - that "the light shines from many different lanterns". Our list below offers titles from both eastern and western spiritual traditions, including Christian, Judaic, Islamic, Daoist, Hindu and Buddhist mystical texts, as well as books on alchemy, hermeticism, paganism, etc..

By bringing together such spiritual texts, we hope to make esoteric and occult knowledge more readily available to those ready to receive it. We do not publish grimoires or any titles pertaining to the left hand path. Titles include:

Abandonment to Divine Providence	Jean-Pierre de Caussade
Corpus Hermeticum	G.R.S. Mead (trans.)
The Holy Rule of St Benedict	St. Benedict of Nursia
Kundalini	G. S. Arundale
The Way of Perfection	St. Teresa of Avila
Q.B.L.	Frater Achad
The Cloud Upon the Sanctuary	Karl von Eckhartshausen
The Confession of St Patrick	St. Patrick
The Outline of Sanity	G K Chesterton
The Teachings of Zoroaster	Shapuji A Kapadia
The Dialogue Of St Catherine Of Siena	St. Catherine of Siena
Esoteric Christianity	Annie Besant
The Wisdom of the Egyptians	Brian Brown
The Spiritual Exercises of St. Ignatius	St. Ignatius of Loyola
Dark Night of the Soul	St. John of the Cross
Moses and Monotheism	Sigmund Freud
The Gospel of Thomas	Anonymous
Alchemy Rediscovered and Restored	Archibald Cockren
The Imitation of Christ	Thomas à Kempis
The Interior Castle	St. Teresa of Avila
Songs of Innocence & Experience	William Blake
The Marriage of Heaven & Hell	William Blake
The Secret of the Rosary	St. Louis de Montfort
Tertium Organum	P.D. Ouspensky
From Ritual to Romance	Jessie L. Weston
The God of the Witches	Margaret Murray

Obtainable at all good online and local bookstores.
View Aziloth Books' full list at: www.azilothbooks.com

Aziloth Books is passionate about bringing the very best in children's classics fiction to the next generation of book-lovers. Renowned for its original design and outstanding quality, our highly successful list has something to suit every age and interest. Titles include:

The Railway Children	Edith Nesbit
5 Children and It	Edith Nesbit
Anne of Green Gables	Lucy Maud Montgomery
What Katy Did	Susan Coolidge
What Katy Did Next	Susan Coolidge
Puck of Pook's Hill	Rudyard Kipling
The Jungle Books	Rudyard Kipling
Just So Stories	Rudyard Kipling
Alice Through the Looking Glass	Charles Dodgson
Alice's Adventures in Wonderland	Charles Dodgson
Black Beauty	Anna Sewell
The War of the Worlds	H. G Wells
The Time Machine	H. G .Wells
The Sleeper Awakes	H. G. Wells
The Invisible Man	H. G. Wells
The Lost World	Sir Arthur Conan Doyle
A Christmas Carol	Charles Dickens
Call of the Wild	Jack London
Greenmantle	John Buchan
Treasure Island	Robert Louis Stevenson
Dr Jekyll and Mr Hyde	Robert Louis Stevenson
Kidnapped	Robert Louis Stevenson
Catriona (David Balfour)	Robert Louis Stevenson
The Water Babies	Charles Kingsley
The First Men in the Moon	Jules Verne
The Secret Garden	Frances Hodgson Burnett
A Little Princess	Frances Hodgson Burnett
Peter Pan	J. M. Barrie

Obtainable at all good online and local bookstores.
View Aziloth Books' full list at: www.azilothbooks.com